I0670724

EVERNIGHT PUBLISHING ®

www.evernightpublishing.com

HIDDEN

DEDICATION

For Sabrina who introduced me to the dream of Iceland,
and Belle who helped me make the dream come true.

HIDDEN

Fire and Iceland, 1

Megan Morgan

Copyright © 2018

Chapter One

Vanessa woke stiff and sore, lying on a cold, hard surface. *I'm on the ground.* She deduced this without even opening her eyes. She was lying on her side, her cheek pressed into—ice? Snow? Whatever it was, the entire left side of her face was numb. Her ribs hurt.

What the hell did I do last night?

With an almighty heave, she rolled onto her back. Her arm had been twisted beneath her and it throbbed. Though she suspected alcohol to be the reason for her current state of affairs, she didn't have a hangover. Or at least, she didn't seem to. No pounding head or queasy stomach. She was a little thirsty, but apart from aching and shivering from being on the ground, she felt fine.

She opened her eyes.

Slate gray clouds hung above her, low enough it seemed she could reach out and touch them. The wind ruffled her hair, which was scattered across her face in matted tangles. She pushed it away and blinked. The light, despite being dull, felt over-bright and made her wince, like she'd been in a dark room for too long.

Somewhere nearby, muffled by the wind, she heard a voice. No, two voices. Men, talking.

She lifted her head and looked around.

What she saw baffled her even more than waking up to find herself on the ground. To say the view was shocking would be an understatement. The land around her was rocky and muddy with patches of green, but it ended in the short distance. Beyond was a broad expanse of water, a few shades darker than the sky. On the horizon was an undulating line of mist-shrouded mountains. Or, maybe they were just hills. They looked too small to be mountains.

This isn't Reykjavik.

Or was it?

During her short stay in Iceland she'd discovered the scenery could shift from civilization to wild, awe-inspiring countryside quite rapidly. But, where were her friends?

Two men stood near her feet. They were tall—or, they just looked tall because she was currently on the ground. One was blond and probably in his mid-twenties, the other a young man with dark hair, perhaps a teenager.

They spoke Icelandic, but she swore she could understand them, so maybe they were also speaking English. She couldn't possibly be translating, because beyond a handful of common phrases and random words she'd learned to make this trip easier, she didn't speak Icelandic.

Her vision blurred. Maybe she *was* hungover. She struggled to hear them over the wind.

"…where she came from…"

"…would have missed her on the boat…"

"…if we should be worried…"

Neither of them looked at her, but instead were glancing nervously around, as though spooked by the situation. She supposed she might feel the same if she found a random girl passed out in the middle of apparent nowhere.

She pushed herself up on her elbows and sat up. Her back ached. Her neck was stiff. She looked down at herself and cringed. Her clothes were filthy. She also realized it wasn't snow or ice her cheek had been pressed against, but cold, sticky mud. It was caked in her hair and smeared down her neck. None of this made sense. She wasn't a heavy drinker. She had never in her life gotten so drunk she couldn't remember the night before. She sure as hell had never passed out on the ground.

The two men were still ignoring her.

She grimaced. "Hey."

They stopped talking and looked at her.

The blond one's curls fluttered against his forehead. He had a chiseled, clean-shaven face, and the sharp slope of his nose and rounded point of his chin gave him an unconventional attractiveness, as did his pale blue eyes. He was what her friend, Jessica, would call *a hottie with character*. The other one had long dark hair pulled back in a ponytail, his eyes dark as well. He couldn't be much past eighteen. Both wore boots and jeans and were wrapped in thick wool sweaters of typical Icelandic fashion: the zig-zag patterned ring around the shoulders, the front zippered.

Just her luck, to wake up from her first-ever blackout, disgusting and covered in mud, in front of two hot guys.

"Um." She shifted from side to side, trying to peel her ass off the cold ground. "Hi, I'm Vanessa. Vanessa Evanston?" She had no idea why she said this. Like they were going to proclaim, *"Ah, yes!*

Vanessa Evanston, of the Connecticut Evanstons!"

The blond one knelt in front of her. He didn't look repulsed, just worried. "Vanessa. How did you get here?" He spoke English for certain now, though it was with a thick Icelandic accent.

She stared at him a moment, woozy. His eyes were so clear she could almost see the surrounding water in them. The gray light washed out his skin but made his face distinct. He wasn't just a hottie with character, he was downright handsome as hell. "I ... was hoping you could tell me that." She tried to stop staring into his eyes. "I don't remember."

The younger one stepped closer. "Are you American?" His accent was not Icelandic. Irish, she thought, though she wasn't an expert on accents.

"Yes, I'm here with my friends on vacation." Panic slowly began to replace confusion as her dominant emotion. "Where's my purse? And my phone?" She patted the ground around her. "Where are my friends? Are they here?"

Handsome Guy narrowed his eyes. "Where were you last night? What do you remember?"

This was surreal. Maybe she was still passed out and having some crazy dream, brought on by one too many cocktails. "I was in Reykjavik." She continued looking around. "But this isn't Reykjavik, is it?" More cringing ensued on her part. "I didn't go home with you guys last night, did I?"

That seemed out of character for her as well. She could barely flirt, let alone pick up a guy, let alone pick up *two* guys. She didn't typically drink or carouse in a way that would put her in this situation, so it was utterly bizarre.

"No," Younger One said. "We just found you out here a few minutes ago."

"Where is here?" she asked.

"Grímsey." Handsome Guy was still gazing at her in concern. "It's an island. The only way out here is by boat."

She struggled to remember the geography of Iceland. She'd been in love with the island for years and they'd made a detailed itinerary of places to visit before the trip. Grímsey sounded familiar, and then it struck her. "Isn't that up north, near the Arctic Circle?" She boggled at him. "It's the northernmost point in Iceland or something." They'd been debating going there just to say they'd visited it.

Handsome Guy shook his head. "This is a different Grímsey, in Kaldrananeshreppur." He pointed across the water. "That's Drangsnes." In the distance, on the mainland, were rows of buildings and houses, what appeared to be a small town.

None of those mouth-filling words sparked any recognition.

Younger One's gaze pierced her. "We're in the Westfjords."

That rang a bell. An area also up north. *Way* up north. "How far are we from Reykjavik?" She almost didn't want to know the answer. Dread filled the spaces inside her where panic had not yet taken root.

Handsome Guy looked up at Younger One. "About, say ... 250 kilometers?"

"A hundred and fifty-five miles," Younger One supplied, apparently for her American benefit.

Terror swept through her, though thankfully she was so stunned she didn't immediately leap to her feet and start screaming. "How the hell did I get here?" She looked to the heavy clouds, as if they held the answer.

Horrible possibilities presented themselves. She could have been drugged and abducted. Her missing purse suggested she was at least robbed. Why would they dump her so far away from where they picked her up, though? Her stomach turned as she also wondered if she'd been violated. However, her clothes, though dirty, were in place, even her boots, and she didn't feel … anything like that down there.

"What's the last thing you remember?" Handsome Guy tenderly touched her calf. "What were you doing last night?"

She swallowed. Her throat was tight and dry. "I was at a bar with my two friends, in the 101 District, in Reykjavik." As she tried to recall the previous evening, she found the memory strangely faded, as though it happened a long time ago. "We came here for a week to sightsee, and we ended our trip in Reykjavik. We were dancing. I was only on my second drink. I don't drink that much, not enough to end up passed out somewhere." Again, she felt queasy. She *had* to have been drugged.

The two men stared at her, their demeanor so intense it made her feel like she was being interrogated.

"It was stuffy inside the bar." She struggled to connect the dots. "I went outside to get some air and I—I don't remember anything after that."

Though she found, in truth, she *did* remember something. She could almost recall a voice, but she couldn't hear the words, or discern if it was a man or woman. Someone calling out to her. One of her friends? She saw herself walking down a street, as if in a dream, but after that it was blank. The memory faded and vanished.

"Someone must have slipped me something." Tears welled in her eyes. "I didn't drink enough to pass out, I swear."

"And they brought you all the way up here?" Younger One sounded skeptical.

She struggled to get up. "I need to call the police. I have to get help." She stopped and looked at them, desperate, frightened. "Please, can you help me?"

Handsome Guy looked at Younger One again. They seemed to be sharing some silent conversation.

"We will take you back to Drangsnes." Handsome Guy nodded in the direction of the town. "No one lives here. Only tourists come out here."

That sounded bad. Whoever brought her here expected her to not be found for a while.

"We thought you might have gotten separated from a tour group," Younger One said. "But they would have missed you on the boat back. Drangsnes is small. News of a missing tourist would be everywhere by now."

She was on the verge of hysterical sobs. "Please help me." Her voice squeaked out tiny and scared. "Someone did something terrible to me."

Handsome Guy reached for her. He grasped her arm. "Come on, let's get you up." He helped her to her feet.

Her legs were stiff and she wobbled. She was freezing, as she only had on the thin blouse and jeans she'd worn to go clubbing. Summer in Iceland, at least in the south, was mild enough she was able to leave her jacket at the hotel. But up here, it wasn't so much. She wrapped her arms around herself, teeth chattering.

Handsome Guy quickly unzipped and slipped his sweater off and draped it over her shoulders. He wore a long-sleeved, formfitting white shirt beneath it. He was only a few inches taller than her, now that she was standing. So was Younger One.

"Thank you," she murmured, and pulled the sweater around her shivering frame. The fabric smelled like fruity cologne.

The two men exchanged glances. Handsome Guy

murmured a word in Icelandic, and the way he said it—with foreboding and dismay—made her ears prick.

"Huldufólk."

Hidden people. She somehow knew what the word was, but not what it meant.

Younger One scowled, his eyes glittering. "You can bet."

She had no idea what they were talking about, but she didn't care. She just wanted to get to a phone, find out where her friends were, and piece together what happened last night.

They led her down a steep and muddy trail cut into the side of the island. The path was wide enough they could flank her and hold both arms, though near the bottom it narrowed and Handsome Guy stayed by her side while Younger One went ahead.

Tears slipped from her eyes and dried on her cold cheeks, but she struggled not to give in to full-on crying. She would fall apart *after* she got help. The fear inside her swelled until she could barely pull in a breath.

At least she had boots on, though they were going-out boots, not meant for rugged terrain. Still, they helped her not slip as the three of them descended to a gravel beach. There, a metal rowboat was tied to a rock and bobbed on the water.

She looked up. The cliff behind them was craggy, the island floor high above. "How did you find me up there?" Birds circled against the clouds. A few more hours, and they might have been feasting on her.

Younger One looked over his shoulder. "We came out to walk the island and we stumbled upon you."

Though it seemed weird they would just walk around this island, she was grateful they had. She climbed into the boat and sat down on a plank across the middle.

Younger One got in behind her, where oars were propped inside the boat.

Handsome Guy untied the rope and hopped in, in front of her at the back of the boat. "It will take about fifteen minutes to cross," he told her. "We will get you some clean clothes and something to eat and drink when we get there."

She huddled into the sweater, the wind whipping her hair around her face. More tears slipped from her eyes.

As Younger One rowed them out into the water, the world expanded in all directions. The sky arched above, the view around her endless. The wind rocked the boat and made small waves break against the sides.

Handsome Guy gazed at her. He leaned forward, bracing his forearms on his knees. His shirt rippled across his broad shoulders and exposed the thick column of his neck. "Vanessa?" His eyes took on the deep gray of the water. "Is that your name?" He spoke the V in her name like a W.

She nodded.

"I'm Gunnar." He extended a hand. "Heimirsson." He nodded to the front of the boat. "He's Aedan."

She slipped a hand from beneath the sweater and it was trembling, though she couldn't tell how much was from cold and how much was elicited by emotion. She shook his hand. It was as cold as hers, but strong, his fingertips rough. She wanted to cling to him out of fear, desperately in need of reassurance and comfort, but she made herself let go.

She turned her head and spoke over her shoulder, trying to make her voice loud enough to be heard over the wind. "Aedan. Are you Irish? I thought your accent sounded Irish." She needed some small talk right now or she'd go insane.

"My Ma was Irish." Aedan grunted out the words as he worked the oars. "I was born here, though." He had a frank, matter-of-fact way of speaking and she got the impression he didn't want to chat.

She turned back around and dropped her gaze to the boat floor, so she wouldn't keep staring at Gunnar's face. In any other circumstance, she'd be happy to meet such an attractive, strapping, and kind man. She might even make some bumbling attempt to flirt.

A thought flashed in her head, from out of nowhere. *You* have *met him before*. She frowned. No, she hadn't. She would certainly remember him. Unless … she had met him last night.

"You're American?" Gunnar asked. "He heard your accent, too."

She looked up.

A faint smile broke his lips, the first crack in his grave demeanor. *He* was trying to keep her from panicking, at least.

"Yes." She pushed her hair out of her face. "My friends must be terrified. After I contact the police, I have to get in touch with them."

"Are you hurt?"

"I don't think so. Just cold and sore."

They sat in silence for the rest of the journey, awkwardly not meeting each other's eyes. She stared across the choppy water and listened to it slosh across the oars. Her mind raced but kept running into walls. Perhaps it was the effects of whatever drug still lingered in her blood.

As they drew closer to the shore, she turned and watched the town approach. Buildings with colorful gabled roofs were scattered across the hillsides above the water. Her stomach knotted as she silently and anxiously urged Aedan to row faster. His arms seemed to never tire, his shoulders working rhythmically. He was like a machine. She noticed when he glanced at her, the glint in his eyes was guarded and cautious.

"You can call from my cell phone," Gunnar said. "It might take the lögreglan time to get here, though. They usually only have to come for poachers."

Lögreglan. That meant "police." Crime was sparse in Iceland, and violent crime barely existent, especially outside of Reykjavik. She'd read about it. Of course, she had to be the one to buck statistics.

They reached the shore, and the beach there was just as rocky as the one they'd left behind. Several other rowboats were tied to a wooden pier. Aedan climbed out and tied theirs up, and Gunnar helped her get out. She was even more unsteady now, the ground seeming to shift beneath her feet.

"We'll take you to our house." Gunnar held her arm. "You can call from there."

"You have cell service here?" She looked up and down the beach at the quaint, modest town.

"Yes, we even have Wi Fi." Gunnar chuckled. "This is a fishing village, but we have a lot of tourists."

Down the jagged shore, to her left, stood a series of—hot tubs? They faced the water and steam drifted off them. People were in them, and more people walked along the top of the breakwater that separated the beach from the higher ground of the town.

Aedan led the way. They followed him up a set of natural stairs to the top of the breakwater and onto a paved road. The sun was starting to peek from behind the clouds, warming the back of her neck.

"This way." Gunnar guided her. "It's not far."

As they walked, what she saw was like most of the architecture she'd already witnessed in Iceland: long wooden buildings, most one story, many roofs painted red, blue, or green. She couldn't tell which structures were houses and which were public buildings, as everything was so nondescript. Salt-bleached light poles lined the chip seal streets. There were no sidewalks, or painted lanes. They passed people as they walked, but she met no one's gaze.

At the back edge of town, where the land beyond rose in steep steps, Gunnar led them to the door of a single-story white house with a red roof. The grass in the small yard was littered with tiny white flowers. In the driveway, two vehicles were parked: a red SUV-style truck with a cap, and a blue car.

Stepping into the warmth of the house was like having a toasty blanket fresh out of the dryer thrown around her, and she almost broke down at the sudden relief. She realized for the first time how exhausted she was, and she'd only just woken up.

"I'll get my phone." Gunnar closed the door behind them. "Aedan, make her something hot to drink."

Gunnar worked his boots off—heavy-duty hiking boots, caked in mud—and dropped them on a mat next to the door. Aedan did the same.

She managed to bend and work her own off, though her limbs were barely functional. Her toes were numb inside her socks. She wiggled them to try to get the feeling back.

Gunnar walked down a hallway opposite the front door. The interior of the house was tidy and cozy. The living room, in which they stood, had broad windows that let in the newly-emerged sun. The furniture was simple, the floor hardwood and scattered with throw rugs. There was also a fireplace. The air smelled of wood smoke and like the sweater she wore.

"You like coffee?" Aedan motioned for her to

follow him through a doorway to the left.

"Sure." She padded meekly behind him. They entered a simple kitchen, as neat and unassuming as the rest of the house. "It's a good thing you guys were out there. I might have died from exposure."

Aedan went to the counter, where a stainless-steel coffee maker sat. In the sunlight, she could appreciate he was quite a handsome young man himself, even if he gave off an odd vibe. His face was softer than Gunnar's, also clean-shaven, his jaw square.

"Not likely." His voice remained flat. "It doesn't get that cold in the summer."

"Lucky me." She gave a humorless laugh and looked around the kitchen. Her gaze settled on a calendar on the wall next to her, with a picture of a landscape much like the one outside. Thank God she *had* come in July, and not the middle of winter.

Aedan moved to the sink and began filling the carafe. "I don't think it's a good idea to call the lögreglan just yet. We need to figure out what to tell them."

Vanessa narrowed her eyes at the calendar. She only vaguely heard him.

Footsteps sounded. Gunnar walked in, holding a cell phone. "What *are* we going to tell them?" He stared down at his phone. "It's an odd story."

Vanessa looked at him, looked at the calendar once more, and smiled uneasily. "You're a man living in the future, huh?"

Gunnar glanced up, a blond eyebrow quirked. "Pardon me?"

She pointed at the calendar. "I'm sorry, is it some sort of Icelandic tradition or joke? I don't mean to poke fun, if it is."

Gunnar looked at the calendar. "What do you mean?"

"That's next year."

Gunnar's expression of concern returned. "What? No, that's this year."

She stared at him. Icelanders didn't live on a different date system. She had never heard of such a thing, and it wouldn't even make sense, if they wanted to interact with the rest of the world.

Aedan stood at the sink, carafe clutched in both hands, and his gaze bored into her. "What do you think the date is?"

Vanessa looked between them as dread made her blood, organs, brain, and entire soul go ice cold.

Gunnar turned his phone around and showed her the display; specifically, the date and time. "That's today's date."

She backed away. "What the fuck is going on?" she whispered.

"What day do you think it is?" Aedan demanded.

Fear flashed in Gunnar's eyes. No one could be more afraid than her, though. This had to be a hallucination, a delusion, or a nightmare.

She stared at the phone. Whatever happened to her hadn't happened last night.

It happened a *year* ago.

Chapter Two

"Have I gone insane? How is this even possible?"

Vanessa sat in a chair in the living room, clicking through websites on the laptop Gunnar had provided her. The Wi-Fi was slow, but it worked well enough she was able to find multiple confirmations of the current date. Somehow, beyond all comprehension or explanation, she had stepped out of that bar a year ago today and possessed absolutely no memory of the time since then. News sites displayed stories about events she had never heard of. She searched "today's date" over and over and came up with the same answer.

"Am I insane?" She kept repeating this rhetorical question. Gunnar and Aedan sat on the couch across from her, in silence. "Someone tell me how this is happening!"

If these two were playing some elaborate prank on her, they had really good poker faces. But why would total strangers play such an awful trick, and how would they even manage it? You couldn't fake the entire internet.

"When the lögreglan get here," Gunnar said, "I don't think you should tell them about this."

She'd called the police, but as Gunnar predicted, they wouldn't get here for a while.

"What?" She looked at him like *he* was the insane one. "I should definitely tell them about this! It's the craziest part of the whole thing."

Gunnar nodded. "Exactly. They might think you're making it up or hiding something. They'll think something suspicious is going on."

Aedan sat back and peeked out the window behind the couch. He'd been doing that often.

"Something suspicious *is* going on!" She tried not to yell, but she was freaking out. "I have to find out where I've been for a whole fucking *year*."

"We'll tell them how we found you." Gunnar kept his voice low and calm. "Tell them what you remember and say you don't know how you got here. But don't bring up that a year has passed. Not yet. Let them investigate first. They might figure it out before you mention it."

She set the laptop on the coffee table between them, next to her untouched cup of coffee. She was still thirsty, but she couldn't stomach anything right now. She got to her feet. "You're crazy. I don't know why on earth you wouldn't want me to tell them I've lost an entire year." She was defensive. They *could* be in on some cruel prank against her.

"Why don't you get cleaned up?" Gunnar stood as well. "Get the mud off you at least, and—"

"No." She shook her head. "I want to wait for the police. If there's anything on my clothes, or any marks on my body that might be a clue, I don't want to disturb it."

Aedan turned from the window and stared at her, with the same scrutiny he'd been regarding her with since they first met. His edginess wound her up even more and she wondered what he was watching for out the window. It couldn't be the police, because they wouldn't be here for some time yet and he knew that.

"All right, that's fine." Gunnar, in contrast, was like a soothing breeze. "We'll just wait."

She gripped her hair. It was tangled and damp, the left side stuck together with dried mud. "I need to call my parents. I need to talk to them, right now. They have to be out of their minds, after a year. They must think they'll never see me again."

Gunnar frowned. "We should wait until after you speak with the lögreglan."

She rushed around the coffee table, hands out. Her fingers and palms were streaked with mud as well. "Please," she begged. "They probably think I'm dead."

Like most people, without her cell phone she was hard-pressed to remember by heart the numbers of anyone she knew. However, she knew her parents' landline number, as it hadn't changed since she was a child. She also knew Jessica's number, as she'd changed it recently and Vanessa had to put it in her phone.

Recently. No, over a year ago.

Gunnar sighed and pushed his hand into his hip pocket. He drew out his cell phone.

"I know it's an international call." She took the phone gratefully. "I promise, as soon as I find my purse I'll pay you for the charges, or I'll have my parents wire me some money." Her hands shook as she gazed at the screen. "I just have to tell them I'm all right."

"I feel like you should wait."

"No, I can't. I'll make it as short as possible."

She typed in her parents' number, tears blurring her vision. Her hand shook harder as she held the phone to her ear and listened to it ring far away on the other end. What if they weren't home? She couldn't begin to work out what time it was in Connecticut right now.

"Hello?" Her father's voice.

She crumpled into the chair, as her legs would no longer support her. A gush of air left her lungs and allowed her to speak. "Daddy." She brought her other hand to her face. "Oh God, I'm so glad you're there. I'm so freaked out right now."

A heavy pause, and then his voice came back, gruffer this time. "Who is this?"

"It's me, Daddy. It's Vanessa." She sniffed,

blinking. "I'm all right. I know this is crazy, but I'm okay, I promise. At least I think I am. But I need help."

Gunnar stood gazing at her, hands in his pockets, his gaze apprehensive.

"Is this supposed to be funny?" Her father's voice turned angry and stilted. "Is this some kind of joke or something?"

"What?" She wiped her cheeks. "What do you mean? Daddy, it's me."

"I don't know who you are" —his words were venomous— "but if you ever contact me again, I'll call the police, you sick freak."

The line went dead.

Vanessa pulled the phone from her ear and stared at it. She put it back. "Daddy? Daddy!"

He was gone. She lowered the phone and gaped at it.

"What happened?" Gunnar asked.

"He … didn't believe it was me." She continued staring dumbly at the phone. "He hung up."

Aedan got up from the couch. "Don't call anyone else."

"I have to call my friend Jessica." Vanessa stood. As Gunnar made to grab for the phone, she shrunk out of his reach. "She was here with me. She was at the bar. Maybe she knows what happened!"

She was baffled and scared. Gunnar watched her with sad, sympathetic eyes, and Aedan stared her down as she struggled to remember Jessica's number and type it in. She turned away from them, head bowed, phone clutched to her ear. It rang.

"This is Jessica Ives."

Vanessa pressed a hand to her forehead, shaking. "Jessica. Oh my God, where are you?"

A pause. "At work. Who's this?"

Vanessa lifted her head. A hole opened inside her, a darkness that was about to engulf her and drag her down into a bottomless pit. Jessica, obviously, didn't work in Iceland.

"It's Vanessa. I know this sounds crazy, but I need you to listen to me. I need help."

Another pause. Then Jessica's tone turned angry, like her father's had. "What the fuck? Is this what teenagers do for fun now? Who the hell is this?"

"It's Vanessa." She turned, hand clutched to her chest. The other two stared at her. "Please, Jessica. I'm so scared right now. I need to know what's going on."

"Good one." Jessica snorted. "Whoever this is, you're a complete and utter bitch. Is this a scam or something? If I find out who this is, I'm gonna come to your house and stab you. Not funny. Fuck off."

She hung up.

Vanessa stood numb, staring at the phone.

Gunnar walked over, pulled it out of her hand, and slipped it back in his pocket. "No more phone calls," he said sternly.

A buzzing filled her ears. Her vision went gray and spotty. She was sure she was about to faint, or at least collapse.

She sank to her knees and was aware after a moment that the strangled shrieking and sobbing she heard came from her. She wrapped her arms around herself and clung, the only thing she had left to hold onto. She had to shake this off. She had to escape.

Gunnar knelt beside her and slipped an arm around her shoulders. "Shh, it's going to be all right. We're going to figure out what's going on."

She was in a nightmare, that's what was going on. And she couldn't wake up.

* * * *

The Icelandic police were more laid-back than the police Vanessa was used to. They talked a little slower and were considerably less intense and imposing, but they dressed the same as American police, and asked her questions like any other police might. The two men who stood in Gunnar's living room spoke English fluently, though with a heavy accent, even more so than Gunnar.

"You don't remember anything from the time you stepped out of the bar until you woke up?" One of them had a notepad, and he asked most of the questions. "You don't remember anyone following you, or anyone in the bar who acted suspicious?"

She recalled the vague memory of a voice. It was so dreamlike, she wasn't even sure it happened. Just another corridor in this labyrinth she was currently wandering through.

"No." She shook her head. "I went outside to get some air. That's the last thing I remember."

Gunnar sat beside her on the couch, so close their shoulders were pressed together.

Aedan stood in the kitchen doorway, sipping from a coffee cup.

"The only way this makes sense," she offered, "is if someone drugged and abducted me. I mean, that could be why I can't remember anything, right?"

She hadn't mentioned the missing year part, not because Gunnar insisted, but because she also had doubts now. It just felt like a bad idea. After the phone calls, she was certain something sinister was going on. What if someone didn't *want* her to tell the police, and what if they were still close by, even in this room? It could be a giant conspiracy that everyone was in on. If she acted dumb, she might still get away.

The officer scratched his cheek with the pen. "And they brought you all the way here to

Kaldrananeshreppur. Are you certain you were in Reykjavik last night?"

No, but yes.

"Yes, I know where I was."

"I ask because sometimes tourists don't understand. The country can overwhelm them. I want to make sure you aren't confused."

"I know I was in Reykjavik." She clenched her hands in her lap. "Right *now,* I don't know where the hell I am, and that's the problem."

The other officer spoke up. "Do you think you were sexually assaulted?" His voice was deeper, and he spoke with a touch of sympathy.

"I don't think so." She'd gone to the bathroom before they arrived and checked herself, though she was reluctant to know. She found no blood or anything else to indicate someone had violated her. She wasn't in pain and all her underclothes were in place and intact.

The officer with the notepad turned to the other one. "Get on the radio. Have them call down to Rey and find out if there's a missing person report."

The man nodded and pulled a radio off his belt. He wandered into the kitchen.

"We should still take you to be examined." The officer's voice softened. "Make sure you haven't been assaulted, and test to see if there's any drugs in your bloodstream. It's plausible that's what happened, but it's odd they would bring you all the way up here."

She tugged Gunnar's sweater around her, as she hadn't taken it off yet. "Unless they dumped me here because they hoped I wouldn't be found right away."

Gunnar leaned away and rubbed her back. "That's not a desert island out there. Especially in summer, tourist boats go out there a few times a day. It wouldn't be a good hiding spot."

"Maybe they didn't know that." She was so tense it was hard to enjoy the backrub. "Maybe they're not from around here. Or, maybe they're not even Icelandic."

While that made sense in her head, it didn't account for the missing year. She couldn't have been drugged for an entire year. Surely, she'd have some ill effects from that.

The officer nodded. "We'll walk around town and ask questions, to find out if anybody saw anything."

The other officer was talking on his radio in the kitchen. She heard her name, and the word "American." She strained to listen, as once again she wasn't sure if he was speaking Icelandic or English. She understood most of it regardless, like she had with Gunnar and Aedan.

Gunnar continued rubbing her back. "We'll keep her here until you return. If you want to go see where we found her, we can take you there."

The other officer returned to the living room. "They're calling."

While they waited for a reply, Gunnar went to the kitchen and got the officers some coffee. She stayed on the couch, her own cup between her hands. It had long since gone cold. She just needed something to keep her grounded in the real world.

Aedan continued to glance out the windows, though he seemed to be trying to make it less obvious with the police there.

Finally, someone came back on the radio, a woman's voice, and she spoke English.

"There are no missing person reports for a Vanessa Evanston." Her voice was crackling and tinny. "At least, not recently."

A chill froze Vanessa's limbs. She looked at Gunnar, who had sat back down beside her.

The officer with the radio furrowed his brow. He

spoke into it. "What do you mean?"

"A year ago, a Vanessa Evanston was reported missing from Reykjavik, by friends she was traveling with. She was an American tourist. But that was resolved."

Vanessa couldn't pull in a breath. She didn't want to hear the rest. She wanted to flee from the room.

"Resolved?" The officer frowned at Vanessa. "She was found?"

"Her body was found, on Esjan. Her death was ruled a hiking accident."

For what felt like the millionth time since she'd opened her eyes on that island, nothing seemed real. She floated somewhere above herself, detached and just watching this unfold.

Gunnar and Aedan exchanged sharp, portentous looks.

The officers stared at her. The one holding the radio spoke absently into it. "Takk fyrir."

Vanessa wasn't sure how she managed to speak, but she forced the words out. "I—she must have had the same name as me. Obviously, I'm ... not dead." Or was she? She might be a ghost. That, somehow, would make more sense than any other possibility.

The officer with the notepad eyed her. "You don't have an ID?"

"No, it was in my purse, which is gone. I swear my name is Vanessa Evanston." She was ready to have another screaming breakdown. "Vanessa is a common name in the US. It's probably someone else."

She wasn't sure about Evanston, though. It might be a coincidence, but given everything else...

"All right." The officer's voice was calm, in sharp contrast to the alarm bells in her head. "We're going to walk around, then we'll come back and transport you to Hólmavík. There's a medical facility there. Maybe we can get some answers."

Despite his professional demeanor, suspicion hid behind his words. It was the same suspicion on Aedan's face, the same suspicion that filled her. This was not right, not right at all.

Gunnar showed the officers out.

The two men murmured to each other as they walked toward their car in the driveway.

She stood next to the couch and stared out the window, watching them go with dread.

Gunnar closed the door and turned. "I'm glad you didn't tell them about the missing year." He drew a deep breath. "Do you have any idea who the dead woman is?"

She couldn't move. She was trembling again. "It's not me," she whispered. "It can't be me." She heard her father and Jessica on the phone, furious and berating her. Refusing to believe it was her.

Aedan cleared his throat, one of those "we need to talk" sounds.

Gunnar glanced at him, then walked to her and touched her shoulder. "Don't panic, we'll figure it out." He gazed into her eyes. "Sit tight."

She couldn't help but panic, and she couldn't do anything but sit tight. After all, what else could a dead woman do?

Chapter Three

LOCAL WOMAN KILLED IN TRAGIC ICELAND ACCIDENT – Durham, Connecticut

It has been confirmed that Durham resident Vanessa Evanston, 24, died while on vacation with friends in Iceland. Her parents identified her body after it was transported to Bradley International Airport early Tuesday morning. Evanston was visiting Iceland on a week-long sightseeing tour when she was reported missing.

Evanston's friends say she was with them in Reykjavik, Iceland's capital, when she disappeared around 9 p.m. local time from a bar. Her friends, believing she had gone outside to get some air, couldn't find her and contacted authorities after she did not return to the bar or their hotel that evening, and did not answer repeated attempts to contact her on her cell phone.

After an extensive search, her body was discovered on Sunday, in a ravine on nearby Mt. Esja, which hosts multiple hiking trails and scenic vistas. It is not clear how or when Evanston travelled to the mountain, as it is not within walking distance of Reykjavik, but can be accessed by bus and taxi.

Her friend, Jessica Ives, says that it was unlike Evanston to wander off without telling them. "She was obsessed with visiting Iceland," Ives says. "She might have been sad that we were leaving the next day and tried to go off and do some more sightseeing on her own. Then she got into trouble and couldn't contact us."

Evanston's death has been ruled an accident.

"There are no signs of foul play," Chief Superintendent Kristjan Jónsson of the Reykjavik police

force told officials. "It's clear she slipped while traversing uneven terrain and was fatally injured. This underlines why it's important in Iceland, especially for tourists, to know their surroundings and use a knowledgeable tour guide when possible. The terrain of this country can be dangerous and change quickly and unpredictably for those who are unfamiliar with it."

Evanston's body was flown back to Connecticut after a coroner examined her remains. Her father, John Evanston, 58, describes Vanessa as a "kind, fun, and studious girl who liked to do sporty things and go on adventures." He said she'd been excited about the trip for months and was looking forward to taking in the sights of the rugged Icelandic landscape.

"She was a bright-eyed girl who liked to try new things," Mr. Evanston told us. "Unfortunately, she was prone to accidents, too. Three years ago, on a family ski trip in Newfoundland, she hit her head and spent three days in a coma. We were so grateful she recovered. This time, she wasn't so lucky."

Ms. Evanston will be interred at Mica Hill Cemetery. In lieu of flowers and gifts, her family has asked for donations in her name to the charities listed below.

Vanessa slapped the laptop shut and stared across the room. Speculation about two Vanessa Evanstons being in Iceland at the same was entirely erased.

This wasn't happening. It wasn't real.

A distant murmur of voices brought her out of her stupor. Gunnar and Aedan were outside, talking. The police hadn't returned yet. The walls around her felt like they were slowly closing in for the past hour, and now they were crushing her head.

She got up and walked to the windows. The words of the article danced in front of her eyes. Durham was her hometown. John Evanston was her father. Jessica Ives was her best friend.

It was her body they found.

She tried to make sense of it. What if it *wasn't* her body? What if the person they found was so mangled or injured they simply misidentified her? She shuddered to think of her father viewing whatever messed up corpse he saw, but it obviously wasn't hers.

Through the thin white curtains, she stared at Gunnar and Aedan. Once again, weirdly, she could make out what they were saying but wasn't positive it was English. They spoke lowly, so she only caught fragments.

She scanned the room in a desperate attempt to find something for her racing mind to latch onto, anything that would help her stay sane right now. Her gaze settled on a photograph on a shelf.

Welcoming a distraction, she walked over and peered at it. It looked antique. The thick paper was cracked and faded, held inside a tarnished gold frame. The picture was color, but the kind of old-school coloring that looked painted on.

The image was of a plain young woman from the waist up, wearing a quaint and traditional black dress with a high collar and flowers stitched into the bodice. She had thick, straight blonde hair that hung past her shoulders and was cut in a fringe across her forehead. She gazed at the camera with eyes of false blue, her skin fair, a tiny smile on her pink lips. Behind her was a stretch of barren rocky terrain and water in the distance. One of Gunnar's relatives, she supposed. She picked up the frame.

In that instant, someone whispered, behind her and near her left ear. She spun around, nearly dropping the picture.

No one was in the room.

Vertigo gripped her. The whispering grew louder and more frantic, but the words weren't clear. She realized the voice wasn't in the room but inside her head. It rose to a shout, and then pitched into a terrified, ragged scream.

She jerked back around and slammed the picture on the shelf. The scream stopped, like switching off a radio.

Breathing hard, heart pounding, she stared wide-eyed at the picture. The woman gazed placidly back at her.

Another voice made her jump, but it came from outside. She looked out the window.

"...tell the police it was a mistake," Gunnar was saying. "...they can't be involved in this."

With a frown, she rushed to the door and yanked it open. They both turned.

"What are you talking about?" she demanded. "I just heard you! What do you mean, you'll tell the police it was a mistake?"

They looked at each other. If these two were part of the conspiracy, she didn't know what she'd do. She'd have to run away, but she didn't know where she'd go. She'd have to try to find the police.

"Vanessa, we need to talk." Gunnar's voice was calm. "And you must listen to what we say, no matter how crazy it sounds."

She glowered at him.

"We might know what's happening," Aedan said. "But you have to let us explain."

She softened and blinked at him. "If you know what's happening, why didn't you say so before now?"

Gunnar walked toward her. "Let's go inside. We'll try to explain."

She went back in the house, because she didn't know what else to do. She could still run, if she needed to. She'd pretend to go to the bathroom and climb out the window.

Gunnar eased her down on the couch and sat beside her, not as close as before.

Aedan stood in front of them, arms folded.

Gunnar touched the back of her hand. He had the air of someone who was about to say something difficult.

"What's going on?" She didn't want to play games. "You realize I'm going crazy right now? Tell me what the hell is happening."

"I can imagine you are." Gunnar stroked her hand. "How much do you know about what Icelanders believe?"

She furrowed her brow. "Believe? Like—what? Your religion? Your political ideology?"

Gunnar locked his hand around hers. "I mean, our belief in supernatural creatures."

She'd read plenty about Iceland over the past few years, since the country had caught her interest and became the subject of her daydreams. She'd read about the people and the countryside, and of course, about Icelandic traditions.

"You believe in elves, so much you even have holidays centered around them. Not to mention museums and tours." She tried not to sound exasperated, though she was past caring if she offended anyone. Her life was in shambles and she didn't have time for this. "You make little houses for them, right? But what's any of this got to do with my situation?"

Gunnar leaned closer. "It's a folk belief now, especially with young people. The way people believe in Santa Claus, you would say. The holidays are for fun."

She shrugged. "But you reroute infrastructure to

avoid their homes. Some of your politicians even believe in them. That seems like more than fun."

Gunnar nodded. "Elves are good creatures, though. They can be mischievous, but they don't harm people. You don't want to disturb them because they might play pranks on you, that's why people are careful. We try to be respectful."

Aedan interjected, his voice as dour as his expression, "And then, there's the huldufólk."

Huldufólk. The word Gunnar had said out on the island.

"It means hidden people," Gunnar said. "If you ask, some will say the elves and huldufólk are the same thing. But others, especially old people, will tell you they're different. The huldufólk aren't helpful, and they're much less forgiving when humans make mistakes against them. Their retribution is less mischievous as downright cruel."

"They don't forgive easily." Aedan loomed over them like a storm cloud. "You have to be careful not to interfere with them. They're not little sprites, like the elves. They look human, and they can deceive people."

She sat back. "Okay, once again, what does any of this have to do with me?" She wasn't in the right mind to listen to folktales, and she had a bad feeling where this was going. She wouldn't be able to shoot it down gracefully if it was.

Gunnar's expression turned earnest. "We think you might have disturbed the huldufólk, and they punished you."

Of course, there it was. Void of answers, they turned to magic. They weren't necessarily in on this. They were just *silly and misguided.*

But she didn't have time for silly right now.

She yanked her hand out of Gunnar's and rubbed

the bridge of her nose. "You're telling me fairies did this."

"It seems the best explanation." Gunnar sounded dead serious.

She pinched her nose hard. "You're saying fairies kidnapped me, killed me, and brought me back to life a year later. That's their punishment? What exactly did I do?" She lowered her hand.

"No." Gunnar looked at Aedan. "They don't bring people back to life, do they?"

Aedan shook his head. "No, but they can do things to your mind. They can erase your memories, or put false ones in. They can make you believe things that aren't real."

She ground her teeth. "Look, I'm not trying to be disrespectful. I know this is what you believe, but I don't. And frankly, it's not very helpful."

"So, there's more plausible explanations?" Aedan snorted. "What, that you've been drugged for a year and somehow can't remember any of it?"

"Yes, maybe!" She flung her hands up. "I mean—what if I was like, I don't know, brainwashed? Or I had amnesia? I was in a coma for a few days three years ago—four, now—what if something from that old head injury made me forget what happened?" She had started to consider this as a possibility.

Aedan rolled his eyes. "And your amnesia conveniently vanished when you woke up on Grímsey, and now you can remember everything up until the point you disappeared last year?"

"Yes!" She didn't mean to get testy, but this was ridiculous. This little punk had no right to talk to her like she was stupid, when he was the one trying to blame this on the supernatural. "I don't know. It sure makes a lot more sense than goddamn fairies, though."

"It's not folklore." Gunnar dragged a hand through his hair. "I upset them too, a long time ago, and I paid the price." He looked down. "I'm still paying the price."

She shook her head. "Right. You pissed off the fairies too. But they didn't steal your memory, right?"

Aedan lurched toward her, his dark eyes burning.

She shrunk back.

"They're not *fairies*." His eyes were bright and strange as he stared her down, his face not seeming so young anymore. "My mother could tell you that, if she were still alive. She came here from Ireland, and here is where she found my father. A huldufólk man."

Vanessa blinked.

"I'm an abomination, the worst kind. I'm half-huldufólk, half-human. So yes, I do fucking believe they exist."

The intensity in his voice almost made her believe him. However, something didn't make sense. "Wait." She held up a finger. "If they hate humans, why would they make a baby with one?"

Aedan drew back.

"Collectively, they dislike humans." Gunnar gazed beseechingly at her, as if his sincerity could somehow convince her. "There are outliers, and when the huldufólk find out they've mingled with humans, they are punished, as well as their offspring."

"I'm only alive right now because we have an agreement." Aedan clenched his jaw. "But they may have decided they no longer wish to honor the terms of that agreement."

Gunnar sighed. "We're afraid you might have been dumped here as a warning. Perhaps they're done agreeing with both of us." He looked up at Aedan. "It's a bad sign."

Suddenly, all their weirdness made sense. They thought she was some kind of omen. That's why they were telling her not to tell the police things. "But why? What do you guys have to do with me?"

She recalled the feeling she'd had in the boat, that she'd met Gunnar before. But she hadn't, she was sure she hadn't.

"We have no idea." Aedan folded his arms again. "They don't explain themselves. But you turning up here can't be a good thing."

"So, you're telling me you're half fai—" she caught herself "—huldufólk." She was incredulous. "And they're punishing both of you. Okay. And now they're punishing me." She struggled to hold back pained laughter.

"I can't do all the things they can," Aedan said. "But I do have some of their magic. They don't like it, but as I said, I live because they allow it."

"They know we're here," Gunnar said. "They never lose sight of us. We have to be careful. We may have made a misstep without realizing it."

She had to get out of here. Her boots were by the door, she could grab them and run. Bad enough crazy things were happening to her, but she'd managed to land with crazy rescuers, as well.

She got to her feet and slipped the sweater off. "I want to thank both of you for finding me and getting me off that island." She tossed the sweater on the couch, on the cushion next to Gunnar. "But I have to leave now. I have to find the police and get real help."

As she tried to step around Aedan, he grabbed her arm. His touch wasn't gentle like Gunnar's. Before she could yank away, he gripped the side of her face. Her heart leapt into her throat and she shrieked.

"Let go of me!"

His hand was hot. Warmth flashed across her skin. His eyes lit up for a moment and then the glow quickly faded, as did the heat snaking through her limbs. He let go of her and she stumbled back.

"What the hell?" She grabbed her face where he'd touched her.

Gunnar stood. "Don't be afraid. It's all right."

She looked down at herself and let out another shriek.

Her clothes were now clean, exactly as they'd been when she'd gone out last night—a year ago—her blouse white, the mud vanished from her jeans. It was gone from her hands as well.

Tentatively, she touched her hair. She turned, toward a mirror over the fireplace, and what she saw made her gasp.

Her green eyes were comically wide. Her face was free of makeup and clean as well. She looked pale, and more than a little stricken, but otherwise like she'd just stepped out of the shower. Her dark brown hair fell around her face and lay in thick waves on her shoulders, the way it looked before she did any styling to it. A short time ago, when she'd been in the bathroom, the girl staring back at her in the mirror was dirty and ragged, her hair a mess, looking like she'd just rolled down a muddy hill.

She looked at her clothes again and ran her hands over them, dazzled and disbelieving. The spot where Aedan touched her face was still warm. Was she hallucinating? Maybe her mind had finally broken under the stress.

No, this was real. Everything she was seeing and feeling was somehow happening.

Holy shit.

She turned, mouth open, unable to speak.

Aedan flashed a brief, smarmy "told you so" smile.

"I know this is difficult to understand," Gunnar said. "But you're in danger, and we're the only ones who can help you. Not the police, not anyone else."

"We're all in danger." Aedan turned and looked out the window. Now it was clear what he was watching for. "I'm sure they'll come to tell us why, very soon."

Chapter Four

Vanessa sat on a set of concrete steps behind the house, wrapped in Gunnar's sweater again. The wind pulled at her hair—her clean hair—and the sun had ducked back behind the clouds, leaving a silvery, dull landscape beneath. She watched Gunnar, a few feet away, as he transferred pieces of cut firewood from a woodpile onto a flat wagon. He sized up each piece in his gloved hands before either tossing it on the wagon or pitching it back on the pile.

"What did you do to make them mad?" Her voice sounded small in the immense surroundings.

Gunnar looked at her. His hair fluttered around his face. Now that her mind had disconnected from reality and she'd gone utterly loopy, she was able to focus on other things, like how pleasantly good-looking he was. She admired the broad width of his shoulders and his thick arms as they flexed beneath his jacket. Might as well get an eyeful while she was down here in the rabbit hole. She might be dead tomorrow, after all. Killed by murderous fairies.

Huldufólk.

A bitter smirk pulled up the corners of his mouth. "I had the audacity to find a nice piece of earth and excavate it, so I could build a house for me and my wife. I didn't know it was their sacred land."

Wife? This house didn't have much of a woman's touch. Maybe in her panic she'd overlooked a few things.

"They punished you for not knowing that?"

"I should have been more careful. They don't separate accidents from malicious behavior, not when it comes to humans." He picked up another piece of wood.

So, that might explain her situation. She didn't

remember *trying* to offend any supernatural people.

"Do you mind if I ask what they did to you?"

He tossed the piece of wood back on the pile and stood still, hands on his hips, staring toward the water. He had a nice form: stocky and muscular, yet graceful.

She'd better kill those thoughts, if there was a wife around.

"They took her away." He said this without emotion, just a statement. "My new bride. We hadn't even been married a year."

She frowned. "They … took her away?"

"An eye for an eye, I guess that was their reasoning. I took something important from them, so they took something important from me."

"Did they—" she hesitated "—kill her?"

He shrugged. "I don't know. They took her away in the night, and I never saw her again."

She wasn't sure how to respond. Now she felt even worse for having those thoughts, somehow. "I'm sorry." Would they take her "away" too? Vanishing into the unknown was a more terrifying prospect than being outright killed.

"And they cursed me." He turned back to the woodpile. "They wanted me to suffer. How dare I spoil their land. How dare I not look for their signs, that it belonged to them."

"Taking your wife away wasn't enough?"

He let out a sarcastic laugh. "Oh, no. They are masters of vengeance." He held up a piece of wood, then tossed it on the wagon. "Their punishment must be long and painful."

"What did they do?" Uneasiness crept in, and she was just getting used to having a break from it.

He smacked his gloves together, knocking dust off them. "The curse was that I should live a hundred years, so I might have plenty of time to miss her. I would have to live with her loss for that long. Wherever she is, or isn't—I've had a long time to think about it."

Despite Aedan's magic trick earlier, doubt was her first reaction. "A hundred years?" She spoke pragmatically. "Uh, wow, that's a long time."

"Yes, but..." He looked around, as though checking to make sure no one was listening. He lowered his voice. "The huldufólk live a very long time. Maybe not forever, but thousands of years. To them, a hundred years of suffering sounds like torture for a human, because our lives are so short. We usually die quickly and that means our suffering ends." He walked over. "They don't understand how human grief works."

She looked around, her skin crawling.

"We're capable of moving on." He squatted down, so they were eye-to-eye. "Did I miss her? Yes. Did I go mad with grief and make desperate attempts to find her? Of course. For the first year, I mourned her. The second. Then five years passed. Then ten. Twenty. Fifty."

She gazed into his clear blue eyes, zoning out for a moment.

"Wait." She blinked. "Fifty? How long ago did this happen?"

He grinned, showing straight, white teeth and a smile that was a little too broad but nonetheless charming. "I have two years left in my sentence."

She boggled. "You're telling me you're ninety-eight years old?"

He lifted a hand and counted on his fingers. "I was twenty-five when it happened, so ... 123, actually."

She bit back the urge to spout *no you're not*. Her doubt intensified.

"It's a very long time." He dropped his hand and

clasped them between his knees. "Sadness and regret may linger, but grief has a much shorter lifespan."

She looked over her shoulder, at the house. "Is this the house that got you in trouble?"

"No, I never built it, and it wasn't here. As you can imagine, living without aging, you have to move around so no one figures it out. I've lived all over the country."

She looked back at him and thought of the picture on the shelf. She titled her head. "Is that your wife in that picture in there?"

She was reluctant to tell him how it affected her, the voice she'd heard when she picked it up. It was too weird, and she couldn't convince herself she hadn't imagined it.

He nodded. A small smile still lingered on his lips, though it was sad now. "If not for that picture, I couldn't remember her face at all." He looked down, then back up. "I've had lovers since. I even lived with a woman for twenty years." He stood. "I think I miss her morc than my wife."

She tilted her head back to look up at him. "What happened to her?"

"She grew old, I didn't." He strolled back to the woodpile.

"She died?"

"No, she's an old woman now, she lives in Akureyri." He started sorting wood again. "She eventually couldn't handle the fact I wasn't growing old with her. It was too strange. I don't blame her." These words were much sadder and more strained than when he spoke of his wife.

"She knew about you?"

"Of course, it's hard to live with someone for two decades and not know their secrets." He studied the pile of wood on the wagon. "And anyway, I thought to keep her safe, it was best she know everything." He dusted his hands on his jeans. "It's a lonely existence. I've had Aedan, at least."

She shifted on the step. Her bottom was getting cold. "What is he to you?"

"My child, in a way. I'm his guardian." He looked at the house. "He's not an abomination, no matter what they say. He stays with me, so I can watch over him. But he does grave work for them, and it haunts him. I can't stop that."

"Grave work?" That sounded ominous.

"I've taken care of him since he was a small child. His mother left him with me."

She wrapped her arms around her knees. "What happened to his mother?"

"I'll tell you about it later, maybe. It's a long story. He's had a hard life. Try not to take the way he behaves as rudeness. He's known nothing but fear, and they're always watching him."

She didn't blame Aedan for being standoffish. If she had to jump through hoops for beings that could erase your memory and would punish you for digging up their land, she wouldn't be the most pleasant person in the world either.

"What did he say to the police to make them go away?" When the police returned to the house, Aedan went out to speak with them and they left, without asking to see her again. Part of her wanted to rush after them, but she knew, if all this was true, there was nothing they could do. They might not even believe her.

"He can't erase minds or plant false memories like they can." Gunnar peeled his gloves off. "But he can make suggestions. He told them everything is fine, it was a mistake, they should forget it. And they will."

Is that what they'd done to her? Erased her mind? Made a "suggestion?"

"We'll find out what's going on, I promise." He tucked his gloves in his jacket pocket. "I know this is terrifying, but we can make contact with them and try to get some answers."

She sat silent, listening to the wind, trying to digest everything. His personal story didn't make her feel any less crazy.

She squinted up at him. "You really can't die?"

He shook his head. "I can't catch sickness or be injured. In times when disease ravaged the countryside, it never touched me. I've had accidents that should have killed me, but the wounds simply heal. I don't age." He heaved a sigh. "To tell you the truth, I'll miss it when it's gone."

She scrunched up her nose. It still sounded far-fetched.

The door behind her opened and Aedan leaned out. He wore his boots and coat. "I have to go." He spoke to Gunnar. "I don't want to, but now is certainly not the time to slack in my duties."

Gunnar's face sagged and his eyes darkened. He nodded. "If anything happens, I'll call you. If I'm able."

Her stomach clenched. She hoped he remained able to make phone calls.

"Keep in contact with me." Aedan swept the empty yard with his gaze. "I'll only be a couple days. Be careful." He turned and went back in the house.

She tried to swallow the fear that climbed up her throat. "Where's he going?"

"To do his work."

Gunnar pulled the wagon to the side of the house. Out front, a car started. The truck from the driveway trundled past on the street and drove down the slope into town. She was scared to watch him go. One less person to protect her.

"What are you doing with the wood?" she asked.

"I have to build a fire tonight." Gunnar looked up at the hills that rose beyond the house. "A big fire."

"Why?"

He didn't answer.

She shifted again. "So, uh, what happens when your curse ends in two years? Are you just going to die?"

He shrugged. "I don't know. I think, most likely, I'll just start aging again. I'll be able to get sick and hurt. I'll live out my life as a normal person. Aedan thinks that's what will happen, anyway."

She looked at the concrete between her feet. That wasn't how most fairy tales ended. It always took something more: a kiss, or the wicked witch being vanquished.

Gunnar bent and opened a toolbox next to the woodpile and rooted around in it. She skittered her gaze to his backside, so nicely outlined in his tight jeans. She looked away, then looked back again.

He stood and turned, and she snapped her gaze out to the water, pretending to be intensely interested in the view. He walked toward her with something in his hand. It was a knife, which he held by its blade. She sat up straight.

He stopped in front of her and motioned for her to stand. She did, wary. He held the knife out handle-first, and though reluctant, she took it. The handle was wood and the blade short and broad. Was this a special huldufólk-killing knife?

Gunnar grinned, tugged up the bottom of his shirt, and rolled it to his chest. His stomach was flat, his abs tight and defined.

She stared in both surprise and appreciation.

"Stab me," he said.

She stared at him. "Huh?"

"Stab me." He smiled his too-wide smile, flashing that bright line of teeth. "You don't believe a word I've said. I'll prove it."

She looked back at his stomach. The lean slope of his hips disappeared into the waistband of his jeans, and a faint trail of golden hair started below his navel. She would have drooled a little more, if she weren't so flabbergasted.

"I'm not going to stab you."

"You're probably feeling frustrated right now. It might make you feel better. It might even make you feel powerful. Like you have some control."

She looked between his face and his sculpted stomach, the knife clutched in her hand. "I'm not going to stab you. I believe you, okay?"

"No, you don't." He stepped closer. "Stab me, Vanessa. Wherever you like. Pick a spot. It won't matter, I promise."

The knife blade was only about three inches, but it would do some damage. She had never stabbed a person in her life. "I can't stab you."

"Do it."

"I can't stab—"

"Do it!" His voice turned commanding.

Her hand shook. Jesus Christ, this was the craziest thing yet.

"Now!" he shouted, so loud it made her jump. Ferocity shone through his kind exterior, something that both scared the shit out of and tantalized her. His eyes blazed. "This is your fault, Vanessa. You trespassed. It's your fault it happened to you."

She scowled. "Are you trying to make me angry? I can't stab you! Stop it."

"Stab me, right fucking now!"

He was so forceful she was terrified to not obey. A voice inside her spoke, a whisper from a place she didn't recognize: *strike hard and fast, don't hesitate.* A scene flashed across her vision: a knife in her hand, dark blood on the ground.

Hard and fast.

With a frightened cry she plunged her hand forward, barely of her own volition, without aim, and unable to look. The sensation of the blade sinking into his flesh was disturbing and too real.

She let go of the knife handle and stumbled back with a shriek, then clapped her hands over her mouth.

Gunnar's face was screwed up in agony and he groaned through gritted teeth. He doubled over, gripping the handle of the knife, which now stuck out of his lower right abdomen.

Oh my God, she'd just killed a man. *A man had asked her to kill him.*

"I thought you were immortal!" she screamed. Her head went woozy.

He straightened a little, still grimacing. "I am," he grunted out. "That doesn't mean I don't feel pain."

With that, he yanked the knife out. Droplets of blood rained on the grass between them, and a gush of it, bright red and thick, pumped out of the gash. Her wooziness intensified and black spots danced in front of her.

Then, what she saw next froze her both inside and out. She stood still, hands cupped in front of her mouth.

The gash sealed itself, swift and smooth, like a zipper closing. Not so much as a scar was left behind. A rivulet of blood ran down and stained his waistband, some that had already escaped, but no more came out.

He stepped closer and rubbed his fingertips over

the spot where the knife had gone in, showing it to her. His smile returned, and he was flushed now. "See?" The blade in his hand was slicked with a pink sheen. "It smarts a bit, but it will pass."

She couldn't speak.

"I'm sorry." He frowned. "That was gruesome, but I had to prove it to you. You need to believe me, Vanessa. You need to trust me."

She wobbled. Her vision tunneled. She was distantly aware of Gunnar dropping the knife and lurching forward. As she crumpled and he caught her, she deliriously, dreamily thought, *wow his arms are as strong as they look*.

Chapter Five

Vanessa didn't realize how hungry she was until she sat cross-legged on the floor in front of the fireplace with a bowl of soup. She tried to show some manners and not just slurp it down, but it was difficult. The soup was a mixture of cabbage, root vegetables, and aromatic herbs in a thin broth, with thick chunks of meat. It made her feel warm and calm inside, and tasted strangely familiar, though she'd never eaten it before.

"What did you say this stuff was again?" she called out.

"Kjötsúpa," Gunnar called back.

She looked down at her bowl and rolled the word around on her tongue. "Kjötsúpa." The meat was lamb, and she of course translated the word in her head. It simply meant "meat soup."

Though it was after eight PM, soft daylight still shone through the windows. It hadn't gotten truly dark the entire time she'd been here. In the dead of night, the shadows lengthened to what could be called deep twilight for a few hours, and the sun sat low on the horizon, but true darkness, the kind she was used to back home, never happened. She was glad for it right now.

Gunnar walked into the living room with a duffel bag. He wore fresh jeans and a tight black t-shirt, since his clothes had been stained with blood from the stabbing experiment.

She tried not to stare at his arms. He had impressive biceps.

Must have lots of time to work out while keeping watch for supernatural creatures.

He dropped the bag on the couch and strode back into the kitchen.

She sucked down more soup. "What do you do here?" She couldn't sit in silence right now. "I mean, for a job?"

Did hundred-year-old people have to work? Surely, it didn't come with unfathomable riches as well.

"I take tourists around the fjord in my boat." He was banging around in the kitchen. "Most people here fish, but I was never very good at it. I cash in on the tourism instead."

She poked at a chunk of meat in her soup. "Do you like it?"

He returned, carrying a flat wooden box. "It's interesting. I've had a lot of odd jobs over the years. As ways to make money, it's not too taxing." He stuffed the box in the duffel bag.

"Does Aedan show tourists around too?"

He paused for a moment, then walked back to the kitchen. "He doesn't have time for it."

"You support both of you?" She looked around the room. The place wasn't a mansion, but it was decent. She couldn't imagine paying the bills with boat rides.

"You'd be surprised the savings one can accumulate over a century." He followed this with a soft chuckle.

"So, you—have a house, and pay the electric bill, and own a car, and go to the store and stuff? Like a normal person?" She wasn't sure why, but that sounded sad. If she lived so long, she'd make better use of her time, or imagined she would.

"I like to think I'm a normal person."

She looked up as he came back in the room. "I don't mean to be rude." She stirred her spoon around in the bowl. "I did just stab you and watch the wound magically close up. You can understand why I have a hard time thinking of you as an average guy."

He smiled wryly. "Even people who can't die need a warm place to sleep."

Though it was true, it was still absurd. Her gaze fell on the picture on the shelf. She thought again of the bizarre hallucination.

"She was pretty."

Gunnar arched an eyebrow. She nodded at the picture, and he looked over.

"I forget that picture is there sometimes."

He continued bringing things from the kitchen and shoving them in the bag: bottles of water, a leather pouch. It was so quiet inside the house, and outside, she could hear the crackle of the flames and his footsteps creaking on the floor. The silence made her tense, as if something might jump out any moment.

"What are you doing?" she finally asked.

"I told you, I have to build a fire."

She didn't think the things he was putting in the bag were for starting fires. She assumed he meant something like a campfire, but maybe it was more complicated than that.

"I'm going into the hills, about a kilometer away. It's a good walk in summer."

She frowned and lowered her bowl. "I'm going with you, right?" He seemed so tall, standing over her, like when she woke up on the island.

"I don't think that's a good idea. You should stay here."

"I'm not staying here alone." She quickly got to her feet. "I don't want to be by myself. What if they show up? I don't know how to defend myself from fairies."

"Huldufólk."

"Whatever." Normally, she wouldn't be so dismissive of someone's culture, but this wasn't about culture. It was about something way crazier. They didn't sound like the sort of creatures who deserved respect. "You can't leave me alone. What if something happens?"

He turned and walked into the kitchen. "It's more dangerous out there."

She followed him. She still wore his sweater. It had become like a protective blanket. It wouldn't work as a shield though, and it wouldn't hide her no matter how tight she curled up in it.

"It's dangerous for me to stay here alone." She plunked her bowl on the counter. "Let me go with you. What are you building a fire for?"

He opened a cupboard above the sink and pulled down a bottle. A bottle of whiskey, in fact. He studied it a moment, then walked past her to the living room.

"Do you really think it's a good idea to toss a few back around the fire?" She spoke sarcastically. "You can't get drunk right now. We need our heads about us."

"I agree." He jammed the bottle in the bag. "You shouldn't come. It's dangerous."

"Yeah, you said that. I agree with the second statement. Not so much the first."

While going out and sitting exposed on some hill wasn't her idea of a good time, she sure as hell wouldn't have more fun here alone.

He turned and looked at her. "I'm going to summon them."

"Them?"

"Them."

She was silent a moment. "You can do that?"

"Maybe." His gaze was fathomless. A chill washed over her. Though he looked the same as any normal person, something in his eyes spoke of his real age. Whatever stood before her—a man, or something else—he was not like any other human being she had ever met.

She swallowed. "A fire will summon them?"

"Possibly, among other things." He ran both hands through his hair, several times. "I want them to appear, so I can speak to them and find out what's going on. Why they did this."

"Well then, I definitely want to be there. I want to know the answer to that too." What did they look like? She could only picture some twisted, terrifying monster. After all, what other kind of being would do such horrible things?

Aedan didn't look like a monster, though. Maybe he had more of his mother's genes.

"It's easy to offend them." Gunnar sighed. "I don't want to make this worse. We might all be alive right now by their grace and I don't want to test that."

"And what if you offend them anyway, and I'm left here all alone, and they come for me next?"

"I know how to talk to them."

"Then let me come with you, and you do all the talking."

He sighed again, his broad chest expanding and shoulders slumping.

"Gunnar." She walked over and gripped his arm. "Don't leave me here. I want to go with you. I want to know who they are and why they did this to me. I have a right to know. I'm so scared, so lost and confused. I need some answers."

He looked down at her hand, then back up. He pulled it off his arm, gently, and held it between his own. "You have to obey what I tell you. If you go with me, you must do as I say."

She nodded, lips pressed together. She was half filled with terror, half expectation.

He squeezed his hands around hers. "They don't

like humans, and most of all, they don't like us arguing with them. If they come, no matter what they do or say, no matter how frustrating, you must not get angry."

She nodded again. "I won't speak, only listen." She considered something. "Will they speak English?"

"If they say anything, they'll make sure you understand." He let go of her hand. "We need to prepare." He looked down at her socked feet on the tile. "You need boots for walking." He looked around, at her dress boots next to the door. "Those won't do."

He went down the hallway and returned a minute later with a pair of hiking boots. They were obviously men's, but he handed them to her.

"Aedan's feet are smaller than mine. They might fit."

She put them on, and they were slightly too big, but not to the point they would be clownish or trip her up. Her toes almost touched the tips. She tied them extra tight to be sure, and even looped the laces around her ankles so they wouldn't slip off.

He brought her a heavy jacket and started coaching her as he put it on her. "Don't speak to them unless they ask you a direct question. Don't address them, don't ask questions. If they want you to speak, do so gently and respectfully."

"Doesn't seem fair, I have to be nice to them when they've done terrible things to me." She shrugged the coat over her shoulders. "A bit one-sided."

"Terribly. But remember, they hold all the power." He grabbed the jacket he'd worn to cut wood and pulled it on. "Sit in silence unless they demand otherwise."

"How can we defend ourselves, if we need to?"

He looked at her, tugging at the sleeve of his coat. "Do you think that's possible?"

"There isn't … anything?"

"If there was, do you think I would have put up with this for a century?"

That was both chilling and depressing.

"There are things that repel them, but you won't kill them." He looked her over. "Are you sure you want to do this?"

"Yes."

Gunnar grabbed his bag and they headed out the door.

She shoved her hands in her pockets and tried to ignore her racing heart. "What—do they look like?" she asked. "Are they scary and ugly?"

He looked back at her. His eyes glinted. "Quite the opposite."

The sun sat low in the sky, resting on the horizon above the walls of the fjord—they weren't mountains, after all. Chilly blue twilight blanketed the land, though the voluminous clouds over the water were tinged pink and yellow. The town was quiet. The wind whistled across the grass and grabbed at her hair.

"Stay close to me." He slung the strap of his bag over his shoulder. "It's a bit of a walk."

She managed to force a smile. "It's okay. The soup gave me my strength back."

Gunnar fetched the wagon of wood and they walked toward the hills. They were green but rocky, and the shadows sheltered thick in every nook and cranny. He led her along a trail, wide enough they could walk side by side. The landscape was serene and impossibly vast. She thought of Jessica and Steph, and all the pictures they'd taken of the scenery in Iceland. Her stomach twisted up in knots.

"What did you say the name of this town is?" She looked over her shoulder.

"Drangsnes." Gunnar's wagon rattled along behind them, and she got the impression he wasn't moving as fast as he was capable. "So, what do *you* do? For a job."

She looked forward. "I'm a pharmacy tech." *Was?* She couldn't imagine her position was still available. Her stomach ached harder.

"You give people medicine?" He walked so close they kept bumping shoulders. "You make prescriptions?"

"It's not as amazing as it sounds. I just put pills in bottles and tell people not to drink on their pain meds. I didn't even need any special schooling for it, just one class."

"Do you like it?"

She shrugged. "I always wanted to do something in medicine, but my parents couldn't afford med school. Maybe I could be an RN or something, one day. I'm still trying to figure out what I want to do with my life." She couldn't believe that had been her biggest concern just yesterday—or, one year ago. Now her worries were much bigger, and significantly more insane. "It pays the bills, so I can live on my own, and..."

She slowed, thinking of her small but cozy little apartment. Her car. The flower boxes out on the balcony that she planted in the spring. The set of crystal wine glasses Jessica gave her for her birthday, sitting on top the cabinet in the kitchen. It was all so overwhelming suddenly.

Gunnar stopped a few steps ahead and looked back at her. "What is it?"

"Everyone thinks I'm dead." She stared numbly into the distance. "They've replaced me at work, probably sold my car, and my place—my parents most likely packed up all my stuff and took it away." Her hands trembled, clenched beneath the long sleeves of the coat. "It's all gone. And for me it was only yesterday."

He walked back and took her arm, carefully. "You'll return home. You'll get your life back."

She looked at him, tears blurring her vision. "How will I explain where I've been?"

He shook his head. "I don't know. Let's find *out* where you've been first." His voice was tender, the worry in his eyes evident even in the dim light. "We'll figure it out."

She wiped her eyes roughly. No falling apart right now. She focused on the path ahead and took a deep breath.

Gunnar urged her along.

They were quiet, then she sniffed. "How did you end up settling down here?"

He chuckled softly. "The wind sort of blew me here."

The path meandered up the hill, and she soon realized both the jacket and sweater were overkill as she began to sweat. She would take the jacket off at the top. Until then, she kept her eyes on the uneven ground and tried not to stumble in her too-large boots. The wind whipped harder as they climbed, adding to the difficulty.

At the summit she stopped to catch her breath, heart pounding and uncomfortably hot beneath her layers. They looked back over the town, the houses now miniature at the bottom of the slope. The water spread out glimmering in all directions. The sun hung red beneath the canopy of clouds.

"What's it like, living so long?" She peeled the jacket off. "You've seen some history, huh?"

The wind ruffled his wild, loose curls. "It's just been my life, nothing more. You see history too, every day. Do you think of it that way?"

The air rushing up under the sweater and cooling the sweat on her skin was bliss. "I guess not. Does it ever get boring?"

"As boring as it is for anyone, I suppose." The sunset caressed his face, turning it golden. "I have things to keep me occupied."

She gazed at him, mesmerized. God, he was handsome. Not pretty, not cute. *Handsome.* Solid and finely sculpted, like carved ice. His eyes held her spellbound. They were so clear, so pale and blue. They reminded her of the glacier she'd walked on with her friends, smooth and bright and so cleanly cold.

A sensation stirred deep inside her, some old, familiar feeling, much like the notion she'd had on the boat that she knew him. It felt as ancient and enduring as the land they stood on. What the hell did it mean? She couldn't grasp or define it.

"Yeah." She pushed her hair back from her face. "You've moved all around the country, fallen in love. You drive a boat. Find passed out strangers." She smiled. "It sounds a lot more exciting than most lives, actually. More exciting than packing pills."

"I've been out of the country, too." He smiled in return. "But not for a long time."

"They let you leave?"

"My body is my prison, not Iceland."

That brought up uneasy questions. Would they follow her home? Would she always be their victim, even when she left here?

"How far does their magic reach?" She tucked her hair behind her ear to keep it from blowing around. "Can you ever escape it?"

"I've never managed to." He turned, toward the flat stretch of land in front of them. Another hill rose in the distance, dark against the deep blue sky.

She draped the jacket over her arm. "I suppose we're going up that one, too?"

"Yes, the place we're going is a place where people don't usually visit."

The grass shuddered in the wind. Apprehension gripped her. "Is this their land?" She kept her voice down. "Are we walking into their territory?"

"I wouldn't be so foolish." He motioned for her to follow as he started ahead. "The place we're going is neutral. A place for both of us. Remember what I told you. Be silent. Don't provoke them. Don't react. Let me lead."

She followed him, behind the wagon. "Why do you think they'll come if you build a fire in this place?"

His voice was grim. "Because they have before."
* * * *

They stopped in a shallow indentation between two hills. The ground was mossy, but a broad, clear spot encircled a dug out firepit. A wooden bench sat next to it, and on this Vanessa waited, the jacket draped over her knees, huddled into her sweater.

The wood in the firepit crackled as orange flames grew from it. Warmth bathed her face and hands. Sparks danced on the air and vanished.

"How do you summon them?" She was afraid to speak too loudly, and she kept glancing into the murky shadows beyond the light of the fire. What if these creatures descended upon them without warning? Would it be disrespectful if she screamed?

"I don't." Gunnar had dumped the odd contents of his bag on the ground next to the fire. "I just try, and wait, and hope they come."

He picked up the flat wooden box, opened it, and deposited the contents on the ground. She stared as the objects clanked into the dirt.

Knives. *Lots* of knives. Most were short and flat, like the one he'd made her stab him with. A few were longer and curved. They were all metal, both blade and handle. He picked up as many as he could in one hand and walked behind the bench.

She swiveled, wide-eyed. She watched as he bent, drove one into the ground, stepped a few feet, then drove another in. He continued doing this until he used up the knives, then walked over and grabbed some more.

"Um." She turned slowly. "What are you doing?"

He held one up in the firelight. "Iron."

She frowned.

"Iron repels huldufólk. As I said, we can't defend ourselves, but we can keep them from getting too close." He went back to driving the knives into the ground. It soon became clear he was making a circle around the fire.

She recalled the myth that iron inhibited supernatural creatures. She'd never imagined it would be real world trivia she'd actually need.

"These are knives I've collected over the years." He worked his way around the circle. "Pure iron is hard to come by now. Some of these are very old."

Each time he spiked another one into the earth, she felt slightly safer. The flames stretched taller on the wood, the warmth getting more intense.

"That doesn't offend them?"

He glanced up, his face flushed from bending. "They think it's cute, like a child playing. Some Icelanders put a horseshoe over their door still." He stood upright and slicked his hair back from his face. "Many only do it out of tradition, and most horseshoes aren't even iron anymore, so they don't help."

He grabbed up the last of the knives. Her gaze fell

on one. It had a thin, curved blade and the handle was cut into a flourish pattern. Before she realized it, she got to her feet and walked over to him. She stared at the knife in his hand.

"What?" he asked.

Incomprehensible thoughts flashed through her head, strange ideas that didn't seem to be her own, like when he'd coerced her to stab him, that moment of certainty how to wield the knife. Again, moving almost unconsciously, she took the knife from him. The metal was cool in her palm and the firelight glinted on the dulled blade.

"I think that's an older one." He frowned. "I don't remember where I got it."

She turned it over, studying it intently. The handle was pretty, and it seemed to fit perfectly in her hand. "Can I have it?"

His frown deepened. "You're not thinking of attacking them, Vanessa. It would not end well for you."

"No, absolutely not. I just—it'll make me feel safer. If I have some iron on me maybe they can't touch me."

He was silent, his expression apprehensive, maybe even a little scared. Slowly, he nodded. "All right, but put it away. Promise you won't do something foolish with it."

"I won't." She lowered it to her side. "There's no way I'd ever be brave enough to do something like that."

"Some can be braver than they think, when they're pushed to it." He glanced at the knife, and her face, then walked away.

She walked back to the bench and sat down. She gazed at the knife between her hands. The swirling designs on the handle were cut all the way through the metal. She rubbed her thumb over them.

What the hell was happening? These creatures must have done something to her brain when they erased her memory. She had never cared about knives. She had never stabbed a person. Yet, something in her head insisted she did and had.

Gunnar finished making the circle. The knife handles stood small and glinting, like a short, useless fence.

"Do you want some water?" He pulled a bottle out of his bag. "It was a long walk." He held it out to her.

She took it and tucked the knife under the jacket. She *was* thirsty. "Do we have to sit here all night?" She twisted the cap off.

"I don't know." He pulled out the pouch.

Again, she was confused by what she saw as he poured the contents into his hand.

The pouch was full of coins—big, small, gold, silver, copper. He walked to the edge of the circle and tossed them into the grass beyond, like scattering birdseed. They twinkled in the firelight as they rained down.

He next pulled out the bottle of whiskey. She gaped at him as he took it to where he'd tossed the coins and plunked it in the grass as well. He did this as though it were the most commonplace thing to do. After that, he got his own bottle of water out of the bag and came over to her. The bench creaked as he sat down. "Now we wait." He twisted the cap. "And hope."

She looked between him and the grass. A few coins glinted there.

"What … was that?"

He quirked an eyebrow and took a drink.

"Why did you just do that? Is it another repellant thing?"

He lowered his bottle and smiled, his eyes

affectionate. "It's a gift. I offer the huldufólk gifts to show my respect. If they choose to come, they will take the things I offer, and hopefully, be pleased."

"So … they like money and drinking? They get torn up and go shopping or something?"

He chuckled. "They like shiny things. Maybe, they just like taking things from us that we enjoy. It's always been tradition to give them alcohol and coins." He shrugged. "That is the way."

These creatures were starting to sound stupid. They wouldn't go near metal and wanted to take people's money and booze. She supposed it was much better than, say, a blood sacrifice, of course.

"It's weird." She tucked her water bottle between her knees. "I'm sorry this all seems so crazy to me."

"It is crazy. Just because I live it doesn't mean it's normal."

She looked into the fire. It had grown large enough the air was toasty warm now, and she peeled the sweater off. "All right, so I guess we just wait?"

"We just wait."

Chapter Six

Vanessa's bottom hurt from sitting on the bench, so she moved to the ground. Gunnar joined her, their backs against it. He'd taken his jacket off too, and she was once more trying not to stare at his arms, all bronzed and sinewy in the firelight.

"It feels like we've been out here forever." She dropped her head back and gazed up at the sky. The clouds had crept in, thick and gray. "How long has it been?"

Gunnar picked up his phone from the ground next to him and looked at the screen. "A little over an hour." He scanned the shadows beyond the fire. "I brought some food, if you're hungry."

She didn't think she could eat. Her stomach was a minefield of nerves. "I'm okay." She lifted her head. Her entire body was tense. She had no idea what was coming, or how they would arrive. Just sitting there was exhausting.

"Do you have a significant other back home?" Gunnar sat with his knees bent, an arm resting on one, hand dangling. He rubbed his index finger over his thumb idly. "A husband or boyfriend? Or … girlfriend?"

"I'm straight." She drew her knees up too and flexed her feet in her oversized boots. "But no." She let out a dry laugh. "I haven't been in a serious relationship in a while. The stars just haven't aligned for me." She sighed. "I actually had this secret idea, when we were planning our trip here. I dreamt of meeting some hot Nordic guy. We'd have a brief but passionate fling, and I'd be sad when I had to go home. We'd have a long-distance thing over Skype for a few weeks until we got bored of each other."

Gunnar grinned. "Sounds like fun."

"It didn't quite work out, did it?" Her eyes were getting itchy from the smoke, but she didn't want to move far from the fire. "I'm glad there's no one back home. He might have moved on by now."

"Silver lining."

"I keep trying to imagine how I'd feel if it had been one of my friends they messed with instead—if it had been Jessica or Steph. If they disappeared and were thought dead, you know? And then they show up a year later. How would I react?"

"People will be stunned." His voice was soft. "But good stunned, I would think. Wouldn't you be happy to see your friend alive?"

She looked at her feet, still flexing them inside the boots. "I can't imagine what they've been through. I can't imagine how my parents have suffered. It must be horrible."

He squeezed her arm. "I'm sorry. This is a bad thing, I know."

She had to stop thinking about it. Once she found out what the hell they'd done to her, and why, she would get out of here and find her way home. All her loved one's suffering would end. And hers.

"What about you?" She looked at him. "The woman you were with, the one who's old now. How long ago were you two together?"

He slid his hand off her arm. "It's been almost ten years, since I last saw her."

"Wow. And there hasn't been anyone since?"

A sad smile touched his lips. "As I draw closer to the end of my punishment, I'm less inclined to bring anyone into it. I don't know what's going to happen. All I know of the huldufólk, really, comes from Aedan's mother."

"His mother?"

He lowered his voice. "She learned things from his father and wrote them in a diary. It's all we have. I think if they knew, they would take it away."

She wanted to ask more, but she realized this was not a good place to talk about it.

"I don't know what happens when a punishment is served." His voice returned to normal volume. "They may let me go, or they may end my life. I hope they think I've suffered enough, but I'm human, so maybe no suffering is enough."

She shifted onto her hip, so she faced him. "Do you still love her, the woman you were with? What's her name?"

He smiled again, still sad. "Eydis. I suppose I do. And I suppose I still love my wife—I remember what it was like to love her, anyway. How being with her made me feel. I worked for her father, herding his sheep. That's how I met her."

She laughed "Herding sheep? Really?"

He turned toward her as well, so they were face to face. "Her father wanted better for her. It was 1918. He wanted her to marry a merchant or a man in government, but instead she found me, out in the pasture."

Vanessa tried to wrap her head around it. *1918.*

"I remember she was strong-willed." He gazed off. "She was rugged, like the land. She ran the farm for her father because he wasn't in the best of health. And she made me laugh." He smiled. "We would sit on the beach and watch the waves. Every once in a while, I remember the little things. They come back, these memories, little sparks of feeling, then she fades into the mist again."

"So they really punished you for digging up their land? For just trying to build a house?"

"I wanted us to have a home of our own, after we married. I swore I'd build it for her. I didn't know the piece of land I bought was theirs. I didn't know it was sacred until I violated it."

"It was an accident." She reached over and touched his hand on the ground between them. "Why wouldn't they let you make amends or something? You could give them, I don't know—a bottle of whiskey? Some coins?"

"I told you, forgiveness is not their strength." His gaze darkened. "I'd already dug and laid the foundation when they came. I should have learned more about the land before I broke into it."

"How does anything get built in this country?" She snorted. "I mean, if you have no idea what land is theirs, and they get upset when you build on it anyway, how do you guys have any civilization at all?"

"Well, even today, building projects get sabotaged—machinery stops working, people get hurt— you read about it all the time. Sometimes, giving offerings helps. But it's their land, all of it. It always was, and it's the price we pay for living here."

It sounded insane. If she had known all this, would she have even come on this trip? A place where supernatural creatures were ready to cut down humans for every unwitting misstep sounded like a nightmare world. And yet, an entire country of people persisted.

She wanted to change the subject, before she got angry and started thinking harder about that knife. "What about Eydis?" She still had her hand over his.

His face softened. "She was a tour guide, but she's retired now. She took visitors on driving tours."

"We went on one of those. It was fun."

"She was restless and outdoorsy. She said she could never work a job that kept her between four walls.

She knows everything about Iceland. I met her in a coffee shop, while her tour group was taking a break. She made me laugh too."

Vanessa moved her leg over and nudged him with her knee. "I guess I better start telling jokes, huh?"

They both laughed. Her cheeks grew hot. That was probably the smoothest line she'd ever used. Where the hell had it come from?

He gazed at her, smiling, but his smile faded. "I'm sorry this happened to you." He touched her wrist and stroked his fingertips across it. "I'm sorry they did this to you."

"I'm glad it was you who found me. If it had to happen, at least someone who had some clue what was going on stumbled across me. I got lucky." Her skin tingled at his touch.

They were close enough she could lean against him if she wanted to. The tension between them was a bright, magnetic pull. If only she had met him under better circumstances. He definitely qualified as that hot Nordic man she'd been dreaming of.

Suddenly, his expression changed. His smile dropped away, and his eyes widened. He turned his head and looked past the fire. She didn't need to ask what was wrong, because she felt it too—the wind turned colder, and at the same time everything around them seemed to fall still, as if the earth paused and the land held its breath.

She was afraid to look. Slowly, she turned her head.

Her heart seemed to stop in her chest and she felt the color drain from her face. Until now, some part of her still clung to the hope that this was all a big prank, despite all evidence to the contrary. That doubt was erased now, as she knew, even from a distance, what she beheld was otherworldly.

A featureless figure stood atop the hill on the other side of the flames, a black silhouette against the gray clouds and indigo twilight. Vanessa could only make out the folds of a gown and strands of fluttering hair so long it was past the figure's waist. It stood perfectly still, and though its face was hidden Vanessa could feel it staring at them. Though the shape was human, the presence emanating from it was anything but.

Gunnar got to his feet, his hand outstretched in a protective gesture in front of her. She rose too, but only to the height of the bench, and sat on it, staring. Gunnar moved closer to her and placed his hand on her shoulder.

"Hello, beautiful one!" Gunnar called out. "Thank you for gracing us with your presence."

Vanessa's head buzzed. As before, she swore he was somehow speaking Icelandic and English at the same time.

The figure moved down the hill—it didn't walk, but appeared to glide like a ghost, like smoke. She cringed closer to Gunnar and he squeezed her shoulder.

"I'm here to beg questions of you." Gunnar sounded much steadier than she could have managed right now. "I would be most honored if you give me answers."

The thing moved into the light of the fire. Until it reached the edge of the circle, the firelight seemed not to touch it. However, as all was revealed, Vanessa wished it had stayed back. At least it stopped, as Gunnar said it would, and didn't step over the knives.

She clutched the belt loop on Gunnar's jeans, clinging to him. "Jesus Christ," she gasped.

Gunnar slipped his arm around her and pulled her against him, perhaps trying to shut her up. "Don't be afraid," he murmured. "She's here to speak to us."

The creature was indeed a woman, but like no woman Vanessa had ever seen before. She was pale and looked like death. And yet, she was hauntingly beautiful. Her face was like alabaster, her dark lips full and her cheekbones high and sharp. She wore a long gray gown and cloak. Her hair was black and hung past her waist. Her eyes were black as well: wholly black, like the eyes of a spider. They gleamed unnervingly in the firelight, and they were so expressionless, her head tilted just so, that Vanessa couldn't tell which one of them she was looking at.

Vanessa couldn't move under that impersonal gaze. She clung to Gunnar, staring back.

"Beautiful one," he spoke again. "I beg you, tell me, have I offended you? Has Aedan offended you?"

The woman briskly knelt, making Vanessa flinch at the sudden movement. She began picking up coins from the grass and pushed them into a pouch at her side. Her hair hung over her shoulders, thick like an ebony curtain.

Vanessa watched mesmerized, the faint clink of each coin dropping into the pouch strangely absurd under the circumstances. They really *did* like coins.

"Have we angered you?" Gunnar asked, louder this time.

The woman kept her gaze down as she collected the coins. She spoke. "No, you have not." Her voice was like the wind over the rocks, airy and emotionless.

Gunnar drew Vanessa closer. She was practically wrapped around him. "Did you bring this woman to us? Did you leave her on the island for us to find?"

Despite Gunnar's closeness, she didn't feel protected. She thought wildly of the knife, in the pocket of the jacket, on the bench nearby. If that thing came at her, she'd surely panic and try to defend herself.

The woman looked up and focused obviously on Vanessa. "My people did."

Vanessa froze. She stared back, trapped between horror and a flare of rage. Here was the answer. It *was* the huldufólk. But why?

"Is she a warning?" Gunnar asked. "Are we in danger of making you unhappy?"

The woman finished collecting the coins, picked up the bottle of whiskey, and rose. Her presence filled the twilight and turned it to darkness. It even seemed to mute the fire.

"She is not a warning." The woman spoke now with pomp and authority. "Her presence here is to punish another, but that is not your concern."

Vanessa untangled herself from Gunnar's waist. Despite her fear, she stood up.

Gunnar slipped his arm around her waist. "I don't understand." He gazed at the woman. "What do you mean?"

Punish another? Who on earth was her "presence" here punishing, except her friends and family? The huldufólk would have no vendetta against them. Apart from her two friends, none of them had ever even been to Iceland.

The woman looked at Gunnar. "Your penance is growing short. Your time of repayment is almost over. She serves a purpose, nothing more. It has nothing to do with you."

Gunnar gazed back at her. "I don't understand. Do you want me to take care of her, like Aedan?"

She was not going to stick around to be cared for, no matter how handsome he was.

"Do with her as you wish." The woman made a dismissive gesture with her hand. "She is not our concern now."

Vanessa's outrage reached a boiling point, and she could no longer stay silent and cowering. She lurched forward. "Where have I been for the past year? What did you do to me?"

"Vanessa." Gunnar gripped her arm. "No!"

"Why did you make it look like I was dead?" Vanessa clenched her fists. "Why have I lost a year of my life? I didn't do anything to you. I didn't even know you existed!"

The woman gazed at her.

Gunnar pulled her back to his side and locked his arms tight around her shoulders. "Don't," he whispered in her ear. "Stop questioning her."

"I deserve a fucking answer!" Vanessa trembled. Let this thing do what it wanted, let it be offended. She couldn't spend the rest of her life not knowing what the hell happened. She couldn't go on like it was nothing.

The woman tilted her head, those black orbs still fixed on Vanessa. She spoke calmly. "You deserve death, but you received mercy, because it was more fitting. You're lucky."

Vanessa was baffled. "What?" She hadn't done anything to deserve death—but then, Gunnar was punished just for trying to build a house. Had she violated their sacred ground too?

"Take your life and treasure it," the woman said. "We will not be so forgiving if you offend us again."

"How did I offend you?" Vanessa tried to soften her voice and speak a little more respectfully, but it was difficult. "I didn't mean to. Did I violate your land? I didn't know it was yours, if I did."

Gunnar gripped her painfully tight. He probably wanted to clamp his hand over her mouth.

"Why can't I remember anything?" she continued, more out of fury than bravery. "Did you erase my memory of the past year? Why don't I know where I've been, or what happened to me?"

"The twisting of your mind was not our doing."

Vanessa narrowed her eyes. "Then who did it?"

"Live your life. Be grateful." With that, she turned away, her hair drifting around her like a black veil.

"Wait!" Vanessa leapt forward, but Gunnar held her. "Where have I been? What the hell are you talking about? I don't understand anything you've said!"

"Don't, don't." Gunnar struggled to hold her. "That's the only warning she'll give you."

Vanessa watched the woman glide away, into the shadows and back up the hill, so swift she was at the top before another word could be spoken. Vanessa was furious. She wanted answers. But the creature left her with even more questions than before.

Like a wisp of smoke, she vanished into the air at the top of the hill.

Vanessa gasped.

One moment she was there, the next she was gone.

"No!" She broke out of Gunnar's grip. "What's happening to me!" She wanted to run up the hill, but she knew it was pointless. The woman was gone, not down the other side but into realms Vanessa couldn't reach.

Gunnar stared into the darkness, his face stony. He looked at her, eyes flashing. "I told you not to speak to them."

She screamed, clutching her hair. "Where the fuck have I been? What did they do to me!"

He grabbed her as her knees weakened and held her.

She sobbed against his chest. What had she done to deserve this, and who the hell was this punishing, if not her? She had to get out of this country. She had to get home and as far away from this horror as possible.

"Shh." Gunnar stroked her hair. "I don't think we'll get any more answers, but we'll try to figure this out."

She wept, clinging to him. "I want to go home," she sobbed.

Chapter Seven

"I have no ID, or passport. I'm dead. I have no money." Vanessa sat on the couch, staring blankly at the dead fireplace. "How the hell am I supposed to get a plane ticket home?"

Gunnar dropped several folded blankets and a pillow on couch. "I can help with the money. The rest, I don't know."

She'd taken off the boots but still wore the jacket, as she could barely function right now. "Is there a US embassy here?" A spark of hope flared in her hollow chest. "Maybe if I talk to them, and I can call my parents again, I can convince them it's really me and there's been a terrible mistake. Maybe someone will believe me."

Gunnar sat down next to her. "We'll go to Reykjavik. We should wait until Aedan comes back, though. It'll be safer if we're all together. We still don't know why this happened."

She sagged. She was drained, and sore, and her mind had turned to mush. Too much stress. "What did she mean?" She spoke softly. "She said this was to punish someone else, but I can't imagine who. The only people it's punishing are my family and friends, and they didn't do anything to the huldufólk. They couldn't have."

He rubbed her shoulder. "Something must have happened, in the past year. Just because the last thing you remember is being outside the bar, doesn't mean it started there."

She looked at him.

"Maybe they erased your memory back to that moment for a reason. Whatever happened, it happened after that night."

She straightened. "She said they weren't the ones

who 'twisted my mind.' Then who did?" She paused. "What about the elves? You said people don't think they're different from the huldufólk, but they are."

He slipped his hand off her shoulder. "The elves are supposed to be helpful and they don't act as cruelly." He rubbed his chin. "And ... I've never seen one."

She frowned.

He shrugged. "I don't think they're real." He said this with sheepishness. "Ævintýrafund."

"What does that..."

Fairy tale.

"Fairy tale." He said it at the same time she thought it. "They're creatures of imagination, unlike the huldufólk."

She rose, rubbing her temples. "Okay, this weird thing keeps happening in my head." She paced next to the couch. "Every time you speak in Icelandic, I understand it. Like, I hear it in English, sort of. I know what you're saying. And I don't speak Icelandic."

He gazed up at her. "Maybe whatever they did to your mind, you do now."

"That's nuts!"

"All of this is."

She stopped and lowered her hands. "I found an article online earlier, about my death. My friends said I went missing after I'd gone outside to get some air. They didn't see me again after that. Whatever happened in that year to start all this, I wasn't with them. They didn't witness it."

Gunnar tilted his head. "But, someone did."

"What do you mean?"

"At least, someone saw what happened that night." He stood too. "You remember which bar?"

"Yes."

"When we go to Reykjavik, we'll go there.

Maybe they have security footage from that night. Especially if you went missing, it might have been saved to give to the lögreglan. They might still have it."

Her spirits lifted, for the first time today. "Yes." She clasped her hands together. "I mean, something had to have happened that night. Where did I go?"

"We'll see."

He was rumpled and wind-blown, and yet lovely, standing there in front of her. She wanted to reach out and rub her hands over his chest but resisted. Instead, she looked at the blankets and pillow.

"I don't know how much sleep I'm going to get."

"You should try." He touched her arm. "I'll heat up some more soup. It'll help."

He also brought her a t-shirt and pair of sweats. She changed in the bathroom, grateful to get out of her jeans and blouse. The clothes were a little big, as they were men's, of course. She sniffed the shoulder of the t-shirt and smiled. It smelled like Gunnar.

While she ate another bowl of soup, he built up the fire again.

"It gets cold at night, even in summer." He stoked the wood with a long metal poker. "And damp. It feels like it will rain tonight." Though it was nearly midnight, dull blue light still pressed against the windows.

"Is that iron?" She eyed the poker and slurped her soup.

He looked over his shoulder and smiled. "No."

She glanced toward the door. "And you don't have an iron horseshoe over your door either?"

"If I did that, Aedan couldn't enter the house. That's why this isn't iron either. He couldn't build a fire."

She paused eating. "Oh, right." She stirred the

soup. "He doesn't look like them. He must favor his mother, huh?"

"Most halflings don't look like them. That's why they're hard to recognize, even for the huldufólk."

She stared at him. "Wait, there's more? There's lots of them born to human mothers?"

"More than should be."

"Hypocrites." She took another bite.

He looked back at the fireplace.

She shrugged. "They hate us. They want to torture us for making simple mistakes, but they like fucking us, apparently."

"I explained, not all of them hate humans." He pulled the screen in front of the fire. "But the ones who do like us suffer for it, when their children are discovered."

Had Aedan's father paid for it? She assumed both his parents had, and that's why Gunnar was his guardian.

Gunnar rose and dusted his hands on his jeans. "We should both sleep. You must be exhausted."

She was, but sleep didn't come easy.

She lay stiff on the couch, gazing through the gauzy curtains over the window above her. The sky was heavy with dark clouds. The lights were off, but the fire filled the room with a flickering orange glow. Gunnar had gone off to his room. Every sound made her twitch: a pop of a log on the fire, a distant rumble of thunder. Every time the wind whistled around the window she held her breath and listened. What if one of them just walked through the front door? What if they were out there watching the house?

Her body ached, and she felt like she'd run a marathon today. Who knew, before this, exactly how much sleep she'd been getting. The idea that she might not have rested well for an entire year disturbed her.

She tried to close her eyes, but in the darkness behind her eyelids she saw that pale creature standing at the edge of the knife circle, her eyes alien and bug-like. She heard her voice speaking like the wind.

Her paranoia intensified, until she could no longer stay put. She felt like a child, quivering in the dark, wanting to run to her parents' room. Truth be told, she'd give anything to run to her parents' room right now. Thinking about that made her want to cry, on top of feeling alone and frightened.

She got up from the couch, grabbed her pillow and a blanket, and padded down the darkened hallway. She knew the door for the bathroom. The others were open, except for one. Hugging the pillow and blanket, still feeling like a little kid, she timidly knocked.

She heard movement inside the room. The door inched open and Gunnar peeked out. "What's wrong?"

"I know this sounds dumb," she said, her voice trembling and tears burning her eyes, "but I'm really, really scared right now. I don't want to be alone." A tear streaked down her cheek. "Can I stay with you? I'll curl up in a corner or something."

He opened the door fully, and the worry in his eyes faded. "It's not dumb at all."

She was momentarily distracted from her distress as Gunnar was shirtless, and his clothes were cruel for covering him up prior to this. His chest was broad, his shoulders wide and the rest of him beautifully toned. Combined with his tight, flat stomach—which she'd seen already—he looked like a damn fitness model. He wore sweat pants as well, which hung low on his hips.

She struggled not to stare. His hair was a mess and he looked soft and huggable. Or rather, climbable.

"Come in." He stepped back so she could enter the room. "I won't make you sleep in a corner."

She walked in. The room smelled like him, like her t-shirt: a manly, musky scent with a touch of his fruity cologne. It was small and contained a double bed with a tall wooden headboard, a vanity-dresser combo, and a TV, next to a closet with a folding door. Across from the bed were two windows, the curtains open. The view looked out on the hills behind the house. She wondered if he left the curtains open to keep watch.

"Um." He brushed against her as he stepped around her. "I'll sleep on the floor, you can have the bed." He started dragging pillows off.

She hesitated. It was his bed, and she had no right to run him out of it just because she was a scaredy-cat. "It's big enough for both of us, I don't mind." She wiped her eyes. "If you don't mind."

He paused in removing the pillows. His eyes gleamed in the dim light. "Are you sure?"

She nodded and walked around to the other side, still clutching her blanket and pillow. "You're a gentleman, aren't you?" She managed a smile. "And I think I'll be more likely to get some sleep if someone is close by. Especially someone who knows about … them. And how to fend them off."

He tossed the pillows back on the bed. "I wouldn't be in this situation if I knew how to fend them off." There was humor in his voice, but it was dark.

She crawled into bed. "Just let me pretend."

The mattress was soft, and she wrapped herself up in her blanket—not because she worried he would touch her, but because she felt safer in a cocoon. He crawled in beside her and slipped under the blanket that was on the bed. There was enough room they had a few feet of space between them.

She wondered if he'd chosen a big bed so he had room for female visitors. One couldn't live a hundred years without some fun.

"Try to rest," he murmured. "Don't worry, they've never entered this house before."

The faint blue light traced the sharp lines of his face, his hair soft against the pillow, eyes glittering. The bed smelled even more like him and it both comforted and distracted her.

"In any case..." He rolled his head so he was staring at the ceiling. "I think she made it perfectly clear she has no more words for us. They won't try to make contact again. We won't see them."

She glanced at the windows, looking out on the murky twilight. Rain spattered the glass.

"Is that why you have the curtains open?" She snuggled down in her blanket.

He didn't respond.

* * * *

Vanessa walked in an alien landscape—and yet, she recognized it. She had been here before, and yet she had never been here. The night was cold and the wind bit to the bone. The clouds were thick and no stars shone through.

She walked down a slope, toward a dark body of water that stretched out before her into eternity. Waves crashed against black sand below, seafoam frothing white between rocks. More rocks, huge and jagged, littered the landscape around her. She had to navigate around them. Mist hung thick and low to the ground, and she walked through it like wading through snow.

This looked like another planet, and yet, she knew where she was. This was Reynisfjara, the black sand beach in the south. The basalt spires of the Reynisdrangar rose out of the sea in the distance, like watchful gods of the night. The ground was stiff with ice beneath the mist. She wasn't far from home, but she was farther than she had ever been.

How could she know this place? She had toured Iceland, and they had come to this beach, but she hadn't walked on any clifftops.

As she gripped a rock taller than her for balance, she was struck by the paleness of her hand on it, by the shortness of her fingers. This wasn't her hand. And was that blood on her fingers?

Before she could examine closer, a sound made her whip her head around and look back up the misty, frozen slope. Someone—something—followed her. She felt and heard it approach.

At the top of the slope, seemingly miles from where she stood, a light flashed, a small glimmer raking across the rocks. Someone was searching—with a flashlight? No, it didn't look bright enough for that.

A lantern.

Was someone calling to her? A voice borne by the wind and flung out over the sea, to be lost forever.

The thing that followed was closing in, though she saw nothing. It crawled toward her beneath the mist.

"Who is it?" she called out. It was not in English.

Nothing answered.

She turned and continued down, faster, gripping the rocks as she passed for support, her feet slipping on the wet ground. She wore a heavy black dress. Her shawl fluttered behind her, offering no real protection. She was so cold she could barely feel it anymore.

I will die here. Her mind raced. *I will throw myself into the sea before I let it catch me.*

She stopped on a snowy ledge overlooking the black sand. The drop was too far. She would perish. She looked back.

The light was gone. The voice, gone. But

something loomed close by, something that glided toward her. She saw it then, tall and black and elegant.

One of them.

She was terrified, and yet her heart pounded with determination. A voice whispered then, a voice like the wind and the crashing waves. *You don't have to suffer. It doesn't have to be this way.*

She lurched back, stumbled, and realized quickly she'd misjudged how close she was to the edge. She gasped as she fell, as the earth disappeared beneath her and she plummeted through the air toward the sand.

This is the end!

Vanessa jerked awake.

Her heart pounded against her ribs. In a moment of fear and disorientation, she struggled inside her blanket cocoon, sweaty and frantic. She sat up, and her surroundings came rushing in.

The light through the windows was brighter now, a golden, pre-dawn light she would typically associate with very early morning. However, she had no real idea what time it was. She didn't see a clock anywhere in the room, and she wasn't about to presume to grab Gunnar's phone lying on a table on the other side of the bed.

Rain still pattered on the window, harder now than when she'd fallen asleep, but not a downpour, only a shower. The hills beyond were obscured in fog.

An ominous sensation filled her. Someone was out there, watching.

Watching *her*, specifically.

She shuddered and tried to shake it off. She was just creeped out by the dream. Was it something they'd planted in her head? She couldn't otherwise explain how she'd known where she was.

The blanket was too hot now and she unwound herself from it. Gunnar was sprawled on his back, his face turned away and the covers around his waist. He drew slow, shallow breaths, obviously undisturbed by her thrashing. She tried not to look at his chest, though it was just—there. Traced by the light, all on display, for her to take in. He was asleep and wouldn't even know she was staring.

She rolled onto her side so her back was to him and pressed her face into the pillow, screwing her eyes shut. She needed some more rest.

As she attempted to drift off again, listening to the rain on the glass, remnants of the dream flitted through her head. The darkness, the rocks, the water. The figure swooping down on her. The lantern light, winking in and out.

The sensation that someone was watching her persisted. No, nothing was out there in the rain, she was just stressed and losing her mind. She tried to ignore it.

Gunnar shifted, sighing and mumbling. His presence made her feel better.

He shifted closer. She snapped her eyes open when he plunked an arm across her and wrapped it around her torso.

"Hera," he murmured.

She blinked, turning her head slightly. He didn't move. He was still asleep.

Hera. That was a name. A woman's name.

She wasn't sure what to do. She lay stiff, staring at the wall. Her heart tripped and her stomach fluttered. This wasn't—bad. Not at all. In fact, it was kind of nice. It had been a while since she'd felt the warm, heavy weight of a man's body against hers.

A handsome, kind, helpful, good-smelling man, *at that*.

Who was Hera, though? He must be dreaming she was someone he'd had in his bed before. It wasn't the name of the woman he'd been with for twenty years. He'd said her name was Eydis. Did it matter?

She could probably wiggle out from under his arm without waking him and save him the embarrassment of realizing what he'd done. Then again, she could lay there and go back to sleep, without feeling like any moment a monster would crawl up under the covers and devour her.

With a smile, she closed her eyes. She even pressed back, just a little. He felt so strong, so protective, even if he was dreaming she was someone else.

The watching sensation receded. So did the shadows in her mind, at least for now.

Chapter Eight

Vanessa sat at the kitchen table, Gunnar's laptop open in front of her. All searches for advice produced little return. The internet didn't have much to offer to people whose dead bodies had been discovered but weren't actually dead. She found some stories about people who had been missing and turned up after being declared dead, but she wasn't exactly *missing*. Her family knew exactly where "she" was.

She thought about emailing her parents and friends, but she feared that would get as kindly a response as calling them had. She didn't want to upset them more.

Despite the temptation, she also stayed away from Facebook. Several times, she started to go there, but the anxiety at the possibility of seeing some sort of memorial was too much. It would be like attending her own funeral, and she'd have a breakdown again.

Gunnar brought her a plate and bowl and set them down next to her. "Did you find anything?"

The rain was gone, and he looked fresh and cuddly in the sunlight streaming through the kitchen windows. His hair was a golden unkempt mess, and he wore sweats and a gray t-shirt. She tried not to think too much about the sensation of his arm wrapped around her.

"Not really. Thank you." She pulled the bowl over. It was filled with thick oatmeal topped with brown sugar. The warm, sweet scent made her stomach growl. The plate held yogurt and berries, and several hearty slabs of toast. She hadn't eaten this good since she lived at home.

She pushed that thought out of her head before it made her sad, and dug into her oatmeal.

Gunnar walked back to the counter and poured a cup of coffee. "Maybe this will resolve itself in a way we're not expecting."

She chewed and swallowed. "What do you mean?"

"You made two calls from my phone." He looked over his shoulder. "What if the people you called get suspicious and have the calls traced? They'll try to catch a scammer and find you alive instead. Maybe you should try again."

She hadn't thought of that. Perhaps, despite the mental trauma it would cause, she should call them back. Over and over. Just keep calling, until they contacted the police.

However...

"That would be super stressful for my parents. Especially when they think I'm in my grave." She looked down at her oatmeal. "And there's no guarantee the police would even care enough to do something about it or be able to trace the calls here." She stirred her spoon around slowly. "I want to try a few other things first."

"I understand."

She looked at the computer screen, wondering if there was anything else she could search. "I could just cut out the middle man and get the police involved again. Tell them the truth—or, well, as much as I can without sounding crazy. I lost my memory, I don't know what happened over the past year, but I'm definitely not dead. We know now that the huldufólk didn't put me here to threaten you or Aedan, so you're not in danger if I do that."

"I wouldn't be so sure." He walked to the table with his cup in hand. "She spoke in riddles, as they often do. I'm not ready to believe we're not *all* in danger, at least in some way." He sat down across from her. "Let's go to Reykjavik first, and see if we can find anything. Then you can tell them your story. Your disappearance is documented in Reykjavik anyway."

He was right. She wanted to see that security footage too, if it existed and was still available.

She continued eating her oatmeal. It was thicker and heartier than American oatmeal, and she liked the texture. Gunnar sipped his coffee and gazed at her over the cup. He lowered it and smiled sheepishly. His eyes were pale in the light, clear and luminous.

"I'm sorry," he said. "About this morning."

Heat flashed across her cheeks. She'd woken up the second time to find him already out of bed. He must have been in the same position when he woke up.

"What do you mean?" She casually sipped her own coffee.

"I was snuggling you in my sleep." He rubbed the back of his neck. "I must have been dreaming. I didn't mean to."

She could pretend she hadn't realized it, but it probably wouldn't be very convincing considering she was blushing like crazy. She avoided his gaze. "It's okay, I didn't mind."

She almost asked him who Hera was, but she didn't want to embarrass him further.

"Still, I promised to be a gentleman, and I wasn't."

He was cute, all bashful and awkward, and it made her feel a little less dumb herself. If he could live as long as he had and still have cringe-worthy moments, she was doing fine. She'd only had twenty-three years to perfect being human.

"You kept me safe and helped me sleep." She smiled. "You were a perfect gentleman. It was exactly what I needed. Thank you."

He smiled too and seemed to relax. "Would you like to go out on my boat today?"

She arched an eyebrow. "Like a sightseeing tour?"

"Yes, I suppose like that. I can take you out and show you the fjords. There's a lot to see this time of year, and to see it from the water is best. Trust me."

She looked at the laptop. Sitting here all day, trying to tell herself not to look up more articles about her death or stalk anyone's Facebook page would drive her right over the edge, which she now stood all too precariously upon.

"Aedan will be back tomorrow." He seemed to read her thoughts. "We can't do much until then. You shouldn't sit here and dwell on things, if you can avoid it. A boat ride will help take your mind off it."

She doubted that but getting out in the fresh air might clear her head.

"All right." She pushed the laptop away, so she could focus on her delicious food. "I've only been on a boat with my dad, when I was a little kid. We'd go to this river near our house, and he'd take his boat so he could fish. I hated putting a worm on a hook. I'd make him do it every time."

Sadness threatened to overwhelm her again. She stuffed it down.

Gunnar smirked. "Don't worry, no worms on my boat."

"I don't want to keep you from your job." She shrugged. "I know this has been a terrible disruption to your life and I'm sorry. I'm sure you didn't expect to have to take care of a lost dead girl this week."

He smiled gently. "When you've been around this long, you need a little excitement now and then." He sat back and sipped from his cup. "You're the most exciting thing that's happened to me in a very long time, trust me." He winked.

He wasn't so awkward now. She grinned and went back to eating.

The yogurt was less like the stuff that came in little cups in the supermarket, and more like a thick cheese mixture, called skyr. She liked the texture of it as well. Icelandic food was wonderful through and through, and evoked a deep response in her, like something she'd been missing for years and didn't even realize it. Though her stomach was in a constant state of nervous agitation, she made herself eat so she'd have strength.

After breakfast, Gunnar announced he was going to get dressed. She needed to as well, and Gunnar said he would give her a pullover sweater as it would be chilly on the water. After he left the kitchen, she drew the laptop back over, unable to resist it.

What was the name of the place in her dream? *Reynisfjara.* She didn't know how to spell it, but she typed out how it sounded and hoped Google would figure it out.

It did. When she clicked on the pictures her heart began to race.

There were the cliffs she'd seen, and the black sand, and the rolling ocean. Three basalt pillars rose from the water. They had spent an hour there on their sightseeing tour, but they hadn't gone up on the cliffs. You also couldn't see the tops of them from the beach.

So how did she know what it looked like up there?

Gunnar came back to the kitchen, carrying several thick wool sweaters. "You can try these on and find one that fits. They will all be big, I think."

She still gazed at the screen. "Thanks." She spoke absently.

Gunnar looked at the laptop. "Are you all right? What's wrong?"

She turned the computer toward him. "Do you know this place?"

He paused for a moment, appearing to hold his breath. "Yes. It's in the south."

"It's called … Reynisfjara?"

"*Reynisfjara.*" He spoke slowly, correcting her pronunciation. "It's—actually where I'm from, originally. At least, near there." His expression turned guarded. "I grew up in a village close by, called Vik. The area is a big attraction now, you probably went there on your tour. Why are you asking?"

"Because I dreamt about it last night."

On top of all the other weirdness, why was she dreaming about the place he was from? Or was it just a coincidence?

He stared at her. "What do you mean?"

She took one of the sweaters. "I had a dream. I wasn't on the beach, though. Yes, we stopped there on our sightseeing tour, and I remember it, but that's not where I was in the dream. I was on top one of the cliffs, above the sand, and it all seemed familiar. I felt like I'd walked there before, but we never went up there."

"What happened?"

She was hesitant to talk about it, as if something might be listening outside the windows. "It was nighttime, in winter, and I was running from … one of them. At least, I think it was one of them. I heard a voice."

He was silent.

"I saw a light." She squinted, trying to see it in her head again. "Like someone was looking for me. I thought someone called out to me, a person. But then I fell, I fell off the cliff and—I woke up."

Gunnar looked stricken, but only for a brief, fleeting moment. His face quickly cleared, and he reached out and cupped her cheek. "It was a nightmare." His hand was warm and gentle. "Of course you were dreaming about them, why wouldn't you? They've put you through so much and frightened you so badly. Your mind put you in a place you've already visited. That's all."

"I didn't visit the tops of those cliffs, though." She stared into his eyes. "It's like how I know what you're saying when you speak Icelandic. I shouldn't know the things I do, but they're just there, in my mind." She shook her head, his hand still on her cheek. "Why would they do something like that? Why would they put all this knowledge inside me—or, whoever did this— what purpose does it serve?"

She had started to consider there might be things at work that were even bigger and more powerful than the huldufólk. Prior to this, she didn't believe in the supernatural, it wasn't even something she thought about. Now, she was forced to consider there might even be gods out there. But what could such entities possibly want with her, and why would they do things to her mind? She was a simple girl from Connecticut. She had never done anything impressive and certainly not universe-shattering that might attract the attention of otherworldly creatures.

"I don't know." Gunnar slipped his hand down to her shoulder and rested it there. "It must serve them in some way, but we may never know the answer. As you can tell from last night, they're not exactly forthcoming."

She tried to imagine spending the rest of her life carrying this mystery. Even if she got home safely and resumed her life in some way, it would eat at her until she really went to her grave.

Gunnar looked at the computer. "It's not such a bad place." He smiled faintly. "When you're not being chased by huldufólk."

"Is that where you herded sheep?"

"No, it was more inland, but near there." He took his hand off her shoulder. "I haven't been back in a long time." A hint of sadness tinged his words.

She looked down at the sweater in her hands. "Maybe it was some sort of osmosis." She looked up at him. "You know, you lying there next to me. Maybe I absorbed your memories or something. Who knows what my messed up brain is capable of now?"

He eyed her playfully. "I don't think I want to ask what sort of things you saw when I had my arm around you, then."

She laughed, and blushed, and for a moment she almost felt like herself.

He handed her the other sweater. "Try them on, find which one fits better."

She collected her jeans from next to the couch and took everything to the bathroom. The one she'd grabbed first fit better, less baggy so the sleeves didn't cover her hands. She also liked the deep green color of it.

When she emerged, Gunnar was in the bedroom with the door closed. She went back to the kitchen, finished up the berries on her plate, and closed the laptop. No more making herself crazier than she already was.

The least she could do was be a good houseguest, so she gathered up the plates and bowls and took them to the sink. As she placed them in, she glanced out the window. The day was sunny, the clouds rolled back to reveal a brilliant blue sky. Remnants of the rain glistened on the grass and in small puddles on the street.

She looked toward the hills. As she did, the same

sensation she'd felt this morning crept over her. Someone was out there, watching. Someone invisible, with their eyes fixed intently on her.

It was too bright and cheery outside to blame her paranoia on the weather. She gripped the edge of the sink, staring into the distance, willing whoever it was to show themselves. If it was one of them, and they had more to say, she wanted to hear it.

There was a quick and sudden movement at the base of the nearest hill, as though something had peeked out from behind the rocks. A figure? A dark figure?

She gasped.

Something touched her waist and she shrieked. She jerked back and stumbled.

Gunnar stood next to her. He lurched back as well, eyes wide. He'd come up behind her and put his hand on her.

"Sorry." She clutched her chest. "I'm a little edgy. You scared me."

"I'm sorry." He held his hands up. "I didn't mean to."

She rubbed her face and looked back out the window. Whatever she'd seen, it wasn't there anymore, and she couldn't even be certain she'd seen it in the first place. "No, I'm sorry. I'm so jumpy. I think going out on the water will do me good. I need to get some air."

He lowered his hands. "You look nice in that sweater. It compliments your skin tone."

She ran her hands over it. "You mean pale as death?" She smiled a little. "Thanks."

"You should wear the boots you wore last night. I don't think your dancing boots will be good on the boat." He headed to the living room. "You should probably pull your hair back, too. It gets very windy on the water and it'll be annoying, all in your face."

"Good idea."

She looked out the window one more time. Hopefully, it stayed nice and sunny today. She didn't know if she could handle the feeling of being creeped on if it turned all gray and gloomy outside.

She followed Gunnar. "Those things can't go out on the water, can they? They stay on land, right?"

Gunnar was pulling on his boots. "They're everywhere. Always be on guard."

She sighed. "Awesome."

Chapter Nine

"This is your boat?" Vanessa shielded her eyes and squinted at it, standing on the creaking dock. "Wow."

She'd been expecting something smaller, like the motorboat her father owned. But this was a broad, long boat, big enough for at least a dozen people. It didn't have a visible motor, but there was a wheelhouse in the front. A green metal railing ringed it, she assumed so people could stand and look at the scenery and not be in danger of falling overboard.

"Yes, this is it." Gunnar was untying the ropes that moored it to the dock. "What do you think?" He grinned. "It's not as big as some tour boats. I only do this casually."

The hull was painted white, but the wheelhouse was red. The word *skoðunarferðir* was printed on the side. That meant "excursion."

Apparently, she could translate even written words.

"It's nice." She lowered her hand from her eyes, wishing she had a pair of sunglasses. "I mean, I don't know much about boats. I didn't assume we were going out in the rowboat, though."

"You can't do much touring in a rowboat." He held his hand out to her. "I'd have to work all day just to make any money."

She took his hand, and he helped her into the boat through a spot where the railing opened like a gate. There were benches, with red cushions. She was glad to see them. She'd be constantly toppling over if she had to stand the whole time.

Gunnar pulled two life jackets from a

compartment next to the wheelhouse. "Safety first." He handed her one.

She took it. "I can swim, but I don't want to try it out here." Though the day was calm, the water was still choppy.

While Gunnar finished readying the boat, she put on her life jacket and looked around. The island loomed in the distance, green and entirely visible, no mist shrouding it today. The walls of the fjord painted the horizon. The wind was light, but it was crisp. Gunnar had supplied her with a waterproof jacket as well, like the one he wore. The sleeves drooped over her hands.

The boat rocked, even in the dock. She carefully sat down on one of the benches.

"You don't get seasick, do you?" He slipped on a pair of sunglasses, then pulled another pair out of his pocket and handed them to her. Her savior.

She took them gratefully and slipped them on. "I don't think so."

He went into the wheelhouse and a moment later, the motors underneath the boat started up. They weren't loud, but they made the floor vibrate, as well as the seats.

He backed them away from the dock slowly, and she gripped the railing. This was going to be fun, dammit. She would get her mind off this madness for a while no matter how hard she had to try.

As they moved out into open water, her thoughts *did* shift. She had never been on a huge body of water before, barring her emotional and frightened rowboat trip from the island.

The wind rushed around her, and she was glad she'd taken Gunnar's advice and pulled her hair back. The engines were muffled by the surge of wind and water. They sped across the murky surface, cutting it into waves of foam on either side of the boat.

They circled wide around the island, and she gazed at it in both awe and trepidation. Birds nested in the walls. The sheer sides and the plateau of green above them made her skin crawl. How had they gotten her all the way up there? Did they levitate or something? The thought made her shudder and she huddled down in the jacket.

They continued out into the wide channel of the fjord. She gazed across the water, mesmerized by the view, overwhelmed by how big everything seemed. This was a country unlike any other, and though she'd met a terrible fate here, she was still enraptured by it.

Eventually, Gunnar slowed the boat, and shortly after, cut the engines. They drifted, the water so vast it felt like an ocean. The incoming silence, apart from the wind, was deafening. High walls of rock and moss towered above them on both sides. She spotted other boats, far off. Some were stationary, others chugging along slowly.

Gunnar stepped out of the wheelhouse. "People come here to fish, too. It's a good spot." He walked over to the side and started turning a huge crank. An anchor dropped into the water.

"How do they know?" She smoothed her hair back. Some of it had come loose in the wind. "It's not like there's signs."

He made his way over to her. "People have been coming here for ages. They tell each other where the best fish are." He sat down.

"So, a long time ago someone got lucky and said, 'hey guys, the fish are over there?'"

"Yes." He turned so he was facing her. "What do you think of it? All of it?"

She looked around. "This is a beautiful land. Despite everything, I still love it." She drew a deep breath. "I don't know how to explain it. I wanted to come here for so long. When we went on our sightseeing tour, it was so amazing I kept breaking down in tears." She chuckled. "I know that sounds silly. My friends kept making fun of me. I felt like I could live here."

Despite that, she now hoped she wouldn't actually become a resident, at least not against her will.

"It's not silly. Iceland is beautiful." He touched her arm. "I understand. Even after all I've been through, I can't imagine living anywhere else. It's my home, even among the huldufólk." She didn't like his sunglasses, because they hid his pretty blue eyes. "That's Hólmavík." He pointed. "It's bigger than Drangsnes, but not much."

Ahead of them and to the left, in the far distance, a small town sat atop the fjord wall.

"Are we going there?"

"No." He took his hand off her arm. "Unless you want to visit the Museum of Witchcraft and Sorcery. It's very interesting."

She frowned.

He chuckled. "I don't know how much is real and how much is made up for fun. I already know too much about magic, and the things I know, they're not in the museum."

It was getting warm under the beating sun, and the wind was mild now. Gunnar undid his life jacket and stood. He peeled off his waterproof jacket and hung it on a hook on the wall next to the wheelhouse. He wore a long sleeved, body hugging white shirt, like he'd had on yesterday when she first met him. It was quite a look. Quite a *good* look.

He put his life jacket back on and noticed she was checking him out. He grinned broadly—that nice, too-wide smile that was nonetheless charming.

She quickly looked away. "Are we going to sit here for a while?" She thought about taking her own layers off, but she didn't want to wrestle with the life jacket right now.

He sat back down beside her. "A short time. It's relaxing, don't you think?"

"Yeah." She folded her arms on the railing and looked down at the dark surface of the water. He said they were everywhere. They weren't under the water, were they?

"How long have you been here, in this place?" She struggled to distract herself from her paranoia. "In Drangsnes?"

He rested his arm on the railing, leaning next to her. "Almost ten years, since I left Eydis. I don't usually stay in one place so long, but Aedan came into my life. I only have two years left. I don't know if I'll move again."

"How old was Aedan when he came into your care?"

He pushed his hair back. The wind had tousled his curls.

She wanted to run her fingers through them, they looked so silky and fluffy at the same time.

"Nine, in human years. The huldufólk age differently. He would still be a child in their world, but he has human blood. I don't know how old he really is, mentally."

"Do you know things like this about huldufólk physiology because of the diary?" She figured it would be safe to talk about it here.

His expression turned strained. "Yes. His mother wrote some things down, the secrets her huldufólk lover told her. There's some information, but not much."

"Do you think this huldufólk man really loved

her?"

"That's what she says in the diary. Shortly after she arrived in Iceland, she wandered into the countryside and got lost. She was homeless, traveling, trying to escape her father. She nearly died from exposure and starvation. The huldufólk man found her and took care of her. And he fell in love with her."

"Do you think they're really capable of that?" She grimaced.

"I don't know. They hid it from his people, of course, knowing the consequences would be terrible. He made a home for her. They met each other in secret, and she eventually became pregnant." He paused. "Aedan was wild, like an animal, when I first met him. He barely spoke. He couldn't read."

"How did you know his mother?"

"She was hiding in the hills near Drangsnes, with Aedan. They'd already killed his father. They burnt him on the summer solstice, beneath a full moon. There's a description in her diary, but—it's rambling and frightened. She watched from a hill nearby."

Vanessa shuddered. It was hard to believe any of them were tender enough for a human to fall in love with.

"When I found her, I tried to help. I felt terrible for them, victims like me. I brought them food and water. She wouldn't come to Drangsnes, though. She was half mad."

"Weren't you afraid they would punish you for helping her?"

"I assumed they let her go because they knew her grief would eventually kill her. If they wanted her dead right away, they would have killed her when they killed him. They discarded her and let her suffer." He gazed across the water. "One night, she brought Aedan to my house. I was surprised to see her. She asked if I would care for him for a few days while she went somewhere. I had a bad feeling about it, she wouldn't tell me where she was going."

Vanessa had a bad feeling, too.

"She flung herself from the cliffs." He looked at the walls around them. "When a body falls into the fjord, it will never be found. It was exactly what they wanted."

Vanessa looked to the cliffs as well, feeling cold inside. She cringed, imagining someone jumping from one of those sheer walls. The pain she must have felt, to abandon her son and do such a thing.

"Wait, how do you know she jumped?"

"Because they told me. They came, a few days later. They wanted to take Aedan away to—wherever it is they take halfling children. I begged them to let me watch over him. I told them I would be his guardian and make sure he didn't reveal their secrets to humans."

"They actually agreed?"

"I had to grovel. And part of the deal was that in five years, when Aedan was older and more capable, they would come and make use of him. I was not to interfere. I think they found my paternal desperation amusing."

Making use of him must mean whatever task was currently keeping him away. His "grave work."

"I won't say any more." Gunnar shook his head. "It's telling his secrets. He's suffered so much. I've raised him like a son. He doesn't deserve this."

She moved closer to him. "You're a good man." She rested her hand on his arm.

He smiled at her.

She still wished she could yank those sunglasses off.

"They've tortured you for a long time," she said softly. "And still, you keep your humanity. You care about other people. You helped Aedan, and now you've helped me."

"I don't know what else I can do. Their punishments don't fit the crimes. It's not Aedan's fault he was born. And digging up their land, I just..." He fell silent.

"What do you think I did?"

He shrugged. "Does it matter? They punish cruelly and without discrimination."

When she mulled over the events of her trip, she didn't recall doing anything that might have pissed them off. She was respectful: she didn't litter, or walk where she shouldn't, or deface anything. She'd picked up a few pretty stones here and there, but surely that wasn't a violation? Unless it was. Maybe she'd accidentally picked up the huldufólk queen's crown jewels or something.

She was pulled out of her reverie by Gunnar gripping her hand on his arm and giving it a squeeze. "I'm sorry this happened to you. You shouldn't have to suffer for an innocent mistake."

Her father's voice on the phone haunted her. It wasn't *her* that was suffering right now. She was here, in a boat on a beautiful fjord, with a kind and handsome man, enjoying the day. Her parents were back in Connecticut, still dealing with the pain of her death. They had buried something that wasn't her, and now they put flowers on that grave.

She blinked a few times to clear her eyes of tears. "I was never content at home." She turned her hand over and entwined her fingers with his. "I always wanted to travel. I put all these pictures on my walls of places I wanted to visit."

"I've never been to America." He rubbed his thumb across the back of her hand. "Maybe I should go, before my time is up."

She gazed at their joined hands. Her skin was pale and his was bronze. He was outside a lot more than her. "I never got to travel much, though," she said. "I figured I'd end up getting married and I'd settle down in that little town, like everyone else I knew."

"Why didn't you?"

She shook her head. "The last serious boyfriend I had was when we went on our family trip to Newfoundland. When I came back, and I was recovering from my injury, things changed between us. He said I was a different person." She snorted. "We'd been together since I was eighteen, I was twenty then. I think he just wasn't ready to stop playing around. He felt like he was missing out, being with me."

"You haven't had a boyfriend since?"

"I dated. It was all bad."

He shrugged. "You just can't find Mr. Right."

"Not for lack of trying, mind you. I'm terrible at flirting. I just focused on work, and I started dreaming of Iceland. You know, I thought maybe I could at least make some of my old travel dreams come true."

"You're not that bad at flirting."

She rolled her eyes. "I'm awful. I'm so awkward."

"That line about telling jokes, at the fire." He grinned. "That was good."

"Yeah, and look, I haven't managed to tell one yet, have I?"

"Well, it's kind of hard to joke right now."

Her hand felt comfortable in his. He kept rubbing, sending little tingles across her skin.

"At least I'm having an adventure, huh?" She propped her other arm on the railing and put her chin on her hand. "So, how did Eydis make you laugh?"

He hummed and tilted his head back. "Like I told you, I met her in a coffee shop. I was standing at the counter, waiting, and she stood next to me."

"Maybe I need to go to coffee shops instead of bars."

"It was late in the summer, early September. I made small talk with her. I said the snow was coming soon, and it was nice weather while it lasted." He smiled, and it was fond and winsome. "She said, 'the east and west are pulling apart.' Because of the continental divide, you know."

She knew what he meant. Iceland was slowly ripping itself in half along the fault where two continental plates met.

"She said, 'I'm going to jump on the part that floats down to the tropics. It should only take a few eons. If I hurry, I can get still get to the shop and stock up on sunscreen.'"

Vanessa giggled, though it was a dumb joke. Gunnar chuckled, but it sounded sad. She supposed, after all this time, it wasn't about being funny but sentimental. Her heart ached for him. She was still trying to wrap her head around him being alive for a hundred years, the things he'd seen, the losses he'd suffered. Though he was undying, he was human.

"So that's how you fell in love?" She kept her tone light. "You fell for her geology joke and it was history?" She was trying to make a pun, but realized it didn't quite connect, history and geology.

"I talked to her until her group left. She gave me her business card, not that I needed a tour. I'd been all over Iceland by then. I saw her again in town a few days later, and we chatted. I asked her out to dinner … and that was that."

"How long did you wait to tell her about—you?"

He tilted his head back again. "Not until we got serious, until I knew it would last. Maybe a year. I didn't want to wait longer. It's a delicate game. How soon is too soon, and how long makes it a terrible secret? She didn't believe me, of course. But I proved it."

Vanessa arched an eyebrow. "Did you make her stab you?"

He laughed. "No, I'm sorry." He looked down at their joined hands, and turned melancholy again. "She's happy. Retired and surrounded by grandchildren. She had two children before we met. I could never get too close to her family, despite how long we were together. They'd know something wasn't right. It's a lonely life."

She eased closer, recalling the comforting words he'd just said to her. They applied to him, too. "I'm sorry this is happening to you. You shouldn't have to suffer because of an innocent mistake."

Their faces were close together. He slipped his sunglasses off, finally. His eyes made her breath catch. Despite all the turmoil, looking into them made her feel calm, like she was looking into the eyes of an old friend.

"Would it be inappropriate," he murmured, "if I…"

She slipped her glasses off as well and leaned in. The world was bright for a moment before she closed her eyes.

His lips were soft and firm. He released her hand and gripped her face instead.

A rush of delight passed through her, chasing away the darkness. She clutched his life jacket and sank into the kiss. The sense of familiarity deepened, the goodness of it so profound she wanted to cry. This was right. The rest of her world was in shambles, but he was all she needed.

He continued holding her face when they broke

apart.

She gazed into his eyes again, his minty taste on her lips. She almost started laughing, thinking how absurd it was that a century-old guy still had to brush his teeth every morning.

He stroked his thumb down her cheek. "What's on your mind?"

"Nothing. Just how strange this all is."

"I've seen a lot of strangeness. You get used to it." He flicked his gaze to her lips. Could they just sit here all day, kissing and pretending nothing else was happening?

She let go of his life jacket and slipped her hand around, onto his side. "This isn't bad, though." She'd let go of him only if this boat sank.

"Should we continue with the tour? There's still much of the fjord to see."

She smiled, and finally thought of a joke. "It can wait for a bit. Then we'll *fjord* ahead."

He rolled his eyes.

"I should stop talking."

"Yes, you should." He leaned in and claimed her mouth again.

She'd never been so happy to be shut up.

Chapter Ten

Gunnar took the boat to the end of the fjord, where it cut deep into the land, and then turned around and headed back. Vanessa stood inside the wheelhouse, where the wind was less sharp. She gazed out the window.

"Are those puffins?" She stared up at a rocky cliff as they skimmed past it. Her spirits, for the time being, were considerably lifted.

"Yes." Gunnar stood behind her, manning the wheel.

"They're cute." She pressed her fingers to the glass, like a child at the zoo. "All fat and fluffy."

"They taste good, too."

She looked over her shoulder.

He turned sheepish. "Sorry, that wasn't funny. I say that because I've been around a while, and—yeah, they're endangered now, so I don't partake anymore, but we used to, a lot."

She smiled. "A hundred years old, and you can still be progressive."

He grinned, so lovely, with the sun streaming in on him, all blond and bronze. Every bit that hot Icelandic guy she'd been hoping to meet.

She looked back out the window. "You guys are really into your fish and fowl here."

"We don't have much else. Our ancestors wanted to challenge God. A barren, inhospitable land covered in ice with volcanoes that intermittently explode? And there's barely anything to eat? Sign us up."

She turned around and leaned against the window. "Do you believe in God?"

His hands rested loosely on the wheel. She was fighting the urge to step over and devour his mouth again, maybe even wrap herself around him. She didn't want him to wreck the boat, though. Also, despite their makeout session things were awkward, strange, and this was probably all horribly inappropriate right now.

"I used to." He gazed straight ahead. "My family was Lutheran, like most Icelanders. We went to church and said prayers. But over the years—I saw more and more things that made it difficult to believe."

"I guess if there is a God, then God made the huldufólk too, and that's scary."

"They might say the same of us."

She narrowed her eyes.

He shrugged. "To them, we're vicious intruders who spoiled the land they possessed for thousands of years. We dig it up, build our houses, and pollute the water and earth. They see us as equally cruel creations of an uncaring God."

"Are you defending them?"

"I'm presenting a different viewpoint." He paused. "I don't excuse or forgive them. How could I? But that's how they think, probably. I've often wondered if there could be a different way."

"A different way?"

"To live in harmony. To respect each other. I don't suppose they'd be open to peace talks, though, and they have an advantage over us. We don't have magical powers." He glanced out the window. "But maybe, like the puffins, they're endangered too."

She turned one shoulder back to the window and gazed out at the water. Both out of fear and respect, she never would have tried to offend such creatures. But she didn't know they were there, and she didn't know what she'd done.

"I'm sorry." He spoke hesitantly. "A hundred years is a long time to think. I'm not saying they're justified. You're freshly wounded, I shouldn't have said that."

"I'm not offended. What you say makes sense." She stepped over and took one of his hands off the wheel and gave it a squeeze. "It says something about your character that you can be so tormented by them and still try to put yourself in their shoes." She frowned. "Do they even wear shoes? I didn't notice." She'd been too busy staring at the woman's freakish eyes.

He smiled and squeezed her hand in return. "It took me many years to build character. Don't give me too much credit."

She attempted to stroll out into the back of the boat, but he held her hand still and dragged her back. Her stomach did a happy flip as he pulled her toward him. They shared a brief but slow and electrifying kiss.

He let go of her hand. "Are you hungry? I'll take you to the guesthouse in Drangsnes. They have good food."

She smiled and tucked her hands in her jacket pockets. "Sure, I could go for some nice fish."

She went into the back of the boat and sat. The sweeping walls of the fjord spread wide around them. Things she recognized came back into view—the jagged coastline, Drangsnes in the distance. Grímsey rose ahead of them, a small rock in a vast bay.

She stared at it, foreboding growing in her. Time to step out of her fantasy world and back into cold, hard reality. As they drew closer, thoughts filled her head, a plan slowly forming.

"Hey, can we stop at the island?" she called over the wind. "Is that okay?"

Gunnar looked back at her. "Are you sure?"

"Yes, I just want to look around."

Gunnar swung out wide around it, then moved in. They approached the side facing away from the town, the side she hadn't seen yet. There was no pier or dock, but a few other boats were moored there. People were climbing trails on the cliffsides and standing on the beach.

At least they weren't alone.

Gunnar cut the engines and eased the boat into a crevasse. She had no idea what it took to drive a boat, much less delicately park one like he was currently doing. After anchoring, he climbed out and tied it to a pole among the rocks. He then offered her a hand, so she could climb out as well. She felt woozy being on a solid surface, like the world was still in motion.

"You don't have your sea legs," he teased. "Don't worry, it fades."

They walked down the gravel beach, hand in hand.

"The tourists mostly stay on this side of the island." He pointed up. "There's a puffin nesting ground up there. They come to see the birds."

The fat, orange-beaked birds were scattered all over the side of the island and congregated in a large group at the top. Tourists were taking pictures of them. A lighthouse stood up there as well, orange and lonely against the blue sky.

"We found you on the other side." He led her toward the mouth of a trail. "But I can't moor a boat as big as mine over there, it's too shallow. The terrain is difficult over there as well, so people don't explore it as much. It's really no surprise a tourist didn't find you first."

That brought up some interesting questions.

"So how did you guys find me?" She let go of

his hand, so he could climb the trail ahead of her. It wasn't too steep, but she could see it would take a while to get to the top. Puffins roosted on the grass and rocks, and stared at them as they passed, fluffing their wings.

"We come out here a lot." No one was nearby and they could speak freely. "The huldufólk leave messages for Aedan."

"The huldufólk come here often?"

"Yes."

"And they bring you messages?"

He trudged ahead of her. She was a little too distracted to enjoy the generous sight of his backside, as other, dark thoughts were starting to occupy her mind.

"They leave them here for Aedan. They don't speak to me. But I come with him, because I worry. We were walking the island when we found you."

She slowed her ascent, and then stopped, staring after him. After a short distance, he looked back, stopped as well, and turned. He frowned. "What's wrong?"

"I *am* a message."

"What do you mean?"

"That woman, she said I wasn't a warning to you. But they left me here, on this island, because they knew you would find me. That means I'm a message instead."

Gunnar's frown deepened.

"If they wanted to get rid of me, they didn't have to leave me here. They could have left me on the mainland. But here, you were the only ones guaranteed to find me. They knew you would come along."

His sunglasses were back on, so she couldn't see his eyes, but the rest of his face suggested that he, too, was having a revelation.

"It's not a coincidence they dumped me here." She looked around. "It was on purpose."

"But why?"

"Your guess is as good as mine." She looked up. "Take me back to the place where you found me."

They climbed to the island floor. The ground was uneven and pitted, and they had to make their way across carefully. The view was dazzling from up here, Drangsnes laid out in front of them and the coastline visible for miles. The sun glittered on the water, the surface ever-moving. The sky was filled with fluffy white clouds.

Such a beautiful place for a tragedy.

Gunnar led her all the way across to the other side. Birds were everywhere, not just puffins but larger and smaller ones, as well. Some circled above, calling. She felt like she was deeper in nature than she'd ever been.

"Here," Gunnar finally said. He stopped on top of an outcropping at the edge of the island, looking down.

She stepped up beside him and looked down as well. There was a flat, muddy area about ten feet below, and she knew immediately it was the spot where she'd lain. She recognized, nearby, the trail they'd taken down to the boat.

She pointed. "You came up that path from the beach, didn't you?"

"Yes. Mostly just fishermen come to this side, other than us."

"Can we go down?"

They had to trek down a steep hillside with no path to get to the muddy spot.

She stopped and stood, staring at it. "Do you come to this spot often?" She spoke quietly.

"Every once in a while. We thought at first you were dead."

Dread filled her like icy water filling a tub. Maybe she imagined it, but something about this place didn't feel right. She swore she felt a presence, or an energy—and it wasn't pleasant. If Gunnar hadn't told her the huldufólk hung out here, she would have already guessed.

"I don't see anything." Gunnar looked around. "No signs."

"What signs do you usually find?"

"Carvings in rocks, or cairns. Sometimes they leave a dead animal, or a trinket. Aedan has to interpret the signs because they don't usually appear and speak directly to him."

The sun vanished behind a cloud, dulling the world. She slid her sunglasses off to get a better look.

He gripped her shoulder. "I don't think we'll find anything here."

The feeling inside her grew more intense. The huldufólk were here, she knew it. She looked at the outcropping above, expecting one to appear, but there was nothing. Were they taunting her? She felt surrounded on all sides, but there was only sky and water.

She lowered her voice. "We're not alone here. Can you feel it?"

"I think they're always here." He lowered his voice as well. "But that doesn't mean anything."

"She lied. She lied about me being connected to you. I'm certain."

"She only said you weren't a warning. That doesn't mean you aren't connected."

She gazed at him, lips pressed together. She wanted the bastards to come out and give her some answers, right now. This was cruel and unfair.

The sun came back out, lighting up the world around them.

"We can walk around some more," he said. "But it might be pointless."

As much as she wanted to get off the island so her skin would stop crawling, she needed to find something that would give her a clue, at least. They made their way back up and he led her around the perimeter of the island floor, as close as they could get to the cliffs. She saw birds, and tourists, and the view continued to take her breath away, but there was nothing else. Gray clouds started to gather in the east, and they crept toward Drangsnes.

"It's going to rain." Gunnar tromped ahead of her. "We should go back soon." At this point, they had been there a good forty-five minutes, maybe an hour.

"I know." She pulled her jacket tight around her. The wind was relentless. "It was worth a shot, right?" Frustration clawed at her.

Gunnar held his hand out. "Come on." His tone was sympathetic.

She took his hand. They made their way back to the side of the island where their boat was. Down on the beach, tourists were starting to get back in their own boats, though a small group remained. They were scattered on the slope, still admiring the puffins.

"We can go to the hot pots after we eat." Gunnar squeezed her hand. "And relax a bit. If you want."

She furrowed her brow. "What are hot pots?"

"Did you see those hot tubs on the shore?"

She recalled seeing them when they first came ashore after they got her off the island. She nodded.

"They're fed by geothermal springs." He smiled. "They're lovely to sit in when it's raining, or even snowing. It'll work the tension out of your limbs."

She smirked. "I don't have anything to wear in a hot tub."

"We'll figure something out."

He let go of her hand, so they could make their way down the trail. She walked behind him, going slowly, careful not to slip. She'd been surprised to discover despite all the tourism, Iceland didn't have much structure. She was used to parks and attractions having paved paths, fences, and security. There was none of that here.

Paths were organic and attractions fully accessible and touchable. Outside of being asked to respect the land, tourists roamed unfettered. She liked that, as she'd gotten astonishingly close to so many wonders. Now she wished there was someone to watch over her. Something to keep her separated from scary things. Maybe then, she wouldn't have offended the huldufólk by—doing whatever it was she did.

About halfway down the cliff, her gaze settled on a woman sitting just off the path to the left. She had her back to them, apparently observing a group of puffins. When Vanessa saw her, her stomach jumped and she nearly stumbled.

The woman had long black hair and she wore a bulky gray sweater.

Vanessa stopped. Her heart was in her throat.

Gunnar kept walking.

Vanessa crept forward, her gaze fixed on the woman. She drew closer to her, her hands clenched and nails digging into her palms, and debated calling out. Did she dare confront one of them, even in broad daylight, even surrounded by other people? She thought of the iron knife Gunnar gave her. It was at the house. She should have brought it with her, just in case.

She tried to force a shout, but her voice was trapped in her throat. Fear pumped through her veins. She managed to clear her throat, making a sound to get her attention.

The woman looked over her shoulder.

Vanessa deflated, the terror draining out of her, to be immediately replaced by embarrassment. If the wind weren't so cold her cheeks would have been blazing hot.

The woman was fair-skinned, but not ghastly pale like the huldufólk. Her eyes were normal human eyes. She frowned curiously at Vanessa. Just a tourist, nothing more.

"Vanessa?"

She started.

Gunnar had stopped and was looking back at her.

She tried to recover, giving a high, false laugh. "Sorry, just looking at the puffins!" She waved to the woman and hustled down the slope. The woman might not even speak English, so it was hardly a save. She felt incredibly dumb.

This situation was putting her way too much on edge.

She caught up to Gunnar. "Sorry, puffins."

Gunnar arched an eyebrow over his sunglasses.

She swallowed and spoke quietly. "Actually, she—spooked me. She has long dark hair, and ... yeah."

Gunnar looked at the woman, then smiled and squeezed her shoulder. "I understand."

They continued down the trail. Vanessa glanced back. The woman stared after them. Vanessa quickly looked forward. Maybe she could just dive right into the water and disappear.

They got down to the beach and walked back to the boat. The wind was whipping up stronger and the water was much choppier now, those dark clouds closer. It was going to be a fun ride back.

She sat in the boat and pulled her life jacket on while Gunnar untied them. He then got in and started the engines. Most of the tourists were on the beach now, heading toward the last boat, but the woman wasn't among them.

"You all right?" Gunnar was pulling on his own life jacket.

She nodded, though she was far from all right. "Let's just get back. This place is freaking me out."

As they crossed the water, she looked back at the retreating island. Something lurked there, she was sure of it, and whatever it was, she could feel it watch her as she left. The answers she wanted, and so very much needed, were on that rocky, jagged piece of land somewhere. But it wouldn't give its secrets up so easily.

Chapter Eleven

Vanessa stood in the little bathroom, listening to the rain patter on the roof. It wasn't a downpour, but it had been gently raining since they got back to shore, and while they ate at the guesthouse. They'd returned to Gunnar's house after the meal and then walked to the hot pots. The little bathroom shack she stood in served as a changing room as well.

She stared at herself in the mirror as she tied the t-shirt she wore between her breasts, turning it into a makeshift bikini top. She didn't want her bra soaked, but she left it on anyway. Mostly, because the t-shirt was white—one of Gunnar's—and everything would be on display once it was soaked. She smirked to herself. Had he planned that?

Well, she was one step ahead of him.

She took her panties off, though. One less thing to dry. She wore a pair of men's swim trunks—also Gunnar's—and she had to tie the drawstring twice so they didn't slip off.

She looked ridiculous and frumpy, but she wanted to sit in the rain in a hot tub with Gunnar. It was the only way she'd be distracted enough to stop dwelling on the island.

Struggling to ignore how self-conscious she was, she left the changing hut and walked across the street. A wooden walkway led down to the hot tubs.

Gunnar waited on it.

She glanced at him, then focused her gaze on the horizon, acting stoically as if the sight of him didn't make her salivate. He wore a pair of red swim trunks. He was shirtless, a towel slung over his shoulder. She gripped her own towel in front of her.

"I look dorky," she said.

"You look fine." His eyes practically glowed in the dull gray light. "It's not a beauty contest."

All his lovely, tight, toned muscles made her curious: if he remained unchanged all these years, could he change *anything* about himself? Did he lose and gain weight? Could he build muscle? Could he cut his hair?

She didn't ask as they started down the steps to the tubs, because there was a couple in one. They all exchanged courteous smiles and nods, but the couple seemed engrossed in conversation and ignored them.

There were three tubs. Two were traditional swimming pool blue, and the other one had murky green water in it. When they first arrived, and she checked them out, Gunnar explained the green one was cooler and suggested they start in it. Steam rolled off all three, but it issued from the two blue ones much more thickly. Rain pattered on the surface of the water.

She eased herself into the green one. It was like lowering herself into lukewarm bath water, not unpleasant at all. Gunnar got in too and sat a few feet away on the seat that ringed the interior. They had a spectacular view. The waters of the fjord were only about twenty feet away, and small waves crashed against the breakwall in front of them. Farther out, the waves were higher and more tumultuous. The island sat to the left.

"We went to the Blue Lagoon on our trip." She sat back against the tub and sank down until the water rose over her chest. "You know, the thermal spas outside Reykjavik? It was nice."

In her mind, that visit only happened five days ago. She could picture the calm crystal blue waters and smell the sulfur on the air. That water was warm, warmer than what she sat in now. Steph kept subtly checking out guys and encouraging Vanessa to go talk to them. A lump formed in her throat. It was an amazing time, and yet, it took place over a year ago. She still couldn't accept that. Her brain shut down when she tried to process it.

"I've been there a couple times." Gunnar stretched his arms out on the back of the tub. "Eydis liked it. I'm not fond of the smell, though. As long as I've been here, I'm not used to the fact most of this country smells like rotten eggs."

She gazed down into the water. Her spirits sagged.

"Hey." He eased closer. "What's wrong?"

She looked up.

He sighed. "I know, everything's wrong." He put his arm behind her. "It still feels like your trip just happened. It must be disconcerting."

She looked down again. Raindrops fell harder, cold as they splashed her face.

"I keep thinking about my friends." She kept her voice down, though the other couple was in the farthest tub. "I've known both of them since high school. We're best friends. We've been through everything together. They must have been so afraid, and then sick with grief when the police found 'me' on the mountain." She shuddered. "They couldn't have seen my body though, it's impossible. There's no way that many people would mistake my identity."

He stroked her shoulder with his fingertips. "Maybe it wasn't a mistake."

"What do you mean?"

"If the huldufólk can do things to your mind, they can do things to other people's minds, too. Maybe, whoever's body that was, they put an enchantment on it, so people would see you instead."

She blinked. "They can do that?"

"They can do many things. Messing with human minds is their specialty."

She hadn't even considered they might have played a trick on everyone else, too. But whose body was it that now rested in her grave in Mica Hill Cemetery?

"Why, though?" It was rhetorical, more than a question to Gunnar. "Why would they come up with such an elaborate scheme? What purpose does it serve?"

"Perhaps it's part of your punishment. Everyone thinks you're dead and it makes your life harder."

That might be a good explanation if not for all the dangling threads: where had she been for a year, and what about the huldufólk woman's words?

"She said they were punishing someone else by doing this, though. Who? And why?" She pressed her clenched hands to her eyes. "This is making me crazy." She dropped her hands and forced herself not to scream in rage and scare the other couple.

Gunnar rubbed the back of her neck. "Maybe we'll find some answers in Reykjavik. Aedan should be back in the morning. It'll only take us a couple hours to drive there."

She watched the waves crash against the rocks. Above the clouds, a shadow seemed to hang over everything, haunting and tormenting her. This magical place of her dreams had turned into a hellscape, and she resented it.

"If we find answers or not," she said, shaking her head, "I'll make someone listen. Someone has to believe me. I'll convince the police. I'll—make them take fingerprints, or something. There has to be a way to prove I am who I say I am."

He rested his hand on her shoulder again.

"And then I'm going home, and everyone will see that I'm alive." She looked at him. "I won't forget everything you've done for me. And, I really want to know what happens to you. We'll keep in touch."

He smiled, a little sadly. "I want to know what happens to you, too."

"Even if I never get answers, thank you, for everything."

They were silent for a while, gazing out at the fjord. The rain slowed again. The couple got out and left. Vanessa tried to refocus her thoughts. Tomorrow seemed so far away.

"Do you come here often?" As soon as the words left her mouth, she laughed. "I don't mean that as a cheesy pick-up line. I mean like, here, to these tubs?"

He grinned. His hair was wet from the rain, dark gold where it stuck to his neck. "Every now and then. It's a nice place to think, especially in the evening. In summer these are usually full of tourists, but the rain must be keeping them away."

Indeed, they were very much alone now. No cars on the street, no people walking around. It was both nice and kind of eerie.

He indicated the other tubs. "Do you want to get into one of the hotter ones now? If it's too much, we'll come back to this one."

The tubs were built flush together, so it was easy to climb into the next one. The water was indeed hotter, like a jacuzzi. It felt nice in contrast to the cool air, though.

She paddled around.

Gunnar sat, facing her, and watched her make her way around the tub.

"I wish we had hot springs back home," she said. "It must be nice, to have them all around."

"You get used to it, then it's not so special."

She drifted toward him. "Like being immortal,

huh?"

He gazed at her.

"I hope they let you live." She spoke softly. "I hope you get to live a long, normal human life. Find a nice woman to marry, have some babies, grow old together."

He smirked faintly. "I don't think I'll ever have a normal life."

She was close to him now, and he reached out and took her gently by the arms. Her heart pounded. She didn't resist as he pulled her to him. Their lips met, his mouth soft and silken as it engulfed hers. She gasped into it as he wrapped an arm around her waist and pulled her into his lap. She settled against him, thighs framing his hips.

He kissed her harder, with a hunger that warmed her insides to the temperature of her skin. She kissed back with fervor, gripping the sides of his face.

Despite everything, she wanted this. She craved connection, comfort, and the safety of his arms. Desire sparked deep inside her. It brightened her senses and cleared her mind. That was what she wanted most—if only for a little bit, to not feel so desperate and scared and lost.

He broke the kiss and gazed up at her, those blue eyes so entrancing she could barely catch her breath. His hands were on her hips. His chest worked against hers.

"I'm sorry." He caressed her back. "I haven't touched a woman in a long time. I know this isn't right and we shouldn't—"

She stopped his words with a kiss, and then looked into his eyes again. "We should. I need something that isn't a nightmare right now. We can regret it later." She hadn't touched a man in a long time either, and her neediness drove her as much as anything else.

They resumed making out. He explored her body, stopping short of anything inappropriate, but she wanted him to cross all her boundaries. She moved her hands over him as well—his arms, his shoulders, his back, his chest. All that delicious supple muscle. He felt like no man she'd ever touched. He felt right. He felt familiar.

As her thoughts raced to the next step, an ominous feeling rolled over her, as grim as the clouds above. She recognized it, that creeping sense of vertigo. The same thing she'd felt when she held the picture, the same sensation when she stabbed him.

What the hell is this?

Someone whispered behind her, like before, but she couldn't make out the words. She didn't want to hear that scream again, but it came anyway. It suddenly filled her ears and she flinched, breaking their kiss.

Gunnar blinked. His skin was pink from the heat of the tub. "What's wrong?"

The voice receded, replaced by the rush of wind and waves. She felt dizzy. She pushed her wet hair back from her face. "Maybe we should get out. This is getting hot."

He smirked and squeezed her hips. "The water, or this?"

She smiled in return. "Both."

They climbed out. The cool air felt good on her skin. Whatever was going on, whatever damage those creatures had done to her mind, she didn't want to deal with it right now. When she got home she'd see a doctor, especially if she kept hallucinating. She could only imagine what scrambling someone's brain with magic did to it.

Gunnar slipped his shoes on—they'd both worn flip-flops, hers borrowed of course and too big for her feet—and she noticed he was carefully keeping his towel in front of his crotch. "We'll go back to the house," he said. "Get dry and warm."

She smirked and wrapped her own towel around her waist. "No need to hide it, I already know."

He took her hand. "Yes, but other people live here. Even in Iceland, free as we are, it's a bit rude."

They walked back to the house, the rain falling gently on them. The heat quickly dissipated from her skin and the cold set in, but she didn't care. They kept stopping to make out in the drizzle, their wet flesh sliding together, his hands in her hair. Everything inside her shifted away from her trauma and focused solely on him, on what they were going to do when they got back to the house. She was so eager for it.

But resentment gnawed at her, as well. This could be the hottest, most romantic thing she'd ever done if not for the circumstance she was in. This was something she'd normally want to gush to her friends about, in detail, later.

But she couldn't.

They only came across one person on the way back, a man hurrying to get out of the rain. The town was theirs for the moment.

When she stepped into Gunnar's house, she kicked the flip-flops off and undid the towel from her waist with a relieved sigh. She'd started to shiver, and it was warm inside.

Gunnar closed the door, and without a word, dragged her back into his arms. She let the towel drop to the floor.

The passion that had been brewing between them all day finally exploded. He helped her yank the soaked t-shirt up over her head, her bra equally wet beneath and slicked to her skin. He wrapped his arms around her and deftly unclasped it as well.

She grinned as he peeled the straps down her shoulders. "You still know how to do that, huh?"

"I've had a lot of practice." He winked.

Her cheeks warmed as he slipped her bra off. She'd always been satisfied with her breasts, but what did Icelandic guys like? Big ones? Little ones? As he gathered them in his hands, she assumed he liked what she had just fine.

She squeaked as she was suddenly pressed against the wall next to the door, and Gunnar dropped to his knees in front of her. She looked down at the top of his blond head. He was pulling her shorts down.

"Should we take a shower first?" she asked weakly.

"No."

He grabbed her hips and pushed her up a bit, and then the hot, velvety touch of his tongue made her gasp, in both pleasure and surprise. He licked her opening and pushed his tongue into her. She hadn't felt that in so long, and she loved when a man ate her out. Her ex hadn't been so keen on it, unfortunately.

Gunnar slipped a finger into her as he focused on her clit, rolling his tongue over it slowly and firmly. He still knew how to do that, too.

She grabbed his hair and twisted her fingers in it, but gently, trying not to hurt him. "Oh … God."

She worked herself against his face as he fingered her deep, the way she liked it. She squirmed between him and the wall, whimpers tearing from her lips, though she struggled not to let them out. She wasn't sure why, since they were alone.

He stopped licking but continued fingering her. Two fingers, now. He kissed up her stomach, his wet lips on her damp skin. She humped his hand shamelessly, because *oh my God,* it felt so good.

"More?" he asked.

Her head swam. Had he said that in English? She nodded.

He stood up, fingers still inside her, and kissed her. His mouth tasted like her. "Let's go to the bedroom."

She shivered. "Should we dry off first? We'll get the bed wet."

"I have a dryer." He slipped his fingers out—making her groan—took her hand, and led her down the hallway. Her knees were weak. She was in a heady, warm haze of want.

In the bedroom, he stripped off his wet swim trunks. She was distracted from her own nakedness by taking him in.

Goddamn, he was beautiful *all* over. Broad, hard, sexy. His hips were a sinuous curve and his thighs were thick and solid. She wanted to climb him. His cock hung long and low between his legs.

Oh, shit. *Yes.*

"You must work out," she said, giddy.

"Farm work is very hard work, I built a lot of muscle."

This made her even more curious as to whether his body could change, but now wasn't the time to discuss it.

They tumbled on the bed together, her beneath him. He felt good on top of her, powerful and overwhelming in the best way. He kissed her, and she begged him with every inch of her body, to take her, to claim her. She would commit this to memory, every moment, every sensation, and someday get to savor it without the black cloud hanging over her.

His hands slid across her flesh. His hips fit snug with hers. Need made her burn and clench inside. She wondered if he had condoms, because she sure didn't.

He pushed his fingers into her again, this time with her knees drawn up and legs spread, so he could go even deeper. He rubbed her clit with his thumb. Her inner walls twitched, the thrill of impending orgasm filling her. She kissed him hard and sucked his tongue, whining into his mouth. Her toes curled and her thighs quivered.

She reached down to stroke him in return. His cock was firm and hot and filled her palm. He was also uncircumcised, which felt fascinating. She'd never been with an uncut guy before.

She pulled her mouth from his, trying to catch her breath. "Gunnar." She squeezed him.

"Shh, just enjoy it," he murmured in her ear. "You first."

She trembled. He was trying to make her come, and he seemed to know, instinctively, just how to do it. Even her ex had a hard time fumbling around the right way to get her off, and they'd been together for years, during which she'd provided plenty of direction.

Despite his insistence this was about her, she kept stroking him. He was slick and surged in her hand.

"Oh God," she gasped. "Gunnar..."

He didn't stop, and she couldn't stop, either. She came with an urgent groan, clenching and gushing around his fingers. Her entire body shook, her hips lifting off the bed. It was so fucking good everything else in the world got shut out for a moment.

Her head cleared. Her thoughts flew away. But as she came down, the whispering started up again, louder and more insistent than before.

Go the fuck *away,* she begged it.

He kept moving his fingers inside her, slow and deep, until it was too much and she gripped his wrist. He slipped them out, a gush following them. She'd never gotten that wet with her ex, either.

"Oh, man." She caught her breath. "That was nice."

He sucked on his soaked fingers. That was sexy as hell. "Yes, it was." He was twitching in her hand, but he gently drew away.

The whispering continued. She closed her eyes and tried to focus on the sound of the rain on the roof.

Then, vertigo swept in. She squeezed her eyes tighter and tried to balance herself. The whispering turned to a scream. She fought to shut her ears against it.

A cold wave crashed over her and dragged her down to black depths.

From the center of the darkness, a scene opened up. This wasn't a dream this time, though. It felt too real. She'd been whisked from the bed and taken somewhere else.

It was daytime, but the sky was gray and heavy with clouds. The ocean roiled to her right. A stepped cliff rose to her left. The wind was cold and whipped at her hair and clothes. Snow frosted the rocks that meandered down the coastline. Winter.

The ground beneath her was black, though. Black sand stretched out in front of her in a broad dark line that cut between the ocean foam and the cliffs.

Reynisfjara.

She walked against the wind, a shawl drawn tight around her. She knew where she was going—toward an outcropping up ahead, where the rock formed a natural windbreak. Someone waited there. Coins jingled dully in the purse hung from her hip, as it clunked against her thigh. This was dangerous, it was madness, but she was determined.

Determined, and in love.

The black sand was soft and cold beneath her

feet, like walking through slush. The water tried to creep up and touch her with each white wave.

How did she know this place so well?

As she drew closer to the outcropping, she saw someone there, tucked into the indentation. Someone in a black cloak, hunched over.

They looked up, peeking from beneath a hood.

It was an old woman, her face deeply lined, her gray hair fluttering around her face. Her eyes were blue, and full of consternation. Her thin lips were pressed tightly together. She was so grizzled she might have been hewn from the rock itself, a statue on the shore.

Vanessa removed her purse and held it out. It was made from soft leather, with laces stitched around the mouth to cinch it.

"Do you have it?" Vanessa asked, but her voice was not her own. It was deeper and throatier. Nor did she speak English.

The old woman reached inside her cloak. She drew out a knife. "I do not think you should do this." She didn't speak English either. "You will only invite misfortune."

"I make my own choices." Vanessa handed the purse off to her. "And I will make my own fortune."

The woman weighed the purse in her gnarled hand, and then, reluctantly, handed the knife over. Vanessa took it. It was heavy and cold.

"This is pure iron?" Vanessa asked. Recognition sparked in her, though it seemed to come from far away. The handle was slim and carved in a flourish pattern, the blade curved. It was the knife Gunnar gave her. Only, it was new and untarnished.

"As pure as can be." The old woman slipped the purse inside her cloak. "I will caution you once more, do not bring heartache and destruction upon yourself.

Rethink your choices. This is the way of folly."

Vanessa turned to the water. She held the knife aloft to the low winter sun, and it gleamed like silver fire. It was not her hand that held the knife, though. This was not her body.

"As I said, I make my own fortune."

Dread rushed in, darkness that blotted out the sea and washed away the scene in front of her. Everything went black again, and then, the world shifted.

"Vanessa!"

The bedroom materialized around her. The transition was jarring, and the sensation of dread only intensified. She realized she was shaking and gasping for air, as though someone had placed their hands around her throat. She no longer felt warm, relaxed, or turned on, but like she had been dunked in ice water.

"Vanessa." Gunnar hovered over her, eyes wide. He cupped her cheek. "What happened? Are you all right?"

She couldn't find her voice. Tears spilled down her temples. Her heart hammered against her ribs.

Gunnar rolled off her and grabbed a blanket. He covered her naked body with it. "Vanessa." He pulled her up, into his arms. "What's happening? Talk to me. You blanked out."

She curled against him and let out a choked sob. "I don't know. I don't know what the hell is happening to me!" She pressed her face against his chest. His heart was beating wildly too. "I keep having these hallucinations. It was the beach again, the black sand beach."

She wept, in fear, in frustration. He held her and stroked her hair. There was no comfort, though. And she'd felt so good, just a moment ago. She'd experienced ecstasy. This was unfair and cruel. It made her cry harder.

"It's all right," he murmured. "Calm down, it's going to be all right."

"It's not." She clung to him. "It's never going to be all right again. What the hell did they do to my head?"

There were no answers, and that made it even worse.

Chapter Twelve

Vanessa jerked awake to the sound of an engine. She blinked blearily and twisted around to look out the window behind the couch, immediately alert.

"It's all right." Gunnar got up from the other end of the couch. "It's just Aedan. He's back."

She sagged against the cushions and into the blanket wrapped around her. Her head felt thick and her eyes hurt. She needed more sleep—or even, any real, deep sleep.

Light streamed through the windows. The room smelled like the fire on the hearth and coffee. She'd always enjoyed both smells, until now. In this moment, they reminded her where she was—and wasn't. Even the scent of Gunnar's cologne was making her feel far, far away from home.

"I'll be right back," he said.

Gunnar went outside to greet Aedan. She rested her head on the back of the couch and closed her eyes with a groan.

She couldn't let herself fall asleep. At least, not completely. She was too worried if she slept, the dreams would come back. Of course, she didn't even need to be asleep to see them now, apparently. Every time she drifted off, she had weird, disjoined visions that jerked her awake, though she couldn't definitively say they were about the beach. She refused to lie down in the bed, in the vain hope that staying on the couch would somehow help.

It didn't.

At least Gunnar stayed by her side. Sometimes, she rested in his arms and felt a little safer. They hadn't gotten sexy again. She wasn't up to it, being too freaked out and disoriented. Maybe they never should have gone so far to begin with. After all, they barely knew each other, and soon, she would be out of his life. Hopefully, anyway.

Starting a romance in the middle of all this was a bad, bad idea.

She rolled her head on the back of the couch and opened her eyes. The picture of Gunnar's wife sat on the shelf a few feet away, gazing at her with those blue, passive eyes.

A thought nibbled at the back of her brain. What if it was *Gunnar* causing her to have these visions? He was from the place she saw. What if she was somehow channeling all this through him, through his memories? After all, both the dream and the vision happened while he was nearby, even intimate with her. Maybe the huldufólk made her psychic.

The door opened, and Gunnar came back in.

Aedan followed. He looked exhausted as well. His hair was loose and messy on his shoulders, and he had dark circles under his eyes. He glanced in her direction and regarded her with the same stoic, distant expression he always had.

She looked away, because she wanted to stare at him and try to pick out his huldufólk features. After seeing one up close, his presence made her uneasy.

"Anything interesting happen while I was gone?" Aedan closed the door and started pulling his boots off.

"Oh yes." Gunnar dragged a hand through his own messy hair. His curls were sticking out all over. "We made contact."

Aedan dropped one boot, then started working the other one off. "You managed to summon them?"

"Just one. She didn't give us any clear answers, though."

"What a surprise." Aedan dropped the other boot.

"We need to go to Reykjavik, if you're up to it." Gunnar looked at her. "We want to go to the bar where Vanessa disappeared. Just an overnight trip. Do you think you can manage it? I'd rather have you with me than not."

"Yes." Aedan pushed his hair back from his face. "I don't think they'll call on me again for a few days."

"Let's have some coffee, and I'll fill you in." Gunnar headed to the kitchen.

Aedan followed.

Vanessa waited until they were out of sight, then she leaned over and tucked her hand beneath the cushion. The knife was there. She'd been checking it compulsively all night. Touching it made her feel a little more in control.

Gunnar had warned her not to attack them, but she was damned if she'd be defenseless if they came. Whatever watched her, she could still feel it out there. Something lurked in the hills beyond the house, and it was keeping a careful eye on them.

She dozed again, vaguely listening to them speak in the kitchen. As always, she wasn't sure what language they were using but she could decipher it. Gunnar was telling Aedan about everything that had happened since he left.

A faint scraping sound jerked her out of half-sleep again. She looked at the shelf above her.

Had the picture moved? Was it turned that far before? She frowned and rubbed her eyes.

Quite possibly, she was having sleep-depravation hallucinations now. She really needed to take a solid nap before they went to Reykjavik, dreams be damned.

Aedan came into the living room with a cup of

coffee. He sat down in the chair across from the couch, next to the fireplace.

Gunnar walked down the hallway.

She shifted under her blanket, curled on her side with her head propped on the couch arm. She stared into the fire, watching the flames dance.

"You look exhausted." Aedan's voice was flat. "It's been rough."

"Yeah." She flicked her gaze to him. "You look exhausted too."

He took a sip of his coffee. His face was hard, his eyes even harder, but vulnerability lurked behind that stony façade. He was dealing with terrible things, even more terrible than what she was going through. He was angry and hurt. She could see it in the way he carried himself.

She cautiously took in his features. He was handsome and pale, his eyes dark, but he didn't look much like them beyond that. She wouldn't guess he was not of this world. "What do they make you do?" she asked.

The worst he could do was not tell her. She was too drained and battered to tiptoe around anyone's sense of propriety.

"Gunnar didn't tell you?" He didn't sound offended she asked.

She shook her head. "He told me about your mother, how he found her, how she left you with him. That's all. I'm sorry."

"Well, I wouldn't have had much of a life with her, so it's altogether better I ended up with Gunnar. Hell, they probably would have killed me otherwise." His demeanor remained sturdy, but pain flashed in his eyes, a grim and icy anguish. "I guess that would be worse."

She didn't say anything. If he wanted to tell her, he would. She wouldn't ask again.

"He told you how my mother and father met? How she came here to Iceland and he found her, lost in the countryside?"

"He said she was running away from her father."

"The huldufólk who do tolerate humans tend to befriend the ones on the fringes of society. Loners, people on their own, or they've just withdrawn in some way. That was her, that's where she was at the time." He paused. "That's what I get from her diary, anyway. I barely remember her. I just read the things she wrote."

She thought of her own mother. She was an outgoing, lively woman who belonged to the tennis club, hosted dinner parties, and participated in every fundraiser in the community. She definitely wasn't the type the huldufólk would seek out.

"Do you think your father loved her?" Vanessa couldn't resist the question. "When he found her and befriended her. Do you think they really fell in love?" She didn't want to imply things, but she couldn't help but wonder if it was coercion, and if he messed with her mind.

"She wrote about him like she loved him." The hurt in his eyes grew more apparent now. "If he felt the same, I don't know. But he was kind to her. He kept her from starving to death and gave her a place to live."

That sounded like entrapment, preying on a vulnerable woman, but Vanessa kept her mouth shut this time.

"Then she had me, and she tried to hide me, but they found out what my father was doing. They caught him visiting us." He rested his head on the back of the chair and gazed at the ceiling. "They burnt him and made her watch. It gets disjointed after that. I think she went mad. I don't know why they let her live, probably for the irony. There's no suffering if you're dead, after all."

"Like Gunnar," she whispered.

He nodded. "Maybe they planned to kill us eventually, or maybe they just expected us to die on our own."

"Gunnar said he found the two of you up in the hills. And then she brought you to him before…"

"She killed herself." He shrugged. "See? They got what they wanted without having to lift a finger."

"They're monsters. I'm sorry, I know it's half of what you are, but so far they haven't endeared themselves to me at all."

He lifted his head. "Do you think I'd disagree with you? They left me alone until I turned fourteen. Then they came back and decided that was a good age to start making use of me."

Did she really want to know this? She had a feeling what he was about to tell her was horrible and would only make her more afraid.

"My mother's story is not unique." He dropped his head back again. "The huldufólk falling in love with humans and having children with them, it happens a lot. I don't know how beings who have such hatred toward us also secretly love us, but it happens."

She noted he was saying "us," classifying himself as human.

She shrugged beneath the blanket. "It's not as if that doesn't happen with humans, too. It's the lure of the forbidden."

He shifted his jaw. "The fruit of that forbidden union is not so loved. Let me ask you something, now that you've met the huldufólk, do you think I'm like them? Do I look like one, or act like them?"

She swallowed. "When you used your magic on

me, of course. But otherwise, no. Not at all. I wouldn't guess. I mean, that is, if I knew about them to begin with."

He sat forward. "It's hard for them to detect my kind as well, because we're not fully of their world. But I can spot someone like me with no problem. I could pick out a human with huldufólk blood in a crowd, just like that." He snapped his fingers. "There's a certain way we hold ourselves, or maybe, I don't know, we're just attracted to each other."

She got an uneasy feeling.

"It takes someone like me to find someone like me."

She sat up a little. "They use you like a bloodhound?" She knew she'd be horrified.

He nodded. "I lead them to the others. Some make it all the way to adulthood without being detected. Some are kids. Some are even … babies." He gazed across the room, his eyes haunted. "When they think they've found someone like me, but they're not sure, they bring me in to confirm or deny."

"And they kill them?" She stared at him.

"I don't know. They take them. They take them away, and sometimes it's quiet and swift, but other times" —he glanced down— "it's loud and violent."

She pictured the huldufólk snatching babies from mother's arms and scooping children off playgrounds. What anguish—and guilt—Aedan must go through. He was betraying his own kind.

"I do this, and they let me live." He set his cup aside. "That's the deal."

She ached for him. However, questions loomed in her mind. "But what…" She hesitated "…is to say they won't get rid of you too, when all the rest are gone?"

Before Aedan could answer, Gunnar appeared in

the doorway. He leaned against the wall. "We don't," he said softly. "We can only hope."

Aedan said nothing. The consternation on his face made him look older, and the glittering light in his eyes intensified it. He was so young, and yet, so unspeakably aged by his task.

"It's not fair." She threw her blanket off and got up. "It's not fair at all. They're punishing you for simply being alive."

Aedan shrugged.

"You didn't do anything." She was too tired and miserable right now to keep her emotions in check. "You didn't ask to be born. I can't understand why they think it's right to punish you for something you had no control over."

Aedan lifted his hands. "I don't know that it's about punishment so much as not wanting more like me out there. If they get rid of me in the end, they do. I expect no less, actually."

"I won't let them," Gunnar said. "Not if I can help it."

She marched toward the hallway. She needed to use the bathroom and maybe scream into a towel. She also needed a shower. Aedan's magic was not a substitute for soap and shampoo.

She stopped beside Gunnar, who gazed at her sadly. "It's not fair to any of us. We don't deserve this, and they should pay." She headed off down the hallway.

After a shower, and some breakfast and coffee, she felt slightly better, at least physically. Her mind was still stuck in the shadows. She'd put her jeans on, and a fresh t-shirt that Gunnar gave her. When this nightmare was over, she would send him money to repay him for everything she'd used, borrowed, eaten, and for all the hardship she'd inflicted on him.

Gunnar took a shower next, and she and Aedan sat at the kitchen table. She finished her coffee while Aedan ate breakfast. "I keep having these hallucinations," she said. "I don't know if Gunnar told you. These—visions. It's why I can't sleep. I dream about things, too." She sipped her coffee.

Aedan chewed and swallowed. "What sort of visions?"

"They're about the black sand beach, in the south."

"Reynisfjara?"

She nodded. "I don't know what the huldufólk have done to my head." She lowered the cup. "Can they give humans psychic powers?"

Aedan swirled his spoon around in his yogurt. "I don't know. My mother wrote down a lot of things about them. She kept notes about the stuff my father told her, but..." He shook his head. "Unless you're half-huldufólk, I don't think you can have any of their powers."

She lowered her voice, though Gunnar couldn't possibly hear from the shower. "I think I'm channeling Gunnar's memories. He said he's from there. Every time I ... get close to him, it happens."

Aedan narrowed his eyes.

She took a sip and avoided his gaze. "It's very strange, and overwhelming."

"What are these visions about? What happens in them?"

She told him about the two clear ones—running from something on the cliff, and on the shore, with the old woman. She thought about getting the knife, she'd hidden it among her things next to the couch, but she didn't want another lecture.

"Other times, I just hear a voice." She played with a strand of her hair. "It's a whisper, and it turns into a scream. It sounds like a woman, but I can't understand what she's saying."

Aedan rubbed his chin. "Maybe you're seeing something that happened in the year you were missing. Maybe it's not a vision, but your own memory."

She hadn't considered that. But why would she have been doing all these things she was "remembering?" Why would she stick around Iceland and not try to go home?

"I don't know what I would have been doing at Reynisfjara." She recalled the hand holding the knife aloft and gripping the rock in the dream. The fingers were shorter than hers. "And I don't think it's me. When I see these things, I don't feel like I'm inside my own body."

"If you think they're Gunnar's memories, do you think you're in Gunnar's body?"

She'd had a dress and shawl on both times. Not men's clothes. "No." She rubbed her temples. "I feel like I'm going crazy." She looked up at the window. "And someone is watching us. Can you feel it?"

He looked toward the window, then turned back around with a shrug. "They're always watching me. I just kind of ignore it now."

"They were watching even when you weren't here." She stared at the window. "Yesterday, we went out to the island to look for clues and I could feel it so strongly. It was like one of them was right behind me and if I just turned around fast enough, I'd catch them."

"Yeah, Gunnar told me." He licked his spoon. "If they're hanging out and watching you, then there's more to this story. More than they want to tell. But you're not going to get them to reveal it. Only if they want to, they will."

Anger flared in her again. This wasn't fair. None

of it was fair.

"They shouldn't be allowed to get away with this." She clenched her fist on the table. "They can't treat us like this. The reason they're tormenting you, the reason they punished Gunnar—I don't know what I did, but based on what you guys did, or didn't do, I can only assume I don't deserve this kind of treatment either. I want answers, and I want them to be held accountable for how they treat humans."

This confident determination was fueled by rage, fear, and something else, something she couldn't quite put her finger on. A fire burned deep inside her, not blazing and vital, but a low-burning heat like coal embers. It made her want to stand up, march outside, and scream down the hills until they showed themselves.

"And how do you plan to do that?" Aedan plunked his spoon in his yogurt. "Do you think I've never had those same thoughts? Even if I'm half huldufólk, and I can use some of their magic, there's nothing I can do to stop them or 'make they pay' like you said. They'd burn me like they burnt my father."

She thought again of the knife. "They're not invincible, though. Gunnar said they can be harmed or warded off with iron."

"Do you think you could get close enough to hurt them with iron?"

"They don't have any other weaknesses? Did your mother write about those things?"

"I guess you can fend them off with salt too, but…" He picked up his coffee and shrugged. "I eat salt, and it doesn't bother me. I think it's just folklore."

"What about non-magical retaliation? They've taken things from us. What if we take things from them, let them see how it feels. They have children too, right? They must. If they want to fight, then we'll fight."

"You want to kidnap one of them?" He gave her an incredulous look. "Are you serious?"

"I don't know." She slapped her hands on the table. "Just something to get back at them. To make them tell us what's going on. You know more about them than me. What are their weaknesses?"

"You can't do anything to them, don't you understand that? Look at what they've already done to you. What do you think will happen if you do something crazy like try to take one hostage?" He leaned forward. "Do you want to go home and forget this ever happened, or do you want to die here, for real?"

She sucked down the rest of her coffee, slammed the cup down, and stood. "This isn't right."

"This isn't your battle, either." He looked up at her. "I know this is scary, and they've put you through hell. But we're going to Reykjavik, and even if we don't find answers, we'll find someone who believes you are who you say you are." He pushed his chair back and stood as well. "And you'll get to go home. You don't have to worry about us. Even if you never figure out what happened here, at least you'll be back with your family, in your own life, safe and sound. Isn't that what you want?" He gathered up his dishes and took them to the sink. "It's what *we* want for you."

She folded her arms and looked at the doorway. She could still hear the shower running.

Aedan walked past her. "I'm gonna get some sleep before we take off. I've been up all night." He walked out of the kitchen.

She sighed and looked out the window. The day was overcast. Not the heavy clouds of rain like yesterday, but somewhere between vague gray and a hint of sunshine. And still, something watched in the distance. Something that sucked all the light out of her and left her black inside.

She walked to the living room, sifted through the pile of clothes next to the couch, and grabbed the knife. She held it up to the light through the window, the way she'd seen in the vision. It was dull, old, and tarnished. She doubted it was sharp enough to cut anything now. She recalled how she plunged the other knife into Gunnar's abdomen. Even dull, all it would take was one forceful strike, like she'd done then. And if the iron itself was the issue, it might cause damage no matter how sharp it was.

"It may not be wise," she murmured, "but if you mess with me, I'm not going to lie down and let you have me. I'll find a way to make you pay, mark my words."

She lowered the knife and looked at the picture on the shelf. She would not be dragged away in the night, like Gunnar's wife. She wasn't going to be the prize in some cruel game. She'd had enough of it.

She slipped the knife into her hip pocket.

"Just try me," she whispered, glaring out the window.

Chapter Thirteen

"How long is it to Reykjavik?" Vanessa climbed in the cab of the truck. It was a big truck, with both front and back seats. She took the back. Maybe she could stretch out and snooze. "I mean, you told me how far away it is in miles, but how long is the drive?"

Gunnar got in too and closed his door. He sat behind the wheel. Aedan climbed in the passenger seat.

"About three hours." Gunnar looked at her in the rearview mirror. "There's a lot of scenery on the way. It won't be boring."

She looked at the house. Hopefully, this would be the last time she saw it, or this town. Though she was glad to leave, it also made her a bit sad.

"Thank you, for all you've done for me, both of you." She was wearing Gunnar's sweater again. "This might be where we part ways."

Gunnar started the truck. "I hope for that, for your sake."

They pulled out of the driveway. She gazed toward the island as they drove the main road, which skirted the water. She might never see that island again, either. Not unless someone wanted to bring her here to investigate where she'd been found. A chill rushed through her as it retreated in the distance. Whatever was out there, whatever watched her, she just wanted to leave it far behind.

Preferably, clear across the ocean. Even that didn't seem far enough.

She glanced at the tubs as they drove past, and then at the back of Gunnar's head. They could have had so much fun, if only. If only they hadn't met like this. If only she wasn't being tormented. If only she wasn't dead.

For a while, the road traced the jagged edge of the fjords, the elevation sometimes higher, sometimes lower. To the left was the water, gray under the gray clouds, the walls of the fjords misty in the distance. To the right were steep sloping hills, craggy and covered in green. It became static. Occasionally, they passed another car, and sometimes she saw a singular house in the distance, but for the most part they seemed very much alone.

The hum of the engine and the quiet—no one spoke, the radio wasn't on—lulled her, and made her eyelids droop. She sagged against the door and stared out at the water, her vision as bleak as the view. Eventually, they came upon a town, almost as small as the one they left behind.

"Hólmavík," Gunnar said, the first word he'd spoken since they left. He looked at her in the mirror. "We still have a way to go."

They didn't go through the town, merely passed by, the houses and low buildings filling in the space for a few minutes. Then, it was back to the same. Her eyes burned. She was miserable. She'd wanted to see this country so bad, and now it was spoiled forever. In another life, she would be alert right now and excited, enjoying every moment of this trip despite the never-changing featureless landscape.

Gunnar turned on the radio, some low music that broke the monotony. She rested her head against the cool glass and closed her eyes. Just to rest, not to sleep.

Her body, however, had other plans. She fell into a much-needed blank, dreamless sleep.

For a while.

When the dreams finally came they were vague and disjointed, flitting past her like wisps of fog. Nothing she could grasp, not even enough to make her aware she was asleep.

But then, she opened her eyes. Only, she didn't really. She saw the interior of the truck in blurred shadows, like the air was full of smoke. She couldn't see Gunnar or Aedan, but she could still feel the road beneath them. She looked at the seat beside her and her heart jumped.

Gunnar's wife sat beside her. Her hair rested on her shoulders, thick and straight and blonde like in the picture. Her expression was passive, also like in the picture. Her eyes were blue and she observed Vanessa with what seemed like pity, or perhaps sympathy. She wore the black dress from the picture, but Vanessa could see all of it now. The long black skirt gathered around her legs. Black lace wrapped around her white wrists.

Vanessa stared at the fabric. Slowly, she realized she was staring at it because she recognized it. This was the dress in her dream, the dress she'd been wearing.

She met the woman's eyes again, and they were now bright and intense. She stared at Vanessa as though they shared a secret and she was encouraging her to remember it.

"I don't know what's happening." Vanessa's voice was small, hard to push out. "Why am I seeing these things?"

The woman swiveled on the seat to look out the back window. She furrowed her brow, frowning, and suddenly seemed angry. Whatever she saw back there, Vanessa felt a sense of dread. Was someone following them? She tried to turn and look as well, but she couldn't move.

The woman spoke. "You won't outrun them. You won't best them." She spoke Icelandic, but the words were clear. "They live for your torture, you know this."

Vanessa *did* know this, she knew it with her

entire being.

"Best to turn and face them." The woman looked at her, and her face brightened, a devious smile curling her lips. "Fight fire with fire. Fire and iron. Show no mercy."

Vanessa stared at her. She could barely speak. "How do I do that?"

The woman jerked her head around, to look at the front seat. Her expression fell and her eyes clouded. "You should not be here. Go, before they catch you!"

Vanessa didn't know who she was speaking to. She turned her head, slowly, laboriously, and through the mist that shrouded the front seat, she saw a face. A pale face, with black eyes, framed in black hair, looming like a ghost. She gasped in horror.

The woman lunged forward and gripped the face, and pushed it back into the mist. She emitted a furious snarl as she did.

"Go!"

Vanessa jerked awake with a yelp. She was still against the door. Her shoulder ached and her arm was sore and tingling. She sat up and looked around wildly.

The truck was stopped. Gunnar turned and looked back at her, frowning. "Vanessa? Are you all right?"

Aedan was slumped against his own door and lifted his head to look back at her as well.

Sunlight streamed through the windows. The world outside wasn't much different except the clouds had cleared and blue sky shone through. They were still near water and hills rolled away in all directions. There were more cars though, and they were at—a toll booth? They were in a lane leading up to a single kiosk, with a lot of signs around in both English and Icelandic.

She rubbed the side of her face. It was cold from being pressed against the window. "Where are we? How long have I been asleep?"

"We're about to go through the tunnel." Gunnar turned back around. "You've been asleep for two hours. You missed the fjords." He looked at her in the mirror and smiled. "I didn't want to wake you. You seemed like you needed the rest."

She had, but she was shocked she'd stayed asleep that long. "Tunnel?" She eased back against the seat. She was trembling. The face from the dream haunted her. It wasn't the woman from the fire, she was certain of it. It looked more like … a man?

"The Hvalfjörður Tunnel," Gunnar said. "It goes under the fjord. It connects the north to the Capital Region."

The Capital Region. That's where Reykjavik was. They were getting closer. To answers, maybe, and help, hopefully.

"Oh." She gazed out the window as they inched up to the toll booth. The hills were higher here, green and lush. It looked peaceful, and the interior of the car was over-warm with the sun. Such a beautiful day to have nightmares.

Aedan was still eyeing her over his shoulder. "What were you dreaming about?" His voice made her twitch.

She didn't want to tell Gunnar she'd been dreaming about his wife. Not right now. The cryptic messages the woman spoke were as bad as the huldufólk, so relaying them wouldn't help either.

"Nothing, just—nightmares." She shook her head. "Nothing I can really put into words."

Aedan continued staring at her, his eyes glittering, but he didn't say anything else.

She focused her gaze out the window and tried to ignore him.

They went through the booth, and a short distance down the road, they entered a tunnel. She snuggled down in the sweater and tried not to let paranoia creep over her as they plunged into darkness.

In the shadows of the tunnel, as they slid between arched rock walls, she kept glancing at the seat next to her, expecting to see her again. The yellow lights cast strange shapes as they flashed by. Any moment, she expected a figure to leap from one of the alcoves along the sides. A figure with long hair and black eyes.

You won't outrun them. You won't best them. Those words had taken root in her brain and whispered over and over in her ears.

She breathed easier when they passed from the tunnel into the bright daylight once more.

"We'll stop shortly," Gunnar said. "Grundarhverfi is just ahead. We'll get some air and stretch our legs. I know it's a long trip."

She almost chuckled. If he thought this was a long trip, he should try a cross-country road trip in the U.S. Iceland was only the size of Ohio.

The land turned flatter, the hills that did rise in the distance much taller, more like mountains. They passed houses and farms, and there were considerably more cars on the road. They'd found civilization. The water was now on the right, though it became more and more distant until she only caught peeks of it on the horizon.

They stopped at a gas station at the edge of yet another small town. Her legs were stiff when she got out. The day was temperate, the wind mild, unlike back in the fjords where it was always trying to knock her over. Farmland stretched out on the other side of the road, beneath mountainous hills. She looked around the parking lot and found that apart from the Icelandic writing on the signs, this could be any gas station in any Podunk town in America.

Yet another illusion of her dream world, shattered.

"Do you need anything?" Gunnar touched her lower back. "It'll only be another half hour to Reykjavik."

She looked at him. His eyes were kind, much like his wife's had been, at first. Blue like hers, but paler. She wanted to throw herself into his arms and rest there for a while, to experience what they were robbed of last night, that sweet intimacy. She was so anxious and knotted up inside, so unsure of what was about to happen. She needed a lot of things: answers, peace, him.

She would have to settle for a Diet Coke.

She stayed outside while Gunnar went in, because she wanted to get some air and stretch her legs while she contemplated her thoughts by walking in slow circles around the truck. Maybe she looked dumb, but it helped.

Aedan stayed in the truck. As she passed by his window, he put it down.

She stopped.

"What were you dreaming about?"

The question was to the point. She wasn't going to get out of it or be able to lie to him.

She glanced toward the station. "I was dreaming about Gunnar's wife."

Aedan looked at her. "His wife?"

She stepped up to the door. No one was close by, but she was still paranoid someone—or something—would hear. "She was sitting next to me on the seat, and she said some weird things. Things I don't understand."

"What did she say?"

"She said I can't outrun them or best them. She told me to turn and face them, to fight fire with fire. Or with—fire and iron, I think that's how she put it."

Aedan just stared at her.

"And I saw one of them. He appeared just for an instant—I think it was a he—and she seemed really angry about it. She told him he shouldn't be there and pushed him away. It was freaky."

Aedan sat up a little. "That is weird."

"I have this sneaking suspicion." She looked toward the station again. "I don't know what they did to my head, if they made me psychic or something, but I don't think it's Gunnar's memories I'm seeing now."

"What do you mean?"

"I think, somehow, I'm seeing what happened to his wife. I'm seeing *her* memories."

Aedan frowned. "How is that possible?"

"I don't know." She clutched the bottom of the window frame. "What do you think happened to her? Gunnar said he doesn't know if she's still alive or dead. It's been almost a century. Do you think she could still be alive somewhere, being held prisoner?" She assumed since they'd kept Gunnar alive so long, they could do the same to his wife. Especially if it meant she got to suffer more.

"I can't begin to say. Just like I can't tell you what they do with the half-huldufólk people. I don't know where they dwell, or if it's even in this realm. These were not things my father told my mother."

She drummed her fingers on the door. "When I had those visions, I was in her body, seeing things through her eyes." She recalled the long black dress. The hand holding the knife. "But in this last dream, I was definitely in my own body. She was sitting next to me."

Aedan kept frowning.

"Maybe she *is* dead, though. Maybe she's a spirit or something, and she's trapped. She's reaching out, trying to make contact."

"Why wouldn't she contact Gunnar, then? Why pick some random tourist from America?"

"I don't know, unless—the way they altered my brain makes me able to pick her up, like some spiritual radio station. She's been trying to reach out to Gunnar, but he can't hear her. Then when I get close to him, I pick up her frequency." She perked, because this made a lot of sense. "What if that's what's happening?"

When she'd had these visions, she was always close to Gunnar. Even in the truck, he was sitting right in front of her. She thought of the overwhelming vision when they'd been getting hot and heavy in bed and cringed. Jesus, was his wife trying to cockblock him from the other side? That only made this more painfully awkward.

Aedan dragged a hand through his hair. "I don't know, I mean, that could be what's happening, I guess. It makes more sense than anything I can come up with."

She was excited to maybe have an answer, but her enthusiasm quickly ebbed. It didn't solve any of her own issues. It didn't explain what happened to her over the past year, or why. Seeing these things, dreaming about his wife, was only a side effect of what was done to her. She wasn't any closer to an explanation.

"I don't think I should tell him about this," she said. "Do you think it would upset him?"

Aedan sank back down in the seat. "I don't know. If she's trying to give him a message, maybe you should tell him. It might upset him, but he deserves to know, doesn't he?"

So far, his wife hadn't really given any messages though. She just showed Vanessa things, and warned her about the huldufólk. If she was dead and wanted Gunnar to know her fate, and she made that clear, Vanessa would tell him. It was the kind thing to do, so at least he would have some closure.

"I'll tell him, but not right now. I'll wait until we say goodbye. It might be better that way."

Aedan just looked at her. She believed she'd be getting off this island soon, but did *he*?

She walked around to the back of the truck and leaned against it.

A few minutes later, Gunnar emerged from the station, plastic bag in hand. He walked over and pulled out a bottle and handed it to her.

"Thanks." She had a lot to say, but none of it really seemed to matter. "Thanks for everything." She met his eyes. "For driving me to Reykjavik. For all the help you've given me."

He pulled out another bottle and stepped closer to her as he twisted the cap off. "I couldn't just abandon you. And like I said, I needed some excitement." He took a drink.

She toyed idly with the cap on her own bottle. "I don't know how I'm going to convince any authority of who I am. Do you think they can fingerprint me or something?" She had never committed a crime or been in trouble for anything that would require her to have fingerprints taken. However, in grade school, they'd had their fingerprints done for a safety project and missing kids thing. Could they still use those? Were they even in any official database?

"You'll have to insist. Just tell them you're not the dead woman they found. Make them contact someone you know to identify you. Your parents would recognize you on sight, wouldn't they?"

They'd also "recognized" her body, which confused her endlessly.

"Where do I tell everyone I've been for the past

year, though?"

"Tell them the truth, that you don't know." He capped his bottle. "They might not believe it, but you're not lying, are you?"

She sighed. The alternative was not going to the police until she figured out what happened—and that might take a long time. It might be never. "We'll go to the bar first. See if they have footage. Maybe there's an answer there."

He squeezed her side, above her hip. "Okay."

She meant to pull away, but instead she moved closer. Aedan could probably see them in the side mirror, but she didn't care. Gunnar dipped down and gave her a gentle kiss. She kissed him back, then drew away. This was really complicated, but it felt so good.

She hoped his wife wasn't watching.

"We better get back on the road." He rubbed her side. "Not much longer now." The stilted tone of his voice told her this was complicated for him too.

She walked around the truck with him and he opened her door. She crawled inside with her cheeks hot, clutching her bottle.

Aedan looked at Gunnar as he slid in next to him. He didn't say anything, though.

She wondered if he would even say something in private. The whole thing was dumb and futile on both their parts, but what was it going to hurt? Except, maybe some ghost's feelings.

Gunnar started the engine. "Tell me what the name of the bar is when we get to Reykjavik. I know the city well."

She looked out the window, across the road at the giant hill that loomed over the farmland. The sun was still out, bathing everything in gold. Such tranquility, and the underlying feel of how ancient and storied this land was, how much old wonder it contained.

But then suddenly, directly behind that feeling was a sensation she knew all too well—it swept over her and made her breath catch.

Eyes upon her. Someone was watching them, again. Still.

She looked around anxiously as Gunnar pulled through the parking lot. Only normal people around, filling their cars, going in and out of the station. Yet, she felt the presence close by, fixed on her. She looked through the back window into the bed of the truck, her heart in her throat, fearing she would see someone back there. It was empty.

If something had been watching them back in Drangsnes, and it was watching them now, that meant it followed them.

Gunnar pulled onto the road. The feeling faded a bit, as if whoever watched didn't advance with them. She still saw nothing unusual as they drove away. She turned back around and settled on the seat, tense.

Aedan looked back at her. "Yeah, I felt it too."

Gunnar glanced up at the mirror. "What? What's going on?"

She wrung her hands around the bottle. Why the hell wouldn't they leave her alone? Maybe they knew where she was going, knew what she was about to find out. If they tried to stop her, she would stop them first. The knife sat heavy in her pocket. Gunnar's wife said fight fire with fire, and iron. Face them.

"We're being followed." Aedan settled into his seat. "It's nothing new, but I don't think it's just me they're watching this time."

She stared out the window at the passing scenery and tried to bolster herself. She repeated what she'd said out loud to them back at the house, this time in her head.

HIDDEN

Just try me.

Chapter Fourteen

Reykjavik was a sharp departure from the desolation that otherwise made up most of the country. Vanessa felt, as she had the first time she'd been here, that she'd passed back into the "real" world. Jumping from sweeping vistas and rolling farmland to modern, cluttered civilization was a jarring contrast.

Once off the freeway, the area they drove into was full of streets that were often narrow and lined with parked cars. Apart from the alien signage, they could have been streets in any city back home. The houses and buildings were colorful and sat tightly together. People lingered in the doorways of bars and shops and walked hand in hand down the street, like normal people, here in reality, where things still made sense.

On the horizon loomed Mt. Esja, the place where her "body" had been found. She got peeks of it between the buildings, ominous and blue, and it made her insides cold.

In her memory, she had only been here three days ago, and some things looked familiar. They were close to the hotel she and her friends had stayed at.

"This is so weird," she muttered. "How can a year have passed?" She asked this of no one in particular, and no one had an answer for her.

Gunnar parked the truck in an empty spot at a curb and her stomach lurched. She realized where they were. She'd told him the name of the place.

And this was it. It looked different in full daylight. Reykjavik's 101 District seemed glamorous and beguiling in the blue twilight of the summer night, lights everywhere, music in the air, people filling the sidewalks. It felt vital and fun, like every party district in every city ever, a siren's call to young people and the adventurous. In the stark light of day, it looked washed out and over-ordinary.

They were near Hallgrímskirkja, the tallest church, and one of the tallest structures, in all of Iceland. The gray tower rose over them to the left. She'd visited it and stood in the courtyard taking pictures before they started their circuit of bars.

She could vividly remember Jessica pointing out hot guys they passed on the street. She remembered Steph's overt attempts to flirt with their server at the restaurant they ate at. She'd been flirting herself, though awkwardly and terribly, with a guy they stood next to at a bar. He had green eyes and a thick accent. He'd slipped away before she could get the courage to ask for his number.

And then she'd stood right there, outside the door of this squat building with the patio on the side, just a few feet away. It was stuffy inside and she was flushed from her cocktail. A guy had stood out there as well, smoking and chatting with a blonde woman. The air was warm, the sky deep blue. Someone drove past and they had an Icelandic hip hop song blaring out their windows.

Only three nights ago.

Gunnar turned and looked back at her. "Is this the place?"

Her hands were clenched in her lap. "Yes."

"They seem to be open. We should go inside and see if we can talk to a manager." He turned off the truck.

She had no idea how they were going to get what they wanted. "Do you think they'll really give us access to their security footage? It's not like we're the police or something. It's going to look strange."

Aedan sat up and stretched. "They'll let us."

They got out of the truck. Standing on that street

again made her feel off kilter. Her mind still wouldn't accept that it had been over a year since she'd been there. As they walked toward the bar, without thinking, she reached out and clutched Gunnar's hand.

He looked at her, then squeezed her hand in return. "It's going to be all right."

Outside the door, she stopped. She looked up at a camera tucked beneath the eaves of the steepled roof. It pointed in the direction of the church. "That's the one we'll need," she said. She let go of Gunnar's hand as they stepped inside.

It was a small, cozy little bar and restaurant, with exposed wood walls and floors and low ceilings. The front was a dining room, and in the back was a bar with huge windows looking out on the patio. It was currently quiet and mostly empty. That night it had been loud and vivacious. She remembered an obviously drunk woman in a short red dress, dancing and hollering near the bar.

They made their way to the back, through the shadowy dining area. The man behind the bar was broad and portly, with short brown hair. She didn't recognize him, but then, she couldn't recall any of the staff, as she'd been wrapped up in other things. Her friends. Her adventure.

The man greeted them in Icelandic. *Good afternoon folks, welcome.* It translated immediately in her head. Being able to suddenly speak Icelandic might have been cool, if not for the circumstances.

Gunnar responded in English. "Hello, how are you?"

The man switched to English. "Great. Can I get you something to drink?" His accent was thick. He glanced at Aedan, probably because he didn't look old enough to be served alcohol.

"Actually." Gunnar slid onto a stool. "We're

looking for some information. We were wondering if you could help us."

Vanessa slid onto the stood beside him.

Aedan remained standing.

"Uh, maybe? It depends on what kind of information you're looking for. What do you need?"

Gunnar looked at her.

She didn't know what to say, so she'd planned to let him do the talking.

"We…" Gunnar looked back at the bartender "…are trying to find some information about a friend. Something happened to her, near here. The security camera you have outside, above the door, we were wondering how long you keep the footage?"

The bartender raised his eyebrows. "Oh, uh." He let out a gust of air and stared thoughtfully across the room. "I'm not sure. It's all digital, you know. I think it's kept in an online archive. The owner takes care of that."

Gunnar sat up straighter. "Is the owner here right now?"

The bartender shook his head. "No, I'm the manager on duty. He won't be in until tomorrow. You could come back and talk to him, if you want."

She started to panic. She couldn't wait until tomorrow. She looked desperately at Gunnar.

"Do you have access?" Gunnar asked. "Could you get in and look at the footage yourself?"

The bartender frowned deeply and folded his arms. "Sure, I could get in on the laptop, probably." He thumbed over his shoulder, toward the back. "I know where it is, I just don't deal with it. What's this about, again?" He narrowed his eyes.

"Like I said, something happened to a friend of ours. We were hoping to find out some things about it." Gunnar spoke amicably, but anxiousness crept into his voice.

"Have you spoken to the police?"

"Yes." Gunnar shifted. "So, do you think you could get in to look at your security footage?"

"Yeah, I can but—"

"Do it," Aedan said.

Vanessa looked at him, wide-eyed.

He leaned against the bar, staring at the man.

The bartender stared back at him, his eyes going blank, then he nodded. "All right." He walked toward a door behind the bar.

Vanessa's skin crawled. "Did you just…"

"I told you they'd let us."

Much as she was glad Aedan was there, and that he had the ability to "suggest" things, it also frightened her. It was the same thing they'd done to her, on a smaller scale.

"Just stay calm," Gunnar murmured.

The bartender came back after a few minutes, carrying a laptop. He placed it on the bar in front of them, open and facing him. He started typing. "I can get into the cameras." He squinted at the screen. "I'm not sure I can find what you want, though."

Gunnar leaned forward and peeked around at the screen. "We're very grateful for your help."

She glanced at Aedan. Was he controlling the man still?

"What happened to your friend?" The bartender's tone was sympathetic, and curious. He clicked around on the laptop.

Vanessa found her voice. "She disappeared."

The bartender looked at her. "From here?"

She nodded. "We're just trying to see if there's any footage from that night. We're looking for clues."

Gunnar squeezed her knee under the bar.

The bartender gazed at the screen, occasionally humming to himself. Finally, he perked. "There we go. Yeah, here are the archives. There's one for each camera."

Vanessa's spirits rose, but this also gave her terrible anxiety. What if she saw something she couldn't deal with?

"When did this happen?" the bartender asked.

Gunnar slipped his hand off her knee. "A year ago. Nearly to the day."

"A year?" The bartender let out a surprised laugh. "I don't know they go that far back." He clicked around again. "I see stuff from a couple months ago, but I'm not sure he'd keep it that long. There's really no need, you know."

Vanessa's spirits sagged again.

"What is the exact date?" The bartender placed his fingers on the keys. "I'll do a search."

Vanessa gave him the date. She sat in stiff anticipation as he typed.

He blinked and looked up at them, obviously startled. "It is here. There's a file from that day."

She held her breath.

"It's—" He peered at the screen. "Actually, just a clip. Oh." He looked up at them, and his gaze turned wary. "It was part of an investigation, that's why it's been saved."

She let out her breath and tried to keep calm. "That would make sense."

He looked between all three of them. "Your friend?"

Gunnar nodded. "Yes, we're assuming."

"Is she still missing?" His whole demeanor was guarded now.

"Yes," Vanessa said softly.

"The police haven't been able to help much," Gunnar said. "We're trying to find some answers on our own."

"Maybe you should talk to them again." He moved to close the laptop. "I'm not sure I'm allowed to do this."

"Let us see it," Aedan said.

Vanessa shivered, but again, she was dubiously grateful to have him there. She didn't look at the bartender so she wouldn't see that blank look in his eyes again.

He turned the laptop toward them.

On the screen was a still video frame of out front. The time stamp indicated it was just after ten PM. The picture was clear, and her heart skipped a beat when she saw herself, standing next to the door. She wore the same clothes she'd woken up in on the island, the clothes she'd put on that evening to go out.

A snag she hadn't considered until this point struck her. If the bartender watched the video, he would recognize her. It wasn't like she'd changed. They couldn't continue claiming it was a "friend" when it was obviously her, unless she made up some preposterous story about it being her twin sister or something. Panic gripped her again.

But Aedan *had* thought this though, apparently. He leaned over next to her, to look at the laptop. "Go do your work," he said dismissively. "Let us look at it by ourselves for a few minutes."

The bartender instantly wandered away.

Vanessa looked at Aedan, pulling in a breath. "Thank you," she whispered.

Aedan shrugged. "Hurry up. It doesn't last long."

There were a set of controls at the bottom of the screen. Gunnar pulled the laptop over and Vanessa huddled close, against his shoulder, staring at the screen.

"You can see up the street." Gunnar pointed to the corner of the video. "Almost to the church. If something happens up that way, we'll see it."

Her stomach was in knots. What were they about to see, and would it help her?

"You ready?" he asked softly.

She nodded.

He started the video.

According to the time bar, the clip was three minutes and twelve seconds long. For the first minute and a half or so, nothing happened. She stood next to the door, looking at her phone. If she peered super close, she could almost make out her texting app—she'd been trying to find something her mother sent her, an article about the top restaurants to visit in Iceland. The guy with the cigarette and the girl were there, almost out of frame at the bottom of the shot. People walked by, but she didn't interact with them.

Then, at roughly the halfway mark, she jerked her head up and looked down the street toward the church, as though there had been a noise or someone called out. Unfortunately, the video didn't have sound.

A surreal feeling swept over her. She didn't remember that. The couple at the bottom didn't react, so whatever had caught her attention didn't catch theirs.

"Did you hear something?" Gunnar asked.

She shook her head. "I don't know."

She lowered her phone to her side and stood still, staring in the same direction. After about twenty seconds, she stepped away from the door and started slowly down the street.

"I don't remember this." She gripped the edge of the bar. She recalled the faint voice in her head, like someone calling for her. "Where am I going?" She watched herself walk down the street, toward the edge of the frame. Then, something else caught her attention and her blood ran cold.

"What is that?" She pointed at the top of the screen.

At the very edge of the camera's vision, she swore she could make out a figure. It was dark like a shadow. Someone seemed to be standing there, waiting.

"It looks like a person," Gunnar said. "But it wouldn't be odd for someone to be on the street, would it?"

Aedan peered closer too.

She watched herself walk up to the figure, stop momentarily as though speaking to them, and then they walked off the screen together. The video ended.

She sucked in a sharp breath. "Play that again."

Gunnar did, several times. Each time, despite the distance from the camera and the ambiguity, she was more and more certain she was specifically meeting up with the figure and they left together.

"Oh my God." She sat back, dumbfounded.

"You don't remember walking away?" Gunnar looked over the laptop, at the bartender who was arranging bottles on the shelves behind the bar.

"I certainly don't remember meeting anyone." She swallowed. "But, I seem to recall—a voice, like someone calling out to me. I don't know what they said, if it was a man or woman. Maybe that's what I heard when I looked up."

Aedan slipped his hand into the pocket of his jeans and pulled out something small and shiny. He handed it to Gunnar. "Hurry up."

A flash drive.

Gunnar stuck it into one of the computer ports.

"You guys came prepared." She was grateful for

that.

"We were hoping they would give us a copy consensually." Gunnar got to work saving the clip to the drive. "You want to have a copy when you go to the police. What better way to prove you are who you say you are?"

She hadn't considered that. All they had to do was look at the video and look at her, and they'd realize she wasn't lying about her identity. Gunnar was kind of a genius. She wanted to throw her arms around him and kiss him.

Gunnar saved the clip, slipped the flash drive out, and turned the laptop back around. The bartender looked over his shoulder, then wandered back to the bar.

She rubbed her sweaty palms on her thighs. "Thank you. You've been very helpful."

She and Gunnar slid off their stools.

Aedan leaned over and gazed at the man.

He stared back at Aedan, looking loopy and dreamy-eyed.

"You won't remember us being here," Aedan said. "Forget about us."

The bartender nodded and gathered up the laptop. "Have a great day, folks."

They hustled through the restaurant and stepped back onto the street. Vanessa looked at the spot where she'd been standing, and then up the street, in the direction she'd walked. If she had her distance right, the figure was standing at the cross street up ahead, adjacent to the church.

"Let's go." She motioned.

They followed her as she marched in that direction. She looked around, but there was nothing strange. Just a summer day, on a quiet street.

"Do you think it was one of the huldufólk?" She

mostly addressed Aedan. "They could have been luring me away."

"It's hard to say," he replied. "It was just a figure."

They stopped at the spot where she was sure the person stood in the video. She stared at the ground, as if there would be some clue there, but found nothing. She looked at Aedan. "Do you see any signs?"

He squinted. "Signs?"

"Gunnar said out on the island, the huldufólk leave messages for you. Do you see anything like that here? Or some indication they've been here?"

Aedan looked around. "No, I don't see anything."

Frustration boiled in her. They were so close, but so far away.

"We're staying there tonight." Gunnar pointed to a white building up ahead, across from the church. "You can come out and look around some more. I thought it would be best to get a room close to the bar."

He truly *was* a genius.

She looked toward the tower of Hallgrímskirkja and the circular courtyard around it. Like the evening she'd visited, clusters of people lingered around the base, taking pictures.

Something—someone—caught her attention there, and she froze.

"What the—" She stepped forward, staring, boggling. Was she losing her mind?

"Vanessa?" Gunnar touched her arm.

"You've got to be kidding me." She took off toward the courtyard, hand pressed over the knife in her pocket.

Chapter Fifteen

In the long shadow of the church, a woman stood, gazing up at it. Black hair tumbled down her back. She wore a gray sweater.

Vanessa circled in front of her, stopped, and stared.

The woman lowered her gaze to Vanessa and frowned. Her eyes were normal, her skin fair but not preternaturally pale.

However, without a doubt, it was the woman from the island—the tourist watching the puffins, who startled Vanessa and made her feel like an idiot. She didn't feel like an idiot right now, though. This was way too much of a coincidence.

"Who are you?" Vanessa demanded.

The woman blinked. "Excuse me?" She didn't have an Icelandic accent.

Gunnar rushed toward them and stopped a few feet away. "Vanessa? What are you doing?"

"You've been following us, haven't you?" Vanessa moved in closer. "Are you the one that's been watching us?"

The woman's frown deepened. "I'm sorry? Who are you?"

"You're one of them, aren't you?"

Aedan had paused at the edge of the courtyard. He stared at the woman too.

"Vanessa." Gunnar grabbed her arm. "I'm sorry, miss. She's mistaken you for someone else."

"I don't think I have." Vanessa pulled out of his grip. "You were on the island. I remember you."

The woman looked genuinely confused and a little frightened, which made Vanessa doubt herself.

Maybe it was just a coincidence, maybe she was sightseeing and this was a random event. However, Vanessa's every instinct told her otherwise. This woman had been following them. She was one of them, even if she looked like a normal person right now.

"What island?" the woman asked. "I don't know who you are, and I don't know what you're talking about."

If she confessed to being on the island, Vanessa might have been even more inclined to think it was a coincidence. But she was absolutely the same woman. She was even dressed the same, though it was a day later.

"Were you the one who called out to me that night?" Vanessa pointed in the direction of the bar. "Did you kidnap me?"

Gunnar looked helplessly to Aedan, who still stood at the edge of the courtyard. Either he recognized her as one of the huldufólk and couldn't get involved, or he understood this was insane and didn't want to spend the night in a jail cell.

"Leave me alone." The woman stepped away. "I don't know who you are, crazy person."

Vanessa lunged forward and grabbed her arm.

"Vanessa!" Gunnar yelped.

"Who are you?" Vanessa jerked her. "Why are you doing this to me? What happened to me, and where have I been for the past year?"

People were looking their way now. She hoped there weren't any police around.

As she'd charged across the courtyard, she'd slipped the knife out of her pocket and up the sleeve of her sweater. She didn't intend to use it as a weapon, unless it came to the point her life was threatened. It rested cold and hard against her inner arm, the tip cupped in her palm.

"Let go of me!" The woman tried to struggle free. "Stop!"

"I want some damn answers."

A rush of whispering filled Vanessa's head. It seemed to come from all around her. The voice of a woman, and she knew now it must be Gunnar's wife. He was close by, and she was trying to come through.

Images flashed in her vision: the beach, in the darkness. Waves crashing against the black shore. She was running, in the cold, on the icy sand, and something was chasing her.

She tried to blink it away. The knife tip bit into her palm.

"Vanessa, stop!" Gunnar pushed between them and tried to pry Vanessa's hand off the struggling woman. "This is a mistake."

It wasn't a mistake, though. That's why she was hearing the voice. It was urging her, telling her to reveal the monster. Face it.

"I deserve some goddamn answers," Vanessa snarled. "You have no right to do this to me."

Gunnar was blocking them from view of the other people in the courtyard. Using that cover, she slipped the knife blade fully into her hand. She yanked the woman's arm forward and pressed the flat of the blade to her exposed wrist.

There was a sound like water hitting hot metal, a sizzle that startled Vanessa even though she expected it. The woman bared her teeth and hissed. Her eyes went black.

Gunnar leapt back.

"I told you." Vanessa was both terrified and elated. "She's one of them!"

The woman yanked out of her grasp and took off running. Vanessa would have gone after her, but people had closed in.

"What are you doing?" a man demanded. "Are you attacking that woman?"

Vanessa quickly lowered her arm to her side, hiding the knife. Her heart thundered in her ears. She looked after the woman as she ran around the church.

"Just a misunderstanding." Gunnar gripped Vanessa by the shoulders and held her in place. "They know each other. Just having a little spat."

"You sure?" The man glared at Vanessa.

"It's fine." Vanessa pushed her hair back. She didn't dare take off after the woman, or someone would probably call the police. And when the woman vanished into thin air, as the huldufólk seemed wont to do, and Vanessa was left standing there with a knife up her sleeve, she would have a lot of explaining to do. "Yeah, just a misunderstanding. Sorry."

Gunnar turned her around and pushed her across the courtyard, toward Aedan. His hands were tight and heavy on her shoulders. The urge to break free was strong, but she forced herself to keep walking in the direction Gunnar moved her.

"I told you," she whispered.

"I know." His tone was terse. "Let's get out of here before we get in trouble."

She slipped the knife back in her pocket.

Aedan stood gazing grimly at her.

"You knew she was one of them, didn't you? You saw it."

He nodded. "I couldn't interfere, though. That would be my death."

"I understand. I'm not angry."

"Let's get out of here." Gunnar took his hands off her shoulders and grabbed her arm, not gently. "We'll get our things from the truck and check in at the hotel."

They didn't speak as they crossed the street and made their way toward the truck. Vanessa's mind was racing, her limbs singing with exhilaration and triumph. She kept looking back, expecting the woman to reappear and follow them, but she didn't. Nor did anyone else from the courtyard, thankfully.

"She could have been the figure in the video," Vanessa said as they approached the truck. "I know she's the one who's been following us and watching us, she must be."

When they reached the truck, Gunnar stopped her with a rough tug of her arm. She turned to face him, frowning. His eyes were stormy, his lips pressed tight together. He let go of her.

"What is this?" He jammed his hand into her front pocket. "What the hell are you doing with this?" He pulled the knife out and held it up in front of her face. "I didn't give it to you to use!"

She snatched it back and pushed it back in her pocket, looking around. "It was just a hunch, that I could use it to expose her. You saw what happened. I only touched her with it, I didn't stab her."

"You can't accost the huldufólk!" He gripped her shoulders. "What the hell were you thinking?"

Aedan stood next to the truck, watching them.

"I was thinking she was following us, and I had to put a stop to it." She flung his hands off her shoulders. "It was her, out on the island. She's been watching us for days, I've felt it. Aedan feels it."

"Then let her watch!" He clenched his fists. "You don't confront them. I warned you about this, weren't you listening?"

"I don't deserve this! None of us deserve what they've done to us. We can't let them get away with it."

"Jesus Christ." Gunnar dragged his hands

through his hair and turned away. "Do you want to get out of this country alive?"

"I want answers!"

He turned back, his eyes still on fire, but there was concern and fear in them, too. "If you anger them, you won't get answers, and you won't get away. They took away a year of your life, they messed up your head. Do you want them to do worse? Because they will. If you throw yourself at them, you will not win. Ask Aedan. He'll tell you that going up against them is never a good idea."

Aedan looked somber. He gazed down at the pavement.

"I'm not going to be helpless if I don't have to be. I will defend myself, mark my words."

He rubbed his forehead. "God, you sound like— someone I used to know." He shook his head. "It didn't end well for her, either."

She wondered if he was talking about his wife. She stepped closer. "How far is Reynisfjara? How long would it take us to get there?"

"Why?"

"We need to go." She looked around again, still on guard. "I don't know why, but we do. I think there's answers there. That's why I've been dreaming about it."

Aedan looked up.

She clutched Gunnar's arm. "You know how to get there, right? You said you lived there."

"I lived there a hundred years ago."

"You haven't been back since, in a hundred years?"

"No." The word was curt.

"We have to go there, I'm sure of it."

"What about the police?" He took her hand from his arm and held it. "Don't you want to go home?"

"It's not far, right?" She tried to remember the geography of Iceland. It wasn't that big, not in American terms. "How long would it take?"

Aedan spoke up. "Two, maybe close to three hours. Less than what we've already driven today."

"And what time is it?" She automatically reached for her cell phone, but she didn't have it, of course. "We've still got plenty of day left, especially since it's summer."

"We should go to the hotel," Gunnar said. "And you should take the footage to the police, so you can prove who you are."

Was he afraid to go home?

"I need to see what's at the beach, first." She pulled her hand away. "Something is calling me there."

Gunnar heaved a sigh. "The black sand stretches for hundreds of miles. It may not even be Reynisfjara you're seeing."

She *was* seeing Reynisfjara, though. Because that was the beach near where Gunnar and his wife had lived, and it was Gunnar's wife she was having visions about. She didn't suppose telling him that right now would ease his anxiety or make him more likely to take her there. "We have to go." She walked around the side of the truck. "Come on." She opened the back door.

Gunnar didn't move, staring at her as she climbed in the back seat.

She shut the door and motioned urgently to him. Maybe she was pushing it and taking advantage of his good graces, but she needed to find out if she was right. If she left Iceland without any answers, it would haunt her for the rest of her life.

And possibly, his wife would haunt her for the rest of her life.

Gunnar turned to Aedan and started speaking to

him. He spoked too lowly for her to hear through the rolled-up windows.

She looked around, twisting on the seat, making sure the woman hadn't returned. She should have gone after her, onlookers be damned. As soon as she revealed herself, Vanessa should have clung to her and refused to let go. She should have held her down and put the knife to her throat until she gave some clear answers.

Since when had she gotten so crazy, or so bold? She'd never been the sort to fight someone, or even confront them. The last time she'd gotten in a fight was high school, and the other girl started it, kept pressing it, and a few smacks were exchanged. Vanessa went home and cried all afternoon and avoided the girl for the rest of the school year. Now she was thinking about tackling someone and threatening their life?

Gunnar and Aedan walked to the back of the truck. She frowned. Aedan opened the back door opposite her. Their bags sat on the floor back there, and Aedan pulled them out.

"What are you doing?" She scooted across the seat. "I'm not asking much, am I? Please!"

Aedan stepped back.

Gunnar looked into the truck. "I'm taking Aedan to check in to the hotel. He's staying here." He didn't sound necessarily angry, but he didn't sound happy, either. "In case they come here to speak to him. You should go with us. Don't sit out here alone."

She considered that, but what if it was a trick? What if Gunnar wouldn't come back to the truck and they forced her to stay at the hotel? She didn't think they would be so mean, but she had also just scared the hell out of Gunnar.

"I'll stay right here." She wiggled back. "I'll keep an eye out."

"After what just happened, I don't think that's a good idea." Gunnar was stern. "If she comes back and wants to punish you, you won't have any help."

"And you can stop her?" She snorted. "If she comes for me, what exactly are you going to do? What exactly are you *willing* to do? You said it's not a good idea to fight them."

Aedan stepped back on the curb, stoic and silent.

Gunnar growled and ran a hand through his hair.

She felt bad, being so difficult after he'd been so kind, but she wasn't going to cower. She wasn't afraid to sit out here, and in fact felt better doing so, because she'd know first if something was coming. She also had the knife.

"I'll be fine." She tried to soften her tone. "Just go get checked in and come back. I'll be right here."

Gunnar scowled. "Get in the front seat and lock the doors."

She got out, and they didn't leave the truck until she crawled in the front passenger seat and Gunnar heard her lock the doors. Could locks keep huldufólk out?

They walked briskly toward the hotel.

"Sorry," she murmured.

While they were gone, she remained fully paranoid, but no one who walked past the truck looked suspicious, or even so much as glanced her way. She stared at the front of the bar, at the spot where she'd stood, checking her phone before something distracted her.

Why? Why did they put her under a spell and lure her away? She had wracked her brain, trying to remember anything she'd done that might have offended them. She didn't disrespect the land. She didn't litter, or go into spots she wasn't supposed to, though she saw plenty of tourists doing those very things. She tried to leave everything as she found it and not trample delicate places. Of course, the huldufólk seemed to dole out punishment for the most ridiculous slights, so maybe she simply breathed their air and it was unforgivable.

After a time, drowsiness made her eyelids droop, the warmth of the sun intensifying it. She must have dozed off, because the door opening jolted her awake.

Gunnar got in behind the wheel. His expression was strained, his eyes glittering with—anger? Worry? Whatever emotions he wrestled with, she had provoked them and her guilt intensified.

She pulled her seatbelt on. "Did you guys get checked in?" Small talk wouldn't help, she had a feeling. "Is it a nice room?"

He turned on the engine and looked at her. "I don't want to go to Reynisfjara. There's a reason I haven't been back. It holds a lot of memories I don't want to dig up."

"I can imagine." She looked down. "That's where they punished you, isn't it? Where it all went down?"

"The place where I tried to build the house was a few kilometers north, but yes, that's where it happened."

"Are you afraid they're still there, the ones who punished you?"

"They're everywhere." He paused. "I know the area has probably changed, but I'll still see it like it was. It will feel like I'm living it all over again."

She leaned over and gently touched his arm. "I'm sorry. I just—think there are answers there. We don't have to go to your hometown, do we? We can just go to the beach."

His eyes were bright. His rush of emotion seemed to contradict how, just a few days ago, he'd told her about the incident and brushed it off as having happened so long ago he wasn't even sad about it. He'd acted like it was no big deal to him anymore.

A hundred years wasn't long enough to get over being tortured by supernatural beings and having the woman you loved dragged away, at least not in her book.

She slipped her hand off his arm. "If you really can't bear it, I won't push you to take me." She wondered if she could book a tour and go there—they'd visited it on their tour, after all. She'd need money for that though, and she cringed at the idea of asking him for it.

"No, you keep having visions of it." He put the truck in gear. "It must mean something. And I should have gone back and faced my demons long ago, I know that."

"Are you sure?"

"Well, it will keep you here a little longer, with me." He gave her a half-hearted smile. "Is that selfish?"

"No." She slid her hand back over and squeezed his thigh. "I kinda feel the same way."

He pulled the truck away from the curb, and they started down the street. She kept her hand there. She was going to miss him.

Chapter Sixteen

Once outside the city the scenery turned flat and scrubby, endless plains that were populated with a few trees but mostly bushes. Mountains rose on the very distant horizon. The sky remained clear and sunny. The road was well traveled, which made her feel less paranoid. She also saw houses and buildings, so they stayed within civilization.

For the first hour, they didn't talk much. She slumped against her door and gazed out the window. She dozed on and off, still so sleepy she could barely think straight.

Gunnar played the radio, adding to the background noise of engine and wheels.

Eventually, she sat up and stretched, trying to wake herself up. The interior of the truck was cool, but the sun made her too warm and she slipped the sweater off.

"I'm sorry about the knife." She finally broke the quiet. "And I'm sorry for what I did back there, grabbing her like that and causing a scene."

He glanced over. The sun shone through his hair, making it almost white, and washed out the blue of his eyes. "I'm very worried," he said. "They'll want to punish you. They won't let it go."

"Well, I don't suppose they're going to leave me alone anyway. Do you really think whatever they did to me, it's over and done with?"

"Do you think they can't do worse? That's why Aedan stayed behind, in case they want to have a word."

She'd acted impulsively, and maybe she acted without consideration, too. After all, they were the ones who had to stay on this island with the huldufólk when she went home. "I never meant to put either one of you in danger. I just couldn't put up with it anymore. It's not fair."

"They don't care about fair."

She thought about what he'd said to her back in Reykjavik, how he'd told her she sounded like someone else he used to know. "Who do I remind you of? Back there, you said I was just like someone else." She hesitated. "Is it your wife?"

He winced. "Yes. She was feisty too. She could never leave anything alone."

Vanessa stared forward. "You said you don't have any grief anymore. That you forgot a lot of details about her. You didn't forget that?"

He heaved a sigh. "You don't get through a century of heartache without lying to yourself a little."

She felt even worse now, for making this hard on him. Of course he still missed his wife. She wouldn't be able to forget her parents, or her friends, not even with a century between them. A frantic thought flashed into her head—what if the huldufólk decided to punish her in the same way they punished Gunnar?

"I told you she made me laugh." His tone was dull and sad. "She did, but she was serious as well. Hera was headstrong and brilliant. I was mesmerized by her."

Vanessa looked at him. "Hera?"

He nodded. "That was her name. Hera Ívarsdóttir."

Hera was the name he'd said in his sleep. Her stomach clenched. This was even more proof that Vanessa was being haunted, and it must be because of her closeness to Gunnar. She needed to be honest with him and tell him everything, and soon. That might make this trip make sense to him, at least.

"I haven't even been this deep into the Southern

Region since it happened." He glanced around. "I didn't think my heart could take it. This is where I came from, where she came from."

"I'm sorry."

"No, it's time I faced the past. I've been a coward. I should have come back years ago and made peace. Maybe things would have been easier."

She touched his arm. "Are you sure?"

He nodded. "You're like her too, in the sense you push me to do things. To not sit. I told you, I needed an adventure, and you brought it to me, like she would have."

She took her hand off his arm. "I've only known you a few days. I wouldn't go comparing me to her too much. And this is one adventure I sure as hell didn't ask for, trust me."

"Still, in that short time, you've gotten me to question things, if not dare go against them." He reached over and took her hand on the seat between them. "Thank you."

She squeezed his hand. "Thank me after we find out if they're going to heap tons of unfair punishment on us." She sighed. "Maybe I'm just too impulsive, I let my outrage get the better of me."

"That's like Hera too."

"She sounds like a catch."

"She was."

The land changed as they continued. They drove over flat wet marshlands and the hills rose out of the earth once more, growing higher and higher until their tops were shrouded in mist. Mountains loomed behind them now. They passed waterfalls cascading down from the hills. The sky turned gray and clouds gathered. Gunnar said it was because they were getting close to the ocean.

Eventually, they stopped to stretch their legs and get some air. She desperately needed a break from riding in a car by that point and was grateful for it. They parked alongside a broad tract of flat farmland with cows grazing. Here, the hills also rose into the mist, but the sun peeked through the clouds. The day was warm and breezy.

Gunnar pointed into the distance, to a spot between the hills where what looked like a flat snow-covered mountain peeked out. "Eyjafjallajökull."

"The glacier," she said immediately. "It covers a volcano." It was one of the places they'd visited on their tour. "We stopped at one of the scenic outlooks and took pictures."

Standing there, gazing at it, it gave her a strange feeling. She hadn't felt it before when they visited, but now it filled her like warm water. It was that sense of comfort and familiarity she'd felt when she ate the lamb stew. She'd been here before—not just sightseeing—and she knew this place and knew it well.

Was Hera feeling through her? This had been her home once. Was she communicating right now, wracked with longing?

She glanced at Gunnar. He leaned against the truck, squinting into the distance. His hands were tucked in his sweater pockets, and they stood close together, shoulder to shoulder.

"How do you feel, seeing it again?" she asked.

The world seemed so impossibly vast around them. All she heard was the wind across the grass.

"I missed it." He rested his shoulder against hers. "It hasn't changed in a hundred years."

She wrestled with a choice. She needed to tell him what she'd been seeing and feeling. It couldn't wait any longer. "Gunnar…" She spoke carefully. "I haven't been completely honest with you, about the visions I've been having."

He looked at her with a concerned frown. "What do you mean?"

"I'm pretty sure they're about your wife. They're visions of things that happened to her."

He turned toward her. "Why do you think that?"

"Because." She fidgeted. "The vision of running through the rocks, on the cliff—I think that was the night they took her away. I think she was running from them. And the vision with the knife…" She slipped it out of her pocket. "I saw her on the black beach. It was winter. She bought it from an old woman."

Gunnar stared at the knife.

"I was seeing it through her eyes. In the vision on the cliff, I saw a light, at the top, like a flashlight, but I—"

"It was me." His voice was intensely quiet.

She blinked. "You?"

"It was my lantern." His face was blank, but his eyes were full of pain. "I tried to chase them, but I lost her in the darkness. She ran. I tried to save her. I never saw her again. Maybe you're seeing my memories."

Vanessa's breath caught. She remembered falling. "No, I'm not. I didn't see it from your perspective. You weren't there on the beach either, when she bought the knife. They aren't things you saw with your own eyes."

"I don't understand."

"I'm seeing these things because you're close to me, but I'm not seeing them *through* you." She touched his hand. "She's haunting me. I'm communicating with her spirit."

He stared at her.

"I saw her in the truck, too, when we were driving to Reykjavik. I dreamt of her. It was the first time

I saw her, not through her eyes. She spoke to me. She told me we can't outrun them, that we have to turn and face them. One of them was there too. He tried to come through and she pushed him away."

His eyes grew bright. "Then she's dead."

Vanessa ached for him. She gripped his hand. "The huldufólk did something to my brain," she said. "I don't know why or how. They made it so I can communicate with spirits, apparently. I made a connection with her because I've been around you." She still cringed at the thought Hera was there when they attempted to have sex.

Damn, girl, I'm sorry.

Gunnar pulled away. He walked alongside the truck, to the front, his hands on his head.

She decided to give him some space. "That's why I want to go to Reynisfjara." She slumped against the truck. "I think she wants me to go there, so she can tell me something. It might be about the huldufólk, or it might be a message for you. Either way, I need to see what's there."

Gunnar didn't speak. He dropped his hands to his sides and leaned against the grill, looking toward the sky.

She walked to him. "I'm sorry," she said softly. She slipped a hand onto his lower back. "I didn't want to keep it from you any longer." She wouldn't tell him how she died, falling from the cliff, unless he asked.

He had his eyes closed. Tears glistened on his cheeks. She snuggled into his arms and held him. He rested his head against hers.

"At least now I know." His voice was strained. "I've wondered if she was gone or trapped in some place, unchanging, with no escape. In a way this is the better fate. Trust me, I know."

She held him tighter. "She's not at peace, though.

I think she needs me to help her find it. Or she needs you."

He wept softly, clinging to her.

She held him as hard as she could. For a moment, all her own anguish and struggle vanished and she focused on him. What monsters, to tear people apart like this. Hera deserved more than peace, she deserved vengeance.

Determination swelled in her. Whatever she could do, however she could defy them, she would. Just let them try to punish her for it.

He pulled back and wiped his eyes. "I'm sorry. I know they're putting you through hell, this isn't about me. I've had time to get used to it, you haven't."

"Don't be sorry." She reached up and stroked his hair. "You've suffered too. And this *is* about me. It's me she's chosen to speak through. Or, she had no choice, I don't know, but she's with me."

He looked up and around, at the sky, the hills, at everything around them. His eyes were red-rimmed. "Maybe she just wanted me to come back here so I could move on. And look at me, it's taken almost my entire sentence to do it."

She clutched his arms. "Maybe she wants to tell me how to get even with them."

He looked at her, and gave a soft, sad laugh. "That sounds like her." He pulled her hands off his upper arms and held them. He looked so sad, so stricken, that she wanted to cry too. "But don't." He turned serious. "Because there's no good outcome of that, not for you. Not for either of us."

She kept her mouth shut.

He continued softly, "No matter what she tells you in your dreams, it's a lie. If she is well and truly dead, that's your answer. She didn't win, did she?"

Vanessa looked down the road, winding away amongst the hills. She could feel the entire world here, it seemed. She felt it breathing, turning. "I still think we should go to the beach," she said. "We've come this far."

He rubbed his thumbs over the back of her hands and nodded. It didn't seem so much resolve as despair, giving in to something he couldn't fight. "Yes, we should keep going. I want to see the beach again too."

They got back in the truck. She was wide awake now, filled with anxiety and nerves.

"I should call Aedan." Gunnar buckled up. "Make sure everything is all right."

A short phone call assured he was fine and hadn't seen any huldufólk. They got back on the road.

Whatever they were driving toward, the expectation inside her was bigger than reality could ever be—or at least, she hoped.

* * * *

For the rest of the drive, Gunnar was sullen and silent, and she didn't try to get conversation out of him or cheer him up. He had every right to be in a bad mood. She gazed out her window and watched the scenery go by, lost in her own thoughts—about home, about the night she disappeared, about what she would say to the police later this evening when they And of course, about Hera and where she was leading them.

The scenery changed once again to broad, flat stretches of farmland and smaller, rolling hills. The sun disappeared entirely behind heavy banks of gray clouds. Gradually, she saw more houses, and they passed more cars. Then, the road turned from paved with lines to a gravelly lane that snaked through the farmland, so narrow two cars could barely pass on it.

"I'm home," Gunnar said. It was the only words he'd spoken in so long it made her start.

She sat up straight, shaking off the trance the silence had put her in. They were surrounded by high, craggy hills. She didn't see the ocean.

"This is the beach?" She rubbed her neck to work the crick out of it. She vaguely remembered coming this way, when they went on the tour, but so much of Iceland looked the same it was hard to discern one hill from another.

"You'll see it soon."

She wanted to ask him how he felt, about being here, but it would probably be a dumb question.

"Nothing has changed." He stared forward. "I don't know why I expected it would. I think it would have been harder if it was different, though. I think this is what I needed to see."

"I won't make you stay here long." Hopefully, whatever Hera had to show her, she would show her quickly.

"I've always been here," he said. "In my heart."

They reached the beach. And, though she had seen it once before, it took her breath away.

There was a parking lot for visitors, and it wasn't paved but filled with black gravel. Quite a few cars were parked there. The beach was also teeming with tourists. She didn't expect they'd be alone here, as there was a visitor center and it was well-traveled. The human world encroaching on nature.

But not by much, because nature was too gigantic for it.

The ocean roiled beneath the heavy gray sky, the water darker gray and capped with white. All of it was so impossibly huge she didn't have words for it, just a deep, pervading sense of awe. The black beach stretched in front of them to the water's edge, smooth in some places, littered with large stones in others. Farther out, toward the water, it became more like gravel until the surf smoothed it over. The hills swept up into towering cliffs, black as well, though they were adorned with thick green grass. At their bases were levels of narrow, step-like basalt columns people often took pictures in front of. Despite the trappings of humanity, it was primal and spoke to her on an instinctual level.

She felt like they'd reached the edge of the world, the edge of the universe. And it sang.

They sat in silence for a moment, gazing out the front window at the ocean.

Like earlier, she experienced a dual sense of familiarity—she'd been here before, with her friends, but she'd also been here in another time and body. She knew it deep in her soul and with all her heart. She had spent time here. Hera's feelings were her own, and it was almost comforting.

"We came here often." Gunnar's voice was full of nostalgia. "We'd walk and talk. She liked to collect stones. Sometimes she'd throw them into the water, because she said they were too pretty for a human to possess and the earth deserved them more."

A warm feeling spread through her chest. She almost wanted to tell him Hera was listening, because she was, but that would only cause him more pain.

"The town where I grew up, it's farther up the coast." He nodded to the left. "Vik. There's a black beach there, too. But she lived in the farmlands behind us, and I worked for her father there. The land I bought to build a house on was in those lands, too."

There was nothing she could say, so she didn't speak.

"I thought if I didn't come back here, ever, the past would seem more like a dream. It would be less real. That was as stupid as thinking I could fool myself into forgetting her."

Vanessa took off her seatbelt. "We should get out. If there's something here for me to find, I want to find it before anyone else does."

He nodded. His expression was glum but winsome, his eyes sad.

They got out. The wind was strong, and much colder. She wrapped the sweater around her. She wished she had a thicker, waterproof coat, like she'd worn the first time. The closer they got to the water, the more the spray would mist them.

They trudged across the gravel and out onto the beach. It was perilous going at first, as there were so many rocks and clumps of errant grass to trip over. She had to watch her feet until they got to the smoother sandy part. People were everywhere, taking pictures, picking up stones, running around. Folks just living their ordinary lives and having a good time. That had been her—a year ago, somehow.

She folded her arms across her chest to stave off the wind. It tore at her hair and made it whip around her face.

Gunnar walked alongside her, hands dug in the pockets of his sweater. His curls fluttered relentlessly. "What are you looking for?" He gazed out at the water. "Any clue?"

"None." She looked toward the jagged sea stacks that rose offshore. Reynisdrangar, they were called. She'd read about them. Folklore said they were the frozen remains of trolls who had been caught by the rising sun. In another version, they had taken a man's wife and killed her, and the husband froze them there in revenge.

A chill passed over her, having nothing to do with the wind. Knowing what she knew now, maybe it wasn't just "folklore."

"Are trolls real?"

He must have realized what prompted the question and looked toward the stacks as well. "I think once, they were. But there haven't been any in Iceland for a while, I guess because of humans taking over the land. Or if there are, they're well hidden, or sleeping." He sounded serious.

She looked at the stacks again. They were positively gigantic. She shuddered. Even more than the huldufólk, she didn't want to meet a real live troll.

"Maybe one day they'll all be gone, all these creatures." Bitterness tinged Gunnar's voice. "Won't that be a fine day?"

This conflicted with what he'd said on the boat, back in Drangsnes. His momentary sympathy and understanding for their plight had apparently vanished. Probably because he was standing, after a hundred years, on the very spot where they'd chased his wife to her death.

"We should walk." She turned in the other direction, putting her back to the frozen trolls. "I'm hoping she'll give me a sign."

"I hope she does too, because this is a big place."

They started down the beach, side by side, and Vanessa had to remember to breathe, even as the wind took her breath away.

Chapter Seventeen

Farther up the beach, the sand turned fine and soft. This was the sand she had walked on in her vision, when Hera bought the knife. "There has to be something." She stopped and looked all around, fruitlessly. "She wouldn't lead me here for nothing." They'd been there a good forty-five minutes at least, and she was cold down to the bone. Her feet ached from lugging the slightly too-big boots on them.

"I don't see any signs of the huldufólk here." Gunnar was huddled in his sweater. "Thankfully."

She looked at him. An idea struck her—why hadn't she thought of it before?

Gunnar must have caught the glint in her eye and frowned. "What?"

They were relatively alone on that part of the beach. They'd walked some distance and the tourists were spread thinner. Besides, she wasn't about to do something obscene or illegal.

She stepped up to him, slipped her hand around the back of his neck, and pulled his mouth to hers.

The kiss was awkward and reluctant. He made a faint surprised sound. She kissed him harder, and he responded.

She squeezed her eyes shut. *Come on, Hera. I'm kissing your husband, speak to me.*

He deepened the kiss, either not realizing what she was doing, or just giving in to the moment. She let herself get lost in it too, almost forgetting why she was kissing him to begin with.

It wasn't working. Frustration bubbled in her. She broke the kiss and opened her eyes.

The world seemed to tilt, the grays and whites

going softer, like she was looking through a fuzzy filter. She blinked, but it didn't clear.

Things changed around her. They were still on the shore, standing on the black sand with the waves crashing to her right. But the air was colder. Snow lay on the cliff faces. It dusted the sand.

And Gunnar stood before her, now in different clothes—old fashioned, like something out of a black and white movie—a long coat and peaked cap. His face was the same, his cheeks wind burnt, and his expression was desperately pained, his eyes pleading.

She stumbled back. Then, she realized she too was dressed differently, in a long dress and shawl. She wasn't in her own body. "I won't abide it," she said, in Icelandic. "Do you hear me? I will not allow it."

"You have to see reason." Gunnar was speaking Icelandic too. "It's too dangerous. Please, don't do this."

"I will not allow it." She gnashed her teeth. "Listen to what I say. *I will not allow it!*"

Her vision blurred, then sharpened again, and she nearly fell over. She was back on the modern-day shore, and Gunnar stood before her, blanched and wide-eyed, dressed in his normal clothes. She realized she'd yelled the last words herself, in English. She clutched her head.

"Oh my God." She tried to steady herself through the vertigo. "I think she came through."

"Stop this." Gunnar grabbed her arms. "Enough."

"I saw her! When I kissed you, I saw the two of you here, on the shore, but it was winter. You were arguing."

He shook her, much to her surprise. Anger flashed across his face. "I said stop it. Quit trying to contact her!"

She blinked at him. "Why?"

He let go and stepped back. "There's more to the story I haven't told you. I should have been honest too, I just—" He clenched his teeth. "It's not easy."

"Tell me."

He stared out at the ocean for a moment, then looked back at her. His eyes shone. "I made a mistake, and they punished me." He hesitated. "But she made a mistake too. I want so much to hold her blameless, and I've tried. I tell myself every day what she did, she did for the right reason. For love. But she wasn't blameless, and I can't convince myself, no more than I can convince myself I don't miss her."

A sense of foreboding crept over her.

"They were going to punish me for a shorter time." His voice was strained. "Five years, that's all they wanted. They were going to take me—I don't know. To their realm, I guess, to imprison me. I was terrified, but willing. It sounded better than death. And I'd be returned at the end of it, allowed to live my life."

"I don't understand." But in truth, deep down, she was starting to.

"I begged her to let it happen." His words cracked. "I told her she couldn't overcome them, that it would only make things worse." He shook his head. "But that wasn't her, to just sit back and let things happen. We were newlyweds, and she refused to lose me. She couldn't live with it."

"She fought them," Vanessa whispered.

A tear slipped down his cheek. "I didn't even know she had the knife. Until today, when you told me about the vision, I didn't know where she'd gotten it."

She touched her pocket.

"She attacked them when they came. She stabbed one of them in the throat."

Vanessa drew a breath. "She killed one of the

huldufólk?"

"I don't know. I never saw if they died. It was all madness." His eyes blazed. "She lashed out, and we both paid the price. Then and there, they brought a verdict down on us. They would take her away, and I would suffer her loss for a century."

Vanessa held her breath.

Anger and anguish, a culmination of years of pain, filled his features and his voice. "She ran, and they chased her, and I tried to find her, but I never saw her face again."

Vanessa thought of the dream.

"Maybe they killed her that night." He trembled. "Their justice was swift."

She remembered the voice then, making a promise. *You don't have to suffer. It doesn't have to be this way.*

"No." She shook her head. "One of them took pity on her, I'm sure of it."

Gunnar clutched her arms again, harder this time.

She almost pushed him off, but he was emotional and had every right to be.

"This is over." He spoke firmly. "You won't try to chase and fight them. You're getting the hell out of Iceland and you're going home, right now."

She opened her mouth, but he spoke over her, louder.

"You're leaving." He shook her again. "Hera fought them, and it cost her life. It cost my heart. Do you hear what I've told you?" Tears slipped down his cheeks, his voice raw and ragged. "I will not let you make the same mistakes. You can't win."

"But—"

"You're leaving, and you're going to put this behind you. You'll never have answers, but you'll have your life."

He let go of one arm, but held the other, and began dragging her back down the beach.

She was so startled she stumbled along after him. "What are you doing?" she demanded.

"We're going back to Reykjavik." He marched along, pulling her after him. "You're going to the police."

She looked wildly around. Had she found what Hera wanted her to? Was it simply about getting the entire truth from Gunnar? "What if I'm missing something!" She tried to pull out of his grip.

He reeled around on her, his face a mask of fury that made her heart leap. He dug his fingers into her forearm. "There is nothing here. There has never been anything here. She's dead! She's gone! It's all gone." Tears continued to streak down his cheeks.

She was breathing hard, tears pricking her own eyes. He turned and resumed dragging her. She didn't resist, though he was hurting her.

"Gunnar!"

"We're leaving!"

Her own tears fell as he led her back to the parking lot. They were like drops of ice on her already cold cheeks, and she wanted to sob—for him, for Hera, for herself. For all of this terrific nightmare she was living.

* * * *

The scenery crawled by, fields and hills, the ocean behind them. The sun was still hidden. Mist lay in the valleys between hills. Everything was so gray it seemed all color had been washed from the world.

Vanessa sat slumped, staring forward, the hum of the engine the only sound.

"I want to see Vik." Gunnar's voice was as bleak

as the world outside. "Might as well."

They'd only been in the truck about five minutes, and she was still cold, her arm throbbing from his grip. They hadn't spoken since they got in.

"That's why I'm driving this way," he explained. "It's only a short distance."

She didn't even realize they weren't taking the same route, as everything looked the same. She said nothing. Much as she wanted to, she couldn't be angry at him. She understood, after all he'd been through. She didn't agree with him on one thing, though: she couldn't leave and never think of this again. That would be as impossible as the lies he told himself about his wife.

"I'm sorry," he said softly. "I didn't mean to be so rough or scare you."

"You did mean to scare me." She spoke without accusation. "It's clear I don't have a healthy level of fear. And I should."

He flexed his hands on the wheel. "I should have told you the truth from the start."

"She loved you. She didn't want you taken from her. Love can make people act crazy."

"I know. I would have done the same for her, probably. That wouldn't have ended well either." He paused. "I struggle with the guilt, of being angry at her for what she did, because I know she doesn't deserve my anger."

"I think such conflicting feelings are natural. I don't blame you."

She was trying to remind herself she barely knew this man, and this situation was complete madness. She *did* want to get home, she *did* want her loved ones to know she was alive. And she sure as hell wanted to put the huldufólk behind her. Whatever the ghost of Hera was making her feel, it wasn't real. It wasn't coming from herself. She had to get her head on straight.

"I don't want the same thing to happen to you," he said. "With all my heart, I don't want it."

She sighed. "I know, and I've been rash. I was thrown into this—yes, a year ago, but to me it only feels like a few days ago—and I'm desperate. I'm terrified. I have no idea what's going on and all of this is new to me. I'm just trying to do anything I can to make sense of it and survive. I'm sorry if I seem crazy, or impetuous. I promise I'm not usually like that, just when I'm being tormented by supernatural creatures who ripped away my memory and a year of my life."

She stilled her words. They were bitter, but the bitterness wasn't directed at him, and she didn't want him to think that.

He took a hand off the wheel and reached over. He gripped her hand and squeezed it. His fingers were cold, like hers. "I understand." He rubbed her wrist with his thumb. "I apologize for freaking out. I should have made everything clear to you. And this place, the memories—they're making me irrational and emotional."

His touch seemed to warm her skin, warm it deep, far below the surface. "We're both messed up right now. Let's just try to calm down and think."

"You'll be leaving soon. The best thing for you—get away from this place, and the danger. Then you'll be able to think."

She still wasn't sure she could leave without answers, and certainly not spend the rest of her life without them. And was she truly safe away from here? What if they could still reach her back home?

"Yeah." She squeezed his hand. "You're right."

Soon, they arrived in a town, and it was clear they'd doubled back toward the ocean. It looked much like the other small towns they'd passed through. Rows of simple, neat houses and buildings, small lawns and short, scrubby trees. The main street was brick.

Gunnar was clutching the wheel again, so hard his knuckles were white. "Vík í Mýrdal." He breathed the words out. "Home."

It reminded her a bit of Drangsnes, in both its simplicity and with the water in the distance. The only difference was the flatter land.

"Does it look the same?" she asked.

He was silent, then shook his head. "Not so much. It's more modern: the buildings, the streets … but it feels familiar."

She couldn't imagine going back to her hometown after a hundred years—and she hoped she wouldn't have to discover how that felt.

He periodically slowed to look at signs and down side streets, but seemed to find his way. He drove them up to a church, on a high hill overlooking the town. It had a red roof and a steeple with a cross on top. A few cars sat in the parking lot, and people were standing outside taking pictures. He parked the truck, facing the most condensed part of the town spread out below.

"This is a good view." He took a deep breath. "Come on."

They climbed out of the truck. The view was indeed spectacular, and the sun had started to peek from behind the clouds again.

She realized they were now on the other side of the cliffs that overlooked Reynisfjara. The town sat at their base. The basalt stacks—the trolls—were visible here too, from the opposite side. The sea rushed up to meet another stretch of black sand that bordered the town. Down the hill in front of them, lush grass and purple flowers grew in abundance. It was an idyllic view: ocean, beach, cliffs, rolling hills at their back. And the feeling she'd had so many times today—familiarity, recognition—welled up in her. They hadn't visited this place on the tour.

Gunnar squinted up at the church steeple. "This is new."

She looked up too. The cross was ornamental, with four points, and sat against the gray clouds.

"Is it?"

He nodded. "There wasn't a church here when I was growing up, and it wasn't here when I left. But we used to come up here to see the view. I understand why they put it here."

She turned back around and gazed at the ocean. It stretched to the horizon, until it became one with the sky.

"It's so different." Gunnar turned back around too. "It's much bigger than it used to be."

It looked like a tiny town to her, so she could imagine how small of a village it must have been back then.

"It's pretty." She folded her arms. The wind was harsh here too. "Where is your house?"

He pointed out into the more densely populated part. "Out there, but I don't see it. I doubt it's still standing. All these buildings are modern. This used to be a place for farmers to congregate, and there were slaughterhouses too. Those times are gone. I look up news from here, from time to time, I can't help myself."

Keeping tabs on his old home like stalking an ex on Facebook. She smiled.

He looked toward the jagged cliffs. "You know, this place is in danger. There's a volcano near here, Katla. It erupted when I was a child. It's under a glacier. If there's a big eruption, it could melt enough of the glacier to completely wash the town away."

That stirred something inside of her, an old

anxiety. Was Hera remembering that fact too?

"I used to be so afraid of it." He chuckled. "Especially after the eruption. I had nightmares about waking up and my bed floating out into the ocean. My parents were ambivalent about it and that didn't help. I wanted them to reassure me it was just a child's silliness. But it wasn't."

She looked at him and smiled fondly. Yes, she was feeling a memory, Hera's memory, and it gave her a cozy, happy feeling deep in her gut. She loved this man, and all his silliness.

Gunnar looked at her and flinched, wariness flashing in his eyes.

She frowned.

"Sorry." He looked away. "A lot of memories in this place."

Did he see Hera peeking out from her mind?

"I want to drive around a bit," he said. "For a few minutes, if you don't mind, before we go back."

There wasn't much to drive around, just a handful of streets and a few winding roads. But she understood his need to see it.

"Of course." She took his arm. "I'm not in that much of a hurry to get back to Reykjavik."

He frowned.

She shrugged. "I've been thinking about it. Maybe I should go to the police in the morning. I need to think up a story. They're not going to believe I lost my memory of an entire year. I need to figure out how I'm going to explain this, without sounding crazy or like I'm lying." In truth, she was stalling, but she didn't know why. She wanted to go home and relieve her parents and friends of their grief, and yet, something made her hesitate.

Maybe if she stayed just a little longer, she'd get

some answers.

"Well, we have the hotel for the night." Gunnar sounded doubtful. "But the sooner you get out of Iceland, the better."

"I'll get out tomorrow, or whenever they allow me to go home. Do you really think they're just going to put me on a plane the second I show them the footage? They'll want to prove I am who I say I am. They might even fly my parents here to identify me." She imagined them arriving here, and it filled her with dread. What if the huldufólk did something to them, too? "I don't think I'll be leaving in a hurry."

This was the first time she felt truly calm with it all. Maybe her mind had finally gone numb. It was much better than constant anxiety and terror, at least.

Gunnar hummed. He reached down and took her hand in his and laced their fingers together. He was quiet for a while as they stared toward the sweeping cliffs. "I wanted to get out of here so badly when I was younger," he said. "I felt like there was nothing for me here. Herding sheep for Hera's father actually sounded like a real opportunity."

"It was. You met your wife, and you would have had a life with her, if not for them."

"I couldn't have foreseen the life I've had."

"It sounds like it's been full, all things considered. You traveled, met another woman you fell in love with, and saw the world change across an expanse of time no other human being could imagine. It's not all bad. I'm sorry you lived through so much pain, but you haven't let it keep you in darkness."

He looked at her and smiled gently. "I guess so."

"I come from a tiny town too, and I've always wanted more. Working in a pharmacy seemed like a big deal to me." She gazed across the land. She still had a fondness for this country, and she loved finally seeing it with her own two eyes. "Who knows how they changed the course of my life as well? Time will tell, as it did with you."

She rested her head on his shoulder. Being with him felt right—and she didn't know if that was Hera or herself, but she suspected a lot of it was coming from her own feelings, and she hoped Hera didn't mind.

"Want to do some sightseeing, then?"

She smiled. "That's what I came here for. It'll be nice to do something normal. Show me your hometown."

Chapter Eighteen

It quickly became apparent that Vik was a place that relied heavily on tourism, like many places in Iceland. She wondered if that bothered Gunnar. She spotted restaurants, guest houses, a golf course, a swimming pool, a campsite, a handful of stores, and several small museums. An inordinate amount of people, given the size of the town, populated the common areas.

"Some of it still looks the same." He drove slowly, his face full of intense concentration. "It's like walking into a house you grew up in, only it's been remodeled."

She realized like with Gunnar's boat, she was easily reading signs on the streets and buildings, though they were in Icelandic. She considered it might be Hera's ghost causing her to understand the language, and not her brain being altered from whatever the huldufólk did to her.

Could ghosts make you multilingual?

The thought made her uncomfortable. In that sense, it was more like Hera was inhabiting her, rather than haunting her. Was she possessed?

They drove past a visitor center, and then, a bit farther up the street, Gunnar pulled the truck into a small gravel lot. They were next to a wooden hut called the Wool Gallery. People were lingering around outside it and going in and out. There was also a ship museum nearby.

Gunnar looked at her. "This is the oldest part of the village, the original Vik. Though I guess it's a town now. There wasn't much beyond this part back then."

He didn't seem disconcerted, but she could tell this was putting him off kilter slightly.

"Progress." She forced a smile.

"Do you want to walk around a bit?"

She nodded.

They got out. They were near the beach, and the wind was relentless. Gunnar looked toward the water, the wind tugging hair, his eyes clear and distant. "I thought I'd fall apart, coming back here," he murmured. "But it feels good. Why did I wait so long?"

"Because it's hard." She took his hand. "Come on."

They walked the streets, hand in hand, and he pointed things out—where buildings had been, how the streets used to look. He said they were all dirt back then. He showed her the places he used to hang out with the other villagers, exchanging news and gossip. He took her to the spot where his house had been. A house stood there still, but it was clearly newer.

"I didn't think it would still be standing." He gazed at it. "Our house was much smaller."

"What … happened to your parents? Were they still alive when Hera disappeared?"

"My mother died when I was twenty, before I met Hera." The sadness in his voice also shone in his eyes. "She had lung cancer I think, but those things weren't diagnosed in those days. The village doctor just called it an infection in her lungs. I moved away a few years after she died, to work on Hera's father's farm. I'd been dragging my feet here, working at trading posts and slaughterhouses, doing odd jobs. I couldn't find anyone to marry. An unmarried man in his twenties without children was an oddity." He chuckled.

She wondered if his mother was buried around here. "And your father?"

He was silent a moment. "After Hera was taken, I couldn't stay around. As far as he knew, and her own parents knew, she just went missing. They thought she'd gotten lost and met some terrible accident out in the countryside. Her parents were grieving and constantly trying to find her body. I went along for the searches and it tore me apart."

She thought about her "body" being found on the mountain after a "hiking accident." She and Hera had some things in common.

"I finally left." Gunnar stared at the house. "I wrote my father from time to time, and her parents. When phones became a common thing, I started calling. He knew my grief kept me away. He died in the 1940's, an old man. I couldn't even bring myself to come back and bury him."

"Did you have siblings?"

He shook his head. "I think my mother had trouble conceiving children, I was a blessing. But my father had his own brothers and sisters, and they took care of him through the years." He squinted into the distance. "I don't know if the old churchyard is still here, and I don't want to look for it. I think I've seen enough."

She sympathized. Just going back home after a year—though it seemed like days to her—would be weird. Had anything changed? Surely, life amongst her family and friends had.

They walked back to the Wool Gallery. She thought it might be interesting to go inside, but there was a line, as the place was tiny, and she didn't have the gumption to be touristy right now.

"I'm going to peek in the window." Gunnar smiled. There was a huge window on the side of the hut. "Wool is a big thing around here, still."

She followed, but as they walked, her attention was drawn to a group of people off to the side, gathered around a man with a bushy white beard. He held something up and spoke in English.

"An iron sheep bell. The clapper is gone, so it doesn't ring."

Her ears pricked at the word "iron." She slowed as Gunnar continued toward the hut. Something stirred inside her, like a dangerous animal awakening.

"These were put on sheep to help find them when they went wandering," the man said. "They're still used today, though they're lighter and made from less rust-prone metals." He held aloft what looked like a large necklace made from a rusted chain, an equally rusted over bell dangling from it. The tourists took pictures.

She stared at it.

"Vanessa?" Gunnar looked back at her.

She held up a finger. "I'll be right there, I just want to check this out." She walked toward the group.

Her movements seemed not to be her own, like her legs were being operated by the other entity inside of her. Sinister thoughts filled her head. She focused on the bell and watched as the man put it down on a wooden table, where a collection of other old items sat.

"Let's walk over here and look at some of the staffs sheep herders used." The man directed the group toward a fence where he had various staffs propped up.

The world seemed to move, elements sliding into place like puzzle pieces clicking together. She was compelled forward, knowing what she had to do.

The crowd walked to the fence, backs to her.

Gunnar was peering in the window of the hut, his back to her as well.

She stopped next to the table and looked at the bell. The chain links were piled together, and it was small enough she could conceal it inside her sweater, maybe, probably. *Pure iron.*

The whispering started in her ears. Her vision

brightened and sharpened.

Take it, Hera said, as clear as if she stood at Vanessa's shoulder.

Vanessa reached out, again feeling like her body wasn't under her control, and grabbed it.

The iron was cold and gritty. She opened her sweater and tucked the bell inside, up under her arm, and quickly closed the sweater across her. She folded her arms. The bell bit into her ribs, and she hoped it didn't make a weird lump. Fortunately, it could no longer ring.

She walked briskly toward the hut. The tourists and their guide were still absorbed in the staffs.

She stepped up beside Gunnar. Inside the hut was an assortment of wool goods: the ubiquitous sweaters of Iceland with their jagged geometric designs, as well as hats, gloves, scarves, and other items. People were crowded in.

"We should go." She struggled to remain calm. "I feel something weird."

Gunnar looked at her. "What's wrong?"

"I think the huldufólk are around." She glanced over at the group. "It's just a strange feeling I have. They haven't been following us, but I think they're here now."

Gunnar looked around.

"Let's go." She gripped his hand. The bell was tucked beneath her opposite arm and she held it against her body with her bicep. "I don't want to see them." She pulled him toward the truck.

Thankfully, he didn't argue. They got in. She had to shift awkwardly to keep the bell in place. She would have to somehow keep it under her sweater and not make it obvious all the way back to Reykjavik. That was going to be interesting.

Gunnar started the truck. "I better call Aedan, check in again."

She nodded. As they pulled out, she watched the group. No one had noticed the bell was missing yet. She hoped it wasn't some valuable antique. *Sorry, dude, hope you have another.* She wasn't even sure what she was going to do with it, though nefarious notions sat in the back of her head.

Hera wanted vengeance, and Vanessa wanted answers. Their motivations meshed.

They drove through town, and Gunnar pulled his cell phone out. She sat in stiff silence while he made the call. It was short.

"He's fine, still nothing." He tossed the phone on the seat and looked at her, brow furrowed. "The last thing I want to do is run into the huldufólk here. I don't think I could endure it, to begin with. You're sure you felt them? They're following us again?"

She nodded. "I think so."

"Bastards."

When they got to the edge of town, she finally managed to relax a little.

Gunnar glanced in the rearview mirror as they drove the road back into the hilly countryside. "I'll visit again, soon I think. It was good to get over my fear. Thank you, for making me do this."

She smiled. "Don't mention it."

* * * *

Their hotel room in Reykjavik was much like the one she'd stayed in with her friends: clean, stark, and simple, a little cramped, but cozy. It had two double beds, and their window faced the church, which she'd been hoping for. She gazed out into the lowering twilight.

"We'll go to the police in the morning," Gunnar said. "Vanessa wants to figure out what to tell them, first."

Aedan was stretched out on one of the beds, propped against the headboard. The TV was on. He'd been watching her since she came in. He didn't respond to Gunnar.

"We can have dinner downstairs," Gunnar continued. "Unless you want to go out somewhere."

The hotel itself was more upscale than the one she'd stayed in before, and historical. She was still tallying up all the money she'd owe Gunnar once she got home.

She turned and picked up the small duffel bag Gunnar had given her to put her things in—which only consisted of her blouse and boots, but he'd given her a few fresh t-shirts too, and another sweater, along with some toiletries. "I'm just going to get freshened up."

Aedan continued to watch her as she walked to the bathroom.

Once inside with the door closed, she slipped the bell from under her sweater and stuffed it in the bag. Somehow, Gunnar hadn't noticed. She had a strong suspicion Aedan knew she was up to something, though.

She washed her hands and face and sorted out her hair. Staring at herself in the mirror, she barely recognized her face. She had dark circles under her eyes, and she wished she had makeup to hide them, but she certainly wasn't going to ask Gunnar for money to go shopping.

She leaned on the sink and stared into her eyes. Did they look different? Could she see Hera behind them? Hera's eyes were blue, or at least they appeared that way in the photo. Her own eyes were green. She thought of the way Gunnar had flinched back at the church, seemingly taken off guard. Had he seen Hera?

"You'll have to leave me," she whispered. "I can't do anything for you. But I can do something for me, can't I?"

A knock at the door made her jump.

"Sorry, Vanessa." Gunnar's voice. "I'm going downstairs to make sure we don't need a reservation. I'll be back shortly."

"Okay." Her voice sounded strange and hollow in her ears.

She looked back in the mirror. As she did, she swore she caught a flash of a figure behind her, a figure with long blonde hair. She spun around. The space behind her was empty.

She shuddered and looked down at the bag on the floor. More whispering in her head, telling her what to do. She snatched up the bag and left the room, trying to leave the ghost behind her.

Aedan had moved to sit on the end of his bed and was staring at the TV. However, he shifted his focus to her, and then to the bag. She carried it over to the bed next to the window and deposited it on the floor, between the bed and wall.

"You didn't find anything at Reynisfjara?" His tone was neutral, but she didn't for one moment think he was stupid.

"No, not really." She sat down on her bed, facing him. "Nothing specific, but she was there."

"You saw her?"

"I had a vision, when I was on the beach." She looked at the TV. Some crime drama was on. "I learned some things about her." She didn't elaborate. She didn't know if Aedan knew the full story of Gunnar's punishment and his wife's abduction, and she didn't want to tell his secrets. "Maybe it was a pointless trip." She shrugged. "But she's trying to tell me how to fight them, I'm certain of it. She wants revenge—for herself, and for me."

"You can't fight them. It won't end well."

"Gunnar has made that clear." The knife was still tucked in her pocket. Hera had buried it in the neck of one of the huldufólk, and that gave her some satisfaction to know. "I can't leave this country without answers. I can't spend the rest of my life wondering what happened here."

"They'll kill you."

"If they wanted to kill me, they would have done that in the year they held me prisoner. They deserve to be confronted for the things they did. Or punished. The way they punish us."

"And you're going to be the one to do that," he said wryly. "An American tourist."

"Maybe. Why not? It seems like everyone here is too scared to do anything about them. You just let them torment you."

His eyes flashed. "With good reason."

"Are you going to spend your entire life as their slave?" She didn't care if she offended him. "Do you want to do their bidding forever, as penance for merely having the audacity to be born? Why do you have to suffer forever?" She had no idea why she suddenly had so much passion about this. She barely knew this man, except that what was happening to both of them wasn't right.

He stared at her, silent.

"They have weaknesses." She got to her feet. "I'm not just talking about iron. I've been thinking it over." She strolled to the window. "If they're so powerful, and they want to punish humans for trespassing on 'their' land, why didn't they just kill all the humans when they first showed up in this country? Why did they let humans take over the island to begin with?"

She stared out the window at the church. People were hanging around it. She didn't see anyone with long black hair, though.

She looked over at him. "Humans didn't swarm this island in droves, in one mass invasion. They came slowly, over time. Maybe the huldufólk made friends with them in those days, maybe they accepted cohabitation."

"But not anymore."

She pondered. "I don't think they're powerful enough to get rid of us. Maybe they're even afraid of us, and that's why they lash out like they do."

He squinted. "What do you mean?"

She walked over to his bed. "Think about it. Their home was overrun by humans, back in the day. And slowly, they were reduced to myths, living in the shadows. We can destroy their homes and sanctity, without even meaning to. Why wouldn't they be afraid of us?" She sat down next to him. "That means they have weaknesses. It means we can hurt them, more than we realize."

"Where are you getting this from?" He frowned. "Aren't Gunnar and I proof enough of how badly they can mess humans up? Trust me, they might have weaknesses, but they don't have any we can exploit."

"I don't know where it's coming from, it's just been on my mind." She stared at the TV. Two detectives were looking for something in a wooded area. "They can't be all-powerful, even with their magic. If they were, they would have just killed us off by now or run us off the island entirely."

"What do you think this weakness is that makes them so afraid?"

"Maybe it's just that—fear. Fear makes people huddle and create defenses against the outside world. It makes insular groups terrified of outsiders. It makes them put on a show, acting like they're bigger and badder than they are."

"So how would that help us? Doesn't that just make them harder to fight? One huldufólk alone can threaten me enough to make me do their bidding, I can't imagine what a group would do."

He wanted to get back at them as much as she did, she could sense it—but he was bound to his obedience, and that was terrible.

"They only threaten you." The wheels in her head were turning. "But you don't know if they're killing the ones like you. What if they're not? And what if they wouldn't kill you either, if it's just an empty threat meant to keep you in line?"

His face was blank, but his eyes held interest.

"What if *all* their threats are empty? What if it's all they have to use against us, and that's why they're afraid? They're afraid we'll find out."

He huffed. "I think Gunnar is proof their threats aren't empty."

She sat back on her hands. "They kept him alive for a hundred years, that's it. They didn't harm him physically." She thought of Hera. She died—but was it at their hands? She fell from the cliff, by accident.

"What about you?" Aedan asked. "Look what they've done to you."

"They messed with my mind, but again, I'm not harmed." She watched the detectives search through the underbrush. "I don't think they have the power to do us real harm. They just have tricks to scare us."

Doubt flitted across his face. She didn't know why she believed this so strongly, but the notion had grown on the drive back, as she cradled the bell against her side like a child. Were they things Hera was telling her? How would Hera know them?

"What are you planning?" he asked bluntly. "You're up to something." He looked across the room, to where her bag was.

She couldn't lie to him. However, she didn't know fully herself what she was up to. "I don't know yet. All I know is, I won't leave here without answers. I don't think Hera wants me to, either." She paused. "Don't say anything about it to Gunnar. He's already angry at me for confronting the woman at the church."

"Does this mean you're not leaving?" He got up. "You're going to stay until you 'punish' them?"

"I'm going home. Make no mistake about that." On the screen, they found a dead body, under a canopy of leaves—apparently, what they'd gone there looking for. "But if I can get information, and payback, I will." She looked up at him. "I don't think I'm the only one who wants that, now am I?"

Aedan's jaw was tight, his gaze hard and intense. He looked away, then back at her. "It's more complicated than you think. What if you're wrong? What if they're not the least bit afraid of you?"

"And what if I'm *not* wrong?"

He walked to the bathroom. "You're taking your life in your hands."

She sat there, staring at the TV. Dramatic music swelled as the detectives shook their heads in defeat and despair. Finding what you were looking for, sometimes, could be dreadful.

"It's my life to hold," she whispered.

Chapter Nineteen

It turned out the restaurant downstairs was more of a lounge without a menu, so they went out instead. Not to the bar she'd visited that fateful night, not even somewhere within sight of it. She had a feeling Gunnar specifically picked one far away from its vicinity and she was grateful.

However, she was still edgy for other reasons.

They sat on the brick patio of the restaurant he'd chosen, and she concentrated more on the people passing by than her food. She scrutinized each one until the task became exhausting. Aedan would of course immediately know and warn them if one of the huldufólk showed up, but she couldn't stop herself.

She also kept expecting her friends to walk by. After all, they were still in the city, right? They must be, it wasn't that long ago.

"How's your fish?" Gunnar pulled her attention from the street.

She looked at him, then down at her plate. She'd barely touched anything, though it looked and smelled delicious. She'd ordered the Arctic Char, mostly because the picture on the menu was nice.

"It's fine." She glanced back at the street. Part of her wished they'd sat inside. Another part of her reasoned it was safer out here, so at least they'd see the danger coming.

"I've been thinking about what you should tell the police." Gunnar attempted once again to draw her attention. "Have you thought about it too?"

He sat across from her, Aedan beside him. Aedan was picking at his food too.

"I don't know what I can tell them that would

possibly make sense." She took a bite and chewed listlessly.

"You can tell them you were kidnapped." Gunnar had eaten considerably more of his dinner than either of them. "The captors kept you isolated and you never saw them clearly."

"That would be pretty unbelievable." She tapped her fork on her plate. "Anything I tell them is going to sound unbelievable, considering I look the same as I did when I disappeared. I don't look like someone who was held prisoner for a year. My hair hasn't grown, my body hasn't changed. I'm not emaciated or beaten up. I've also still got the same clothes I disappeared in, and they're clean."

"We can get rid of your clothes. We could cut off your hair or something."

She went back to eating and tried to keep her eyes off the street. Eventually, she spoke again. "I'm just going to tell them the truth, that I don't remember the last year or what happened to me."

Gunnar looked good, despite everything. In the low lighting on the patio, he was starkly handsome and his eyes seemed to glow, and it would have been more distracting if she wasn't already horribly distracted. She was also trying not to think of him that way anymore. Soon, she'd be gone, and whatever flared between them would be forgotten.

It was for the best.

"They're probably not going to believe I am who I say I am, anyway." She put her fork down. "Even with the footage. I've been declared dead. Someone identified my body."

Aedan broke his silence. "And you'll be hounded and questioned for as long as you live."

"I suppose that's my punishment." She gazed at

Gunnar. "Unless I find a way to escape it." She picked up her glass and took a drink. Gunnar had ordered a bottle of wine, but she didn't want booze, and stuck to water instead. She needed her mind clear.

The meal was uneventful, thankfully. They weren't approached by anyone, and neither did she notice anyone watching them. They walked back to the hotel, and she stared at the church. The sun sat on the horizon in the west and the sky behind the church was deep blue, a few stars splashed across it.

"I want to go walk around," Aedan said. "Check out the shops and galleries and stuff. We hardly ever get to Rey. I'll be back in a bit."

Gunnar smiled. "Okay. You have a key to get back in, yeah?"

Aedan nodded. He tucked his hands in his jacket pockets and loped off down the street.

She watched him go. "Is he going to patrol?"

Gunnar's smile widened. "No. He rarely gets to be a real person. I need to get him out of the house more."

She felt bad for Aedan. He was a young man, and half huldufólk or not, he should get to do things people his age did—drink, go to parties, meet girls. But they'd made a prison for him. Did he even know how to be a "real person?"

"Are you sure you don't want to go to the police tonight?" Gunnar took her hand.

She shook her head. "Tomorrow. I have to get things sorted out first."

They went into the hotel, but she looked back over her shoulder at the church again as they stepped inside.

Upstairs, the room was quiet. The moment was awkward, and heavy with things that needed to be said.

She didn't know how to start any of those conversations.

She stepped up to Gunnar and looked into his eyes. "I know today must have been hard for you," she said softly. "I'm sorry."

He rubbed her arm. "I'm actually more at peace with it than I thought I would be. Seeing my home again was cathartic."

"And finding out your wife is dead?"

He took a slow, deep breath. "It's good to have an answer, I guess." He flashed a small, tight smile. "I always suspected it. In two years, this will be over, and then—I don't know. Maybe I'll get her remains back or something."

She eased closer, and though it was foolish, she rubbed his chest. "You didn't deserve any of this. And neither did she."

Though she knew she should pull away, instead she leaned in, and so did he, and they kissed. Lingering, deep, with a lot of heat behind it. There was comfort in this, created by a shared bond of misery and fear.

When they broke apart, she stayed close to him.

He put his hand over hers on his chest. "This isn't a good idea," he said. "Not least of all because my dead wife is watching us."

"And the fact I'm not going to be here much longer, huh?"

Despite their sensible protestations, he slipped an arm around her waist. She didn't resist. Nor did she stop him from kissing her again. She melted into it, in fact. The magnetism was irresistible. He smelled so good it made her head swim. How could he smell so good after a full day of driving? She didn't feel like figuring it out, she just wrapped her arms around his broad shoulders.

In the back of her mind, she begged Hera to stay away. She didn't want to hear her whispers or be swept off into some vision. This felt good, and right, and she was determined to stay grounded in the moment and enjoy it.

"A really bad idea," he murmured between kisses, as their lips met again and again. "I don't know when Aedan will be back, either."

Once again, it didn't stop them from walking to her bed and working their shoes off. It didn't stop them from tumbling onto it, entwined, still kissing. It didn't stop him from climbing on top of her or her locking her legs around his hips. She'd been so long, before yesterday, without the weight of a man on top of her, the touch of skin, the scent of a man. Desire swept away all rational thought. Need blossomed hot inside of her.

And of course, the vertigo swept in. She squeezed her eyes shut and fought it back. *No, stay away, stay away.* She tried to concentrate on his mouth on her neck, his soft curls brushing her cheek. She would stay right there, in the bed, underneath him. She held on with a pulse of anger. She was still alive, and she was tired of being cockblocked by a dead woman.

She tried to reason silently to Hera that she could at least feel her husband again if she let this happen. It was a creepy and bizarre thought, but it seemed to stabilize things. Vanessa didn't hear the whispering. Her mind and vision both settled, and she came back to the moment.

Gunnar lifted his head and gazed down at her. His eyes glistened in the twilit room. "Are you okay?"

She nodded. "Yeah, I think she might mind her own business this time."

It went unspoken that this *was* her business—but acknowledging it too much would make it strange. A hundred years had passed. Hera was dead, and Gunnar was perfectly single. Vanessa might not be here in a few days, but that didn't mean they couldn't have what they wanted while she was still here. It didn't mean they couldn't seek solace in each other.

Gunnar looked toward the door. "Like I said, I don't know when Aedan will be back." He looked down at her. "I don't think he's ready for that much real life."

She gripped his shirt in the back and dragged it up. "Guess we better make it quick, then." Despite all the danger and potential embarrassment, she thought she might go crazy if they didn't actually do it this time.

His eyes glittered, and a devious smile curled his lips. "All right, then." He pulled her shirt up too.

"We probably shouldn't get fully undressed." She struggled out of it. "Let's just make this happen."

"A woman who knows what she wants. I like it." He kissed her.

Yes, she did know what she wanted, for once in her life, and she was going to have it. She was in control. What she wanted was right here on top of her, and she wasn't going to let any ghosts or other supernatural creatures interfere.

Not this time.

In a flurry of heat and giggles, they undid their jeans and worked them down. She had to completely remove a leg from hers, as well as from her underwear, to make it work. He stroked his fingers up her slit and then licked his fingertips.

"Already wet."

"Already hard." She gave his stiff cock a stroke. His jeans and underwear were around his knees. "It seems we're compatible." *That*, at least, was a decent joke.

She noted they didn't have protection—she certainly didn't, and she didn't guess Gunnar had brought any with him. She found she didn't care, though. She kept glancing at the door, ears pricked, praying that Aedan would stay out and have a good time. They couldn't pause to run out and buy a box of condoms.

Gunnar grabbed her leg still in her jeans and hauled it up around his waist. He didn't seem concerned either, as he slid that nice long cock right up into her, in one smooth, precise thrust.

She gasped, her eyes going wide. *Holy hell,* that was good. He filled her up, completely, way up inside where she was aching for it. She groaned against his ear.

"Don't worry," he gasped. "I don't think this is going to take long."

She didn't care how long it lasted, it was happening. This was bliss. She clung to his shoulders and begged him with every inch of her body to fuck her.

They stayed intensely quiet, listening, so much they were nearly holding their breath. The bed squeaked as he worked into her. Breathy whimpers passed her lips, and she clung even tighter. It felt good, so good, but something niggled at the back of her brain. She wanted it different, but she wasn't sure how.

Gunnar caressed her face and hair. He rocked his hips against hers, and his cock opened her up over and over, filling that ache. She could hear how wet she was around him.

"Gunnar…"

An urge rose in her, not unlike the urges she'd been getting from Hera, and maybe it did come from her. She pressed her hands to his chest, stopping him. Then, with more strength than she knew she had, she forcefully rolled him over, so she was on top of him.

He stared up at her. She slid back down on his cock, slowly, and groaned in satisfaction. Yes, this was what she wanted. She started riding him.

His cock hit just the right spot. She slid up and

down on it, taking him in, letting it slip back out. Perfect. She placed her hands on his chest and was no longer able to keep quiet as she rode him hard, hard enough the headboard banged against the wall.

His face sagged in a mask of helpless pleasure, his mouth slack, eyelids drooping, but something shone behind them—he looked somewhat cautious and confused. She didn't question it and kept riding. She was going to come like this.

"Gunnar." Her voice was a growl and didn't sound like her own. She slammed her hips down. "*Já!*"

Her pussy clenched around the hard shaft buried inside her. She pressed it all the way up into her and dragged her nails down his chest as she came. Her legs shook. Her inner walls throbbed.

He groaned and grabbed her hips, then started pounding up into her. She shrieked. The headboard slammed into the wall.

"Yes, fuck me," she snarled. "Fuck me, fuck me!"

He came, panting, moaning, his fingertips digging into her hips. His cock pumped hot, thick wetness up into her and she didn't try to move off him. She still clenched as he filled her with his release. She was soaked, inside and out.

It felt wonderful. It felt amazing.

She slumped over on him, cheek pressed to his chest. They were both slick with sweat. His cock twitched inside her and she dripped around it. She shivered. She was never that damn wild during sex. Maybe she just hadn't been with the right guys.

"Jesus," she gasped. "I don't know—what came over me. I just wanted to ride you."

He stroked her back with trembling fingers. His heart thumped beneath her ear. "Hera liked it like that," he whispered.

She swallowed, gazing at the gauzy curtains over the window. "I think she still does."

It was weird, but it was what it was. And it was damn good sex, anyway. She'd finally gotten to have him without being swept away. If Hera was inside, making her act like a freaky porn star, that wasn't such a bad thing, was it?

She'd believe, at least for right now, it wasn't.

* * * *

The room was silent, the deep blue of not-nighttime shining in. The curtains were open, so she could stare at the church pressed against the sky. Lights lit up the arch of the spire, filling it with a gentle glow, so it did indeed look holy. It appeared to be early evening outside, but the clock next to her said it was two AM.

Like back in Drangsnes, she was rather glad the sun didn't set. The darkness would be terrifying.

She turned her head on the pillow and looked over at the other bed.

Gunnar was on the side closest to her, on his back. Judging by the slow rise and fall of his chest, he was asleep.

Aedan lay on the other side of him, his back to her.

Her pillow smelled like Gunnar's cologne. She wished he could have slept in the bed with her. However, part of her was glad he couldn't. It made things easier.

She sat up, slowly and quietly. She'd dozed for a few hours, but the noise in her brain kept her from completely falling asleep. That was good too.

That noise continued now, a voice urging her. It wasn't the whispering, but it was still Hera—her presence compelling her, commanding her. She didn't even fully understand what Hera wanted, but the compulsion she instilled in Vanessa moved her limbs, like a marionette.

She slipped out of bed. Gunnar definitely wouldn't approve of this, because it was fucking crazy, and she might just be putting herself in the worst danger yet.

She'd worn a pair of Gunnar's sweats and a t-shirt to bed. The ill-fitting clothes added to her sense of displacement.

She grabbed her duffle bag and went into the bathroom, where she fished her jeans out and changed into them. Much easier to move if she didn't have to worry about her pants falling down.

She slipped her own boots on, too. They had low heels, but she could run much better in them than the clunky boots. If she got the chance to run, that was.

Next, she drew the bell out, and straightened out the links of the rusty chain. She gave the chain a hard tug. It was still solid, despite years of decay. It wouldn't break easily.

The urge inside her intensified. Would she do this of her own free will, if nothing dwelled inside her? She wasn't certain. Part of her was deeply terrified, but another part, maybe not wholly herself, was profoundly enraged and wanted what she deserved. It burned in her like hot coals, scorching her guts.

She pulled the knife out of the bag and pushed it into the pocket of her jeans. A glimpse into the mirror, into her own eyes, and they seemed darker somehow, filled with quiet determination and fury.

No one stirred when she slipped back into the room. From this angle she could see Aedan's face, and he appeared to be asleep as well. She grabbed her sweater and the room key. The key went in her pocket opposite the knife, though she didn't believe she'd be creeping back in. She pulled the sweater on and tucked the bell up under her arm once more.

No one called out to stop her as she left the room—part of her expected them to, at least Aedan. She shut the door quietly, paused a moment to listen, then started down the hallway.

The hotel was silent. The light was stark and strange in that empty space. Her feet seemed to move of their own accord, her thoughts consumed with Hera's will.

There was no one at the front desk, the lobby empty. She left the hotel.

Outside, a chilly breeze blew. No one was out on the streets near the hotel, either walking or in cars. The bars and restaurants around them were silent and dark. However, she caught the faint sound of music and activity in the distance. Some of the bars were still open, deeper in the district. She supposed if it were the weekend this might be harder, as there would be more people outside in her immediate area.

The sun still peeked over the horizon in the west, painting the sky deep red and brilliant orange.

She folded her arms across her chest to keep the bell in place and walked across the street, focused on the church.

The courtyard was empty, bathed in the gentle glow of the spire lights. She didn't think it was illegal to be there, even at this hour, but she still hoped she didn't meet an officer on patrol. They would definitely misunderstand the situation.

If there was a situation.

She stopped in front of the church and tilted her head back. It towered over her, breathtakingly tall, touching the blue sky. The world tilted, and the whispering started. She wasn't scared this time, and she didn't try to shut it out.

Yes, I know. I'm here, and I'll wait.

The minutes ticked by. She stared at the closed doors of the church. The breeze stirred her hair and crept under her sweater. Every sound around her made her tense—the distant hum of a car, the skittering of a piece of trash across the pavement, a remote shout or voice. The whispers came and went, keeping her feet planted on the cobblestones.

She slipped the bell from beneath her sweater and clutched it between her hands. The links filled her palms, cold and gritty. Her vision tunneled.

When the minutes had accumulated so long she started to doubt herself, she heard another sound.

This wasn't a human sound. It was so faint as to barely be perceptible, a soft *whoosh*, and she knew immediately it wasn't something natural. She shifted her gaze to the side, toward her shoulder, but didn't look back yet.

"You are more stupid than I could have imagined." The soft female voice didn't even make Vanessa flinch. She'd been expecting it. However, her flesh crawled. A wave of cold swept over her, and yet, the embers inside her burned hotter yet.

She turned slowly, at the same time moving her arms, and the bell, behind her. She clutched it tight behind her back.

The huldufólk woman was dressed the same as the last two times, but her dark hair hung over her shoulders. This time, she didn't hide what she was. Her eyes were black and alien. Even in the warm glow of the church lights, her skin was ghastly pale. Disturbingly, Vanessa could make out similar features in the angular shape of her face that Aedan possessed. He had that regarding, regal way of holding his head, too.

"Am I?" Vanessa gazed at her. "Perhaps you're the stupid one. Did you come to spirit me away again, like you did on this very street a year ago?"

The woman stood a few feet away. If she could sense the iron, she didn't react.

"I wasn't the one who spirited you away."

"I don't believe you. Why are you following me, then?"

"You were given the gift of keeping your life." Her lips seemed to barely move as she spoke. "Why don't you take it and go? Do not tempt fate further."

Vanessa tilted her head. "Yeah, that's the thing. Why *did* you spare my life? Why do you spare anyone's life? I'd think you wouldn't be so merciful, big and powerful as you are. It sure would teach humans a lesson about messing with you, if you just killed them off."

The light glinted on the obsidian surface of her eyes. "Do you think it's wise to mock us?" Her tone didn't change, but danger lurked behind those words.

Vanessa had already come too far to care.

"I don't think it's *un*wise." Vanessa shrugged. "I don't think you're as powerful as you pretend to be. You're scared. You subsist on smoke and mirrors, hoping it's enough to scare humans into leaving you alone."

The woman sneered. Her teeth were straight and white, but abnormally large. "You should mind your words. Trespassing against us is dealt with harshly, and you are making your own sentence."

"What are you going to do? Make me live a hundred years? Make me hunt down babies?" She strolled closer. "You've lost your power, haven't you? All these years, losing your lands and your domain inch by inch to humans. Did it sap you? Or were you ever that powerful to begin with?"

Something flashed into Vanessa's mind then, and she had no idea where it came from, but she was certain of it. Perhaps it was a knowledge Hera held.

"You get your power from the earth, don't you?" Vanessa stopped in front of the woman, so close. "And you don't have much earth left."

The woman hissed in her face, like a snake.

Vanessa didn't react. Inside, she recoiled and screamed, but the other part of her—the part that was being fueled by Hera—just laughed.

"What do you want?" the woman snarled. Her eyes seemed to pulse. "Why would you pursue me twice and endanger yourself like this?"

"I want answers." Maybe she, too, was a terrifying sight to this woman. "I want to know why you kidnapped me, and where I've been for the past year. I didn't do anything to deserve this."

The woman drew back, and her lips quivered, as if she meant to sneer again, but it faded. "You deserve it more than you know. Be happy you have no recollection. It could be so much worse."

Vanessa felt, once again, this was an empty threat. "I want to know what happened. Tell me that, and I won't persist. I'll leave you alone. Trust me, it can be so much worse for you, too."

The woman gave a harsh laugh. "What could you do to me, foolish human girl?"

Vanessa clutched the chain harder, the weight of it powerful in her hands. "Tell me what happened," she insisted. "This is your last chance."

The woman sneered again, this time cruel and taunting. "You should walk away. Next time you dare to confront me, you will pay the price. Take your precious life and leave this land."

And with that, like the foolish creature she was,

she turned away, her hair flowing around her. It was a flounce and meant to dismiss Vanessa entirely. Instead, it provoked her and drove her forward. This was the moment, the one she'd been waiting for.

Vanessa lunged forward, whipping the bell from behind her back. The woman was slightly taller, but with a leap she managed to easily fling the iron necklace over her head. Vanessa gripped it by the bell, twisted, and yanked.

An unholy shriek tore from the woman's throat but was quickly muffled, as it turned into a garbled, desperate whine. Vanessa was shocked at how quickly she went down. She expected more of a struggle. Instead, the creature crumpled to her knees, scrabbling at the chain. Vanessa didn't tighten it enough to choke her, but still the woman's strength seemed to immediately diminish. Vanessa had to bend over her to keep her grip.

"I warned you," Vanessa said. "Did you think I would come out here defenseless? You've got good reason to be afraid of us." Hera cackled in triumphant glee inside her head.

The woman squirmed feebly. She made wheezing, choking sounds.

Vanessa bent to her ear. "Now, bitch, let's get some answers out of you."

Chapter Twenty

Vanessa didn't expect to come out on the winning end of this. Even if the woman couldn't hurt her while restrained, she would eventually have to let her go. Vanessa accepted she might be attacked when she'd made the choice to go through with this.

However, things turned more complicated than she expected.

"Jesus Christ, Vanessa, *why?*" Gunnar's voice echoed, enraged and despaired, across the courtyard. She was afraid he would draw attention to them.

"Because I'm tired of being a victim." She held the knife beneath the woman's jaw. She didn't know if she had it in her to cut someone—but Hera did, and Hera was all over this.

Gunnar stopped in front of them. His hands were in his hair, his eyes wild, face blanched. He looked like the world had just crashed down on him.

Aedan stood a few feet behind Gunnar, staring at the woman. He was the one who probably heard, or at least sensed her go out the door and woke Gunnar. It didn't matter now.

"Let me go," the woman snarled. "You will pay for this. Others will come." She fought weakly, seething and hissing. Her hands were red from touching the iron and thin rivulets of blood trickled down her neck. A raw, rank smell hung on the air, like burnt flesh.

Vanessa was almost horrified enough to stop, but she didn't, because Hera was like an anchor inside of her. "Call to them, then," Vanessa taunted. "Summon them."

"Did you hear anything I fucking said today?" Gunnar yelled, arms out. "The things I told you? They killed Hera for this. Do you want to die?"

Vanessa jerked the chain. "Did you see Hera Ívarsdóttir die?" she questioned the woman. She pressed the blade to her flesh. "Did you drive her to her death?"

The woman's lips were pulled in a grimace and though her eyes were black and blank, they conveyed pure rage. The rest of her face, however, radiated fear. Vanessa knew her assumption was correct. This creature had no power to hurt them, and no one was coming to save her.

"I wish I had," the woman wheezed out, her voice full of venom. "You will not torture our secrets out of me, you waste of life."

Vanessa chuckled darkly at the insult. She'd never been called that one before. Also, what did she mean by "I wish I had?" Did she wish to be the one who knocked Hera off the cliff?

Blood streaked down the woman's jaw from the blade, though Vanessa wasn't pressing hard enough to cut.

"Vanessa!" Gunnar's voice cracked. "Let her go, please."

The woman looked at Aedan.

His expression was stony and tense, though he didn't seem as upset as Gunnar.

"Abomination," the woman snarled at him. "Make her release me, or you will pay the price!"

Aedan flicked his gaze to Vanessa.

Vanessa shook her head. "They don't have the power to hurt you. If they did, they would have killed you as a child. Don't be afraid. You don't have to bow to their command like they've made you think." She hoped he believed her, because she wasn't sure she could fight him off and keep the woman restrained at the same time.

"You don't deserve this." Vanessa spoke calmly to him. "Help me, Aedan. Get some payback."

His face softened, reminding her of the look he'd had back at Gunnar's house, when he'd been talking about his fate. He suddenly looked his age, vulnerable and uncertain.

"Vanessa." Gunnar choked out a sob. "You're going to die."

"She's not going to kill me." Vanessa curled the chain in her hand, tightening it. "Look at him, you monster. Look at both of them. You and your kind have been terrorizing them for years, but it ends now. You're not going to mess with them anymore, and you're not going to mess with me. If I let you live, you're going to call your dogs off. That's the deal."

The woman wheezed. "I will not do anything for you."

Gunnar rubbed his face and eyes. "Vanessa, you have to see reason."

She was seeing reason, already. A plan was forming in her head. If the woman wouldn't talk, fine. *Someone* would. Having one of them hostage was an advantage in their favor. For the first time since she woke up on that island, she felt like she was in control.

"I guess we'll have to find someone willing to have a discussion with us." She nodded at Aedan. "If this one doesn't have anything to say?"

Aedan gazed back at her.

Vanessa wanted to hurry this up. If someone saw them, they'd have bigger problems. After all, she currently had a woman restrained with a knife to her throat.

"What are you planning?" Aedan asked.

"We're taking her back to Drangsnes." It wasn't a suggestion, or a plea. It was a statement. "You said the huldufólk visit the island. So, let's invite them for a conference."

"What?" Gunnar gaped at her. "We're not taking her anywhere!"

The woman squirmed. "No, you are not!"

"We take her to the island." Vanessa ignored them. "We draw them out."

"No." Gunnar slashed his hands through the air. "This is over. Let her go, Vanessa. The last thing you want is to call them out. What, summon more of them? That's insane."

"You will die!" The woman seemed suddenly anxious. "You cannot draw them to you."

"Can't I?" Vanessa peered at her. What was she afraid of? "Do you have things you want to say, then?"

Gunnar gave a wild laugh. "This is not going to work!"

Vanessa dragged the edge of the blade across the woman's cheek. "Someone talks, or you die."

"Idiot," she gasped. "They will not negotiate with you!"

Aedan spoke up. "What if they swarm us? That island is their domain. Bringing a hostage will only provoke them."

"Then we kill the hostage. I don't think they can afford to lose any more of their people."

Gunnar was visibly trembling.

She didn't mean to give him flashbacks, but she was also beyond caring at this point. She would have what she wanted.

"They could mess with your mind," Aedan said. "They might not be as strong as we think, but they're very capable of that. What if they do something to make you release her?"

Vanessa bent to the woman's ear. "Are you going to mess with my mind? Go on, do it. Do it right now."

She struggled again, but it was still a weak fight

and she didn't come close to escaping. "Release me!"

"We take her to the island," Vanessa said. "And demand they give us answers, on threat of her life." She tried to imagine actually spilling huldufólk blood, to show them what she was capable of. She found it surprisingly easy to visualize.

"We're not taking her anywhere." Gunnar was near tears. "You won't win any negotiation with them. Let her go, I'm begging you."

She wasn't addressing Gunnar with her plans, not really. She could see the shift from doubt to consideration in Aedan's demeanor, and that's where her hope was. If Gunnar wouldn't drive, they'd find their own way back. She wondered if cabs charged more for transporting supernatural beings and almost laughed.

Aedan looked at Gunnar. "I think we should take her back," he said.

Gunnar turned sharply to him. "What? Are you insane?"

"Abomination," the woman gritted out. "You will die as well."

Aedan ignored her. "I think Vanessa is right. Look at her, she's weak. Why isn't she doing anything to us, if she has so much power? Why aren't her people rushing in to save her and kill us?"

Aedan was getting the gist of it now.

"It doesn't mean they won't!" Gunnar grabbed him by the arms. "They'll certainly kill us if we take her to the island. They'll rip us to pieces. They won't negotiate, that's not their way."

"Why haven't they killed us yet, then?" Aedan spoke calmly. "Why didn't they kill me when I was a child? If they could actually harm us they would have done it by now."

Gunnar shook him. "They killed my wife!" His

voice was ragged. "I haven't told you the entire story. She attacked them and they took her away and they killed her." He sucked in a breath. "That's why I've been punished like this. The original sentence was shorter, but because of her, this is what happened! Because of her impulsiveness, she died, and I was left to suffer."

Aedan stared at him. He looked young and vulnerable again. "How do you know they killed her?"

"Because she's haunting Vanessa." He let go of Aedan and stepped back. "And I tell you, that's why she's doing this now. That's why she's gone mad. Hera's ghost is possessing her."

Vanessa sighed. "They didn't kill her, Gunnar..."

He looked at her, eyes bright and full of fear. "She fell from a cliff, by accident, while she was being chased. I saw it."

The woman in her grip hummed and scoffed, and it was an amused sound, a sound one made when somebody said something so untrue it was funny. Vanessa looked down at her. Her black eyes danced and a pained smile curled her lips.

Vanessa frowned. The woman's previous words echoed in her head. *I wish I had.*

Vanessa looked around the courtyard, and the world seemed to come into focus. Her own thoughts and emotions came forward. She looked back down at the woman. "Hera isn't dead, is she?"

The woman's smile remained.

"What?" Gunnar said.

"She's not dead." Vanessa yanked at the chain. "Where is she?"

She was baffled. If Hera wasn't a ghost, then she'd developed mind-possessing powers and took over Vanessa from afar. Maybe for a prisoner trapped amongst the huldufólk, that wasn't unusual. After all, in one short year Vanessa had gained the ability to pick up those signals.

"I will not tell you anything." The woman's voice was gravelly. "It is not my place to share our secrets."

Gunnar stepped toward them, staring down at the woman.

"We'll take her to the island," Aedan said. "If nothing else, we can get them to tell Vanessa what they did to her and why."

Gunnar turned back to him. "Do you want to suffer more?"

"I want to suffer less!" It was the first time she'd heard true emotion in Aedan's voice. "I don't want to spend my entire life on their leash. We have a chance to maybe escape our fate. Don't you want to be free of them too?"

Gunnar shook his head. "That won't happen. They won't bargain over one woman."

"They might." Aedan's eyes shone. "It's worth a shot, isn't it? It's worth trying, before I go fucking crazy. The last time I was hunting, I just…" He stumbled over his words. A tear streaked down his cheek. "Do you know how many times I've thought of jumping, like my mother?"

Vanessa ached for him. She knew that desperation in his voice. One thing the huldufólk *were* good at was inflicting mental distress.

"Aedan." Gunnar's voice softened. "I know you suffer. But I don't want you to die. You're my son."

"And you're my father." Aedan's voice was thick. "And I can't stand to see what they've done to you, either."

Vanessa's legs burned with the strain of kneeling. She was ready to haul the woman up and get on with this.

"We can't stay here much longer. We have to do this, now."

Gunnar looked at her. "This is madness," he whispered. "This won't turn out the way you want, mark my words."

It wasn't permission, but he wouldn't fight.

She nodded to Aedan.

Aedan wiped his eyes and strode over. He helped Vanessa haul the woman to her feet. She was light, but she sagged and wobbled. Vanessa kept her grip on the chain.

"Fools!" The woman wailed. "Do you crave death so much? Do not do this!"

"Pull your shoelaces out," Vanessa told Aedan. "Tie her hands behind her back." She couldn't let go of the chain until the woman was incapable of getting away.

Aedan dropped and began to pull out his laces. They weren't tied, his shoes probably slipped on in a panic to get out here. Gunnar watched him, standing there helpless.

"Shoelaces aren't going to keep her hands tied," he pointed out. "They're not iron."

Vanessa lowered the knife to her side and smoothed her thumb along the blunt edge of the blade.

"Don't worry, I'll keep them in place."

* * * *

The drive was tense, silent, and overwhelmingly unpleasant, but Vanessa expected no less. The fact she was spaced out and physically exhausted from lack of sleep didn't help. Hera, or Hera's messages, kept her eyes open and her nerves on edge. They were speeding toward some great unknown, and she would sleep when it was over.

Or else she'd be dead, and it wouldn't matter.

The sun climbed as they drove. It would be nearly

six AM by the time they arrived back in Drangsnes, full daylight. The sky brightened from inky blue to pink and orange. The only clouds in the sky were gathered on the horizon. The road was empty. They rarely passed another car or saw a person, even as they drove through the small sleepy towns along the way. The world was holding its breath.

Vanessa twisted and looked through the back window into the bed of the truck, for the hundredth time. Paranoia clawed at her insides, and she feared any moment she would feel hands around her throat from behind.

The woman hadn't moved since they left Reykjavik. She was curled on her side, her black hair spread around her. The chain was secured around her neck. Her arms were wrapped behind her, the shoelaces binding her wrists.

Vanessa had tucked the knife between her wrists, so she wouldn't have the strength in her arms to break the laces. She didn't know if it would work, but so far, it had. Vanessa was reluctant to give up her weapon, but even if the woman could find a way to wiggle free, she wouldn't be able to wield the knife since it was made of iron.

She turned back around and eased into her seat. "I hope she isn't dead." She spoke into the silence, so thick her words seemed muffled. "She hasn't moved an inch."

Aedan was driving. He glanced in the rearview mirror. The reason he drove wasn't because Gunnar refused to, but more a safety issue. Gunnar was human and prone to the effects of sleep deprivation far more than Aedan was. He might fall asleep behind the wheel.

"I don't think she is," Aedan said. "Iron only weakens them, it doesn't kill them through touch. She's just immobilized."

Vanessa peeked into the bed again and tried to pick out if there was any blood pooling beneath her head or behind her back where her hands were. It was too shadowy with the cap over the bed of the truck to tell.

"I almost feel guilty." She turned back around. "I'm torturing her." Hera whispered in her head. *She could have saved herself by telling you what you want to know.*

Aedan glanced in the mirror again. "They're torturing us. They've been torturing us for a long time."

Gunnar was slumped against the passenger door, his head on his arm. He might have been asleep, but she got the feeling, like her, rest wasn't possible for him. He seemed both resigned and full of silent anger and panic. She was surprised he even allowed them in the truck.

But, maybe it was hard to say no to his son.

"Everything's going to change." She looked out the window. "One way or another."

The landscape was all hills and farmland. Sometimes the hills were massive, like mountains, and sometimes they were gently rolling. The farther north they went, the craggier and bleaker the land became. She saw fewer farms, and less civilization. The water appeared, to their right. This was the scenery she'd missed on the first drive while she was asleep, majestic as the rest of Iceland, but she could barely concentrate on it. It flashed by in a meaningless blur.

Gunnar spoke eventually, and it was so sudden it made her start.

"What makes you think Hera is alive?"

She looked at the back of his head, his curls a matted mess. She thought of last night, the touch of his hands, the taste of his mouth, the way he filled her. She didn't want to lose him, or his trust. She didn't want him to hate her.

"It's something the huldufólk woman said."
Vanessa looked out the window again. "She said 'I wish
I had' when I asked if she saw Hera die. I thought she
just meant she wished she'd been there, but it wasn't
that. She was smiling about it. I think she meant she
wished Hera was dead, period."

"You think she's been alive all this time, like
me?"

"If they can extend your life, they can extend
hers. If they wanted you to live as punishment, they'd
want her to live as punishment, too."

"That's why we're doing this," Aedan said.
"Look at what they've done, to all of us. To your wife."

Gunnar lifted his head. The morning sun traced
his profile. "You won't get vengeance. We're going to
die."

Aedan didn't reply.

Vanessa pressed her lips together. Maybe the
huldufólk *did* have more power than she assumed.
Maybe they *would* punish them horribly, even kill them.
But she would go down fighting, and she wouldn't
cower.

Gunnar was silent again, for a while, then he
spoke once more. "Where is she, then? If Hera's alive,
where are they keeping her?"

Vanessa propped her arm on the door, and her
head on her hand. "I don't know, but I still hear her.
Even clearer than before. I feel her out there. It's
something else we're going to demand from them, I
promise."

Could she really kill one of them? Could she kill
many of them? They were barely human in her eyes,
twisted monsters who only wanted to see her suffer—and
yet, she'd never been the type to inflict violence. They
were beings who looked like her, talked like her, and

they had motivations other than sadism and spite, surely. She hoped they did, anyway, and would want to save one of their own.

Hopefully, Hera would give her the strength to do the dirty work if it came down to that.

They drove across the fjord lands, through ancient landscapes, and the sun grew warmer and brighter. It was a beautiful day.

A battle loomed on the horizon.

Chapter Twenty-One

"I'm going to beg you one more time not to do this."

Gunnar's eyes were tired and red-rimmed. His face was blanched with trepidation and terror. And yet, she wanted to drag her fingers through his curls, kiss him on the mouth, and whisper that it would be all right, that she had this under control.

But that was kind of bullshit.

Vanessa pulled her sweater around her. It was cold here with the wind blowing off the water. "Do you think if we let her go now, they wouldn't punish us for what we've done? We can't turn back."

Aedan had placed the woman in his row boat, the one they'd rescued her in. She looked deathly, but she was alive. Her breath was quick and shallow, her face fixed in a grimace. Blood stained the front of her sweater and painted dark streaks down her neck. Her hands were also covered in blood. Vanessa wanted to take the knife back but hesitated to do so. If she freed the woman's hands she might get the chain off her neck.

"Nothing good will come of this," Gunnar said. "Vanessa, please." His tone was anguished. "Both of you need to stop and think."

"I am thinking. Don't you want to know where Hera is?" She didn't mean to hurt him, but she would do what she had to do. "If you don't want to go to the island with us, you don't have to." She touched his arm. "You can stay here."

He huffed. "You want me to stay here while you two go out there and face the huldufólk alone?"

"If something happens to us, it might be easier for you."

He shook his head, looking away from her, out toward the island. His eyes glinted. "No, it won't be easy. Don't you understand that?"

Aedan stood next to the boat, waiting. This early in the morning, the beach was empty. They seemed to be the only people in the world. Just them, and the angry, wounded thing in the boat.

"We should go," Aedan said. "Before the tourists start heading out there."

Vanessa certainly didn't want any innocent bystanders getting caught up in this. "Come on." She held her hand out to Gunnar. "If you're coming with us, then come."

Gunnar pointed at Aedan, glaring at her. "You're giving him false hope. They won't show mercy on either of you. You're filling his head with ideas that he can really fight them."

"What if he can?" She still held her hand out. "What if he has that choice and he doesn't take it? Do you want this to be his life?"

Gunnar looked at her hand, then turned and walked stiffly toward the boat.

She sighed and followed him.

Aedan had put the woman on the floor between the front seat with the oars and the middle plank. Vanessa sat on the plank facing her. Aedan and Gunnar pushed them off, then Aedan splashed into the shallow water and jumped in the front. Gunnar got in behind her. The boat rocked as they drifted out on the choppy water.

The woman didn't move. She was curled up, her head resting on the side of the boat.

Vanessa leaned over her. "Why hasn't anyone come to help you? Are they afraid, or do they just not care about you?" She was using the fact they hadn't been ambushed, more than anything, to fuel her courage. If the huldufólk hadn't set upon them yet, there must be a reason.

She just hoped that reason wasn't because they were amassing the troops.

The woman turned her face up to Vanessa, and her skin was ghastly pale, like a corpse. The sun shone on her black eyes.

"They do not know I was watching you." Her voice was thin and wheezy. "Do not do this."

Vanessa blinked.

"Why not? Why didn't they know you were watching us?"

Aedan began to row. They bobbed across the small waves.

"Do not summon them." The woman's raspy voice was hard to hear over the lapping water and the wind. "I am forbidden to tell you anything, but if you do not draw their attention to me, I will give you clues to find the answers yourself."

Vanessa was startled to hear her strike such a bargain.

The woman twisted, as if trying to look around outside the boat, but she could barely move. The dried blood on her skin was nearly black.

"Why do you not want us to summon them?" Vanessa narrowed her eyes at Aedan.

He gazed back at her, stony-faced.

"I will help you." She tried to squirm again. "I will tell you where to look."

It might have been tempting, but Vanessa was intrigued now why the woman didn't want the other huldufólk to show up. What had she been doing that they didn't know about? Was spying some forbidden act?

"Tell me why you don't want them to come." Vanessa stared down at her. "And I'll consider your request."

The woman was silent, her chest heaving with ragged breaths. Her lips were almost as pale as her skin.

They glided across the water, the island growing ahead of them.

"It won't take long to get there." Vanessa pointed at it. "You'd better speak up."

Suddenly, the woman's eyes snapped from black to normal brown human eyes. They were much like Aedan's. Her face seemed less monstrous now.

"I was not supposed to be watching you." Bitterness tinged her words. "The edict given was that you were to be released and we were to have no further contact with you. We were never to make ourselves visible to you again, even if you wanted us to."

Vanessa furrowed her brow. "Released from where? And why would I want you to?"

Her human eyes looked tired, and frightened. She didn't speak.

Vanessa leaned over. "Where have I been?"

"I cannot tell you these things, especially given the rule. But I will guide you to the answers."

Gunnar spoke up. "And how will you do that?" He seemed much more interested in the situation now, possibly because it was clear this was a lone huldufólk without backup. "You just said your kind aren't to make contact, so how is she going to get answers?"

The woman didn't answer.

Vanessa suspected she was bluffing—she would coax them to remove the iron and she'd be gone in a flash. "Why are you watching us if you're not supposed to?" she asked. "You seem afraid they'll punish you if they find out. Is that true? Would they?"

She grimaced. "We punish our own much more harshly than we have ever punished you." The bitterness in her voice was overwhelming now.

Vanessa thought of the story of Aedan's father, burnt alive on the solstice. They let his human mother flee, though.

"Then why would you risk it?" Vanessa pushed her hair back from her face. The wind was ripping it out of the ponytail. "Why would you risk being punished?"

The woman tried to look around again, straining her neck. "I was trying to protect someone."

This was getting interesting.

"Who?"

The woman sagged against the boat. "My brother."

That wasn't an answer she expected. Vanessa hadn't considered these creatures might have families. Suddenly, she remembered the face in the truck, in her dream—it was a man.

"What are you protecting him from?" Gunnar asked. "And how is watching us protecting him?"

The woman was silent again.

Vanessa stared at the approaching island. The water lapped the rocky beach. Birds circled above it. She nudged the woman with her foot. "Are you going to answer our questions?"

"I cannot." She gritted her teeth. "It is part of what I am forbidden to tell you. Let me go. I swear, I will lead you to the answers."

Gunnar leaned forward and spoke near Vanessa's ear. "Maybe you should consider her offer. It's saner than summoning a bunch of huldufólk who will already be angry she disobeyed them."

Vanessa weighed her options. She squinted at the island. "She's lying. She can't lead me to any clues. Like you said, if they want no contact with me, how is she going to help?"

Gunnar sat back, and she heard him sigh.

"Keep rowing," Vanessa told Aedan. "If she won't talk, someone will."

The closer they got, the more the woman struggled. Fat tears slipped from her eyes.

Vanessa tried not to look at her, so she wouldn't feel sorry for her. After all, it might just be lies and manipulation.

They reached the shore, and Gunnar jumped out to pull the boat up on the beach. Aedan put the oars down and hopped out too. Vanessa gazed up at the craggy cliff in front of them. Puffins rested in the crevices and hopped over grassy outcroppings. She didn't see anyone around—human or huldufólk.

She stood and stepped up onto the plank she'd been sitting on, so she towered over the woman. "This is the side of the island where you found me, isn't it?" she asked Gunnar and Aedan.

Aedan nodded. "Yes. There's a path." He pointed it out, a meandering line up the cliff face.

"Let's take her up there." She jumped over the side of the boat onto the beach. "It seems to be a spot they like to visit."

Gunnar didn't move, but Aedan dragged the woman out.

She was still crying, now moaning pitifully as well.

"Listen." Gunnar held his hands out. "Why don't you give her a chance? If she's willing to help us, you don't have to summon more of them and put us all in danger. Maybe she *can* lead you to the answers."

Aedan held the woman up.

She sagged in his arms.

Vanessa stood before her.

The woman's pupils were dark in her wet human

eyes.

"All right." Vanessa folded her arms. "If you answer all three questions I'm about to ask you, I'll let you go."

Aedan frowned.

She didn't expect the questions to be answered, though.

The woman gazed back at her.

"Who are you protecting your brother from?" Vanessa asked.

The woman was still, then she looked up at the cliff. She looked back at Vanessa. "You."

Vanessa was both surprised to get an answer, and at the nature of that answer. "Me?"

"I am protecting him from making contact with you. He is an idiot." She twisted her neck, teeth bared in agony. Her skin was raw beneath the chain. "He will be put to death if he breaches the rule and they find out. He may be foolish, but he is still my brother. I must save him from himself."

Vanessa was confused. Instead of asking her second, original question, she changed it. "Was it your brother who kidnapped me that night, outside the bar?"

"No, it was one of the Council."

Gunnar stepped up beside Vanessa. "The Council?"

"I can say nothing else." She turned her face away. "I am forbidden." Vanessa looked at Gunnar, frowning.

The woman writhed in Aedan's grip "That was two questions. Ask your third."

Vanessa didn't plan to release her, even if she answered. But, things might go in a different direction.

Vanessa moved closer.

"Where have I been for the past year?"

The woman glared at her. She kept her lips sealed, the expression on her face one of fury and despair. Her eyes snapped back to black. It was a question she couldn't, or wouldn't, answer.

"I told you, she's bluffing." Vanessa turned and motioned for Aedan to follow. "Come on, let's go." She trudged across the rocks toward the cliff face.

"Wait!" Gunnar called out. "Vanessa, she told you. She's forbidden to say certain things!" He hurried after her and grabbed her arm.

"That doesn't help me." She flung his hand off. "I didn't come here to play games."

The woman struggled as Aedan tried to pull her along. He stopped, picked her up, and flung her over his shoulder. She let out a shriek.

"Aedan!" Gunnar pleaded.

Aedan plodded past him after Vanessa.

"Show me the way up," Vanessa told Gunnar. "Lead us to the spot."

Gunnar didn't move. They stopped and looked back at him.

"You can stay here, then." Vanessa was trying not to be angry or impatient, despite the need for haste. She understood his reluctance. "Aedan knows the way up, I'll let him go ahead."

Gunnar gritted his teeth. "We are all going to die."

She looked at the woman hanging over Aedan's shoulder. He held her effortlessly.

"No." Vanessa shook her head. "They don't have the power to kill us. Torment us, yes, but nothing more."

The woman ceased her noisemaking, and from where her head dangled next to Aedan's hip, she looked at Vanessa. This seemed to be confirmation.

"There's been too many times in the stories

you've told me when they could have killed a person." Vanessa opened her hands. "But they didn't. If they're so powerful, and so deadly, they certainly fail to flex it when it would benefit them the most."

Gunnar walked toward her. "You don't know them as well as you think you do. You haven't lived here for a century, in their presence."

"Fear is their only weapon. I'm not afraid. Not anymore."

Gunnar clenched his hands at his sides. He looked as angry as the huldufólk woman.

"I'm going up." She pointed at the cliff. "And you can come with us or not. I'd rather have you there, truth be told. I'd feel a lot better with you at my side."

He looked up, then back at her. They gazed at each other, and her heart ached, with a profundity she couldn't deny. His expression didn't change, but he moved past her and trudged toward the path. She nodded at Aedan. They followed.

* * * *

They walked the uneven path up the cliff face single file. Vanessa tried to concentrate on her feet, so she didn't stumble in her dress boots. Despite his load, Aedan moved deftly ahead of her. Huldufólk blood was good for something, at least.

The woman occasionally cried out, but they ignored her.

The view was beautiful: the morning sun spread orange and gold across the water, the sea encircling them, and the shore stretched in the misty distance. The sky was clear and blue, and apart from the wind, it was temperate. The verdant green rocks of the cliff teemed with puffins, who watched curiously as they passed by. It was a surreal, idyllic backdrop for this strange, protracted drama.

It took them about ten minutes to reach the island floor. Gunnar led them to the grassy spot where she'd been found. Being back there a third time still made her skin crawl.

"Put her down here." She pointed at the spot where she herself had lain.

Aedan slipped the woman off his shoulder and dumped her on the ground.

She flopped on her back, growling like a feral dog. "This is your last chance to let me go!" Her voice was weak and strained.

Vanessa looked at Aedan. "Do you see any sign of the huldufólk here?"

Aedan looked around. The wind pulled at his hair. He shook his head. "No."

Gunnar stood with his hands in his sweater pockets, gazing dully at the woman.

Vanessa pulled her up, onto her knees.

She hung her head.

"Here we are!" Vanessa called to the wind. "Come out. We have one of your kind!"

Gunnar stared at her, then looked around. He was pale.

Vanessa bent and gripped the handle of the knife between the woman's wrists. She pulled it out. If she tried to free herself, that was fine. She wouldn't get far. "Come out, or I'll kill her!" She pressed the knife beneath the woman's jaw.

No response. No one appeared.

"Do you want her to die?" Vanessa demanded to the air. "I will spill her blood on this island."

Minutes passed. Vanessa's hand was steady around the knife handle. What if they didn't care? Or they weren't listening?

Then, suddenly, something seemed to change, the

air itself taking on a different quality. The wind picked up, and it was colder. A chill rushed across Vanessa's skin and crawled up under her sweater. The back of her neck prickled.

Aedan shifted. "They're here," he whispered.

Vanessa looked around, her senses sharp. Hera whispered in her head, furious and frantic.

The woman let out a sigh, a sound of both despair and fear. Perhaps she would be better off if Vanessa just killed her.

Vanessa looked back at Aedan. "I don't see anything." She felt their presence though, descending on the island like a black fog. "Where are they?"

Aedan pointed upward.

Vanessa looked up. Her breath caught. Her heart pounded in her ears.

On the outcropping that looked down on the spot, two figures stood, dressed in gray robes. Their black hair fluttered in the wind. They gazed down at them with black eyes and stony white faces.

"You got your wish," Gunnar said, weakly.

Vanessa swallowed back her fear. "Not yet, we haven't."

The creatures glided down to where they stood, moving like ghosts.

Vanessa kept the blade to the woman's throat. As the two figures approached, she narrowed her eyes. She recognized both—or, all huldufólk looked the same.

The one who came forward first, a woman, was almost certainly the one who had visited them before at the fire. The one who followed her was a man, and Vanessa was sure it was the face Hera had pushed away in the truck. Was this the brother?

Vanessa stared at him. Something stirred deep inside her, a definite sense of recognition that went beyond remembering a face in a dream. He gazed back at her, or seemed to, as it was hard to read his expression with his black eyes.

Aedan and Gunnar flanked her. Aedan was defiant, chin tilted up. Gunnar fidgeted and held his breath.

"Good of you to show up." Vanessa spoke as boldly as her tightened throat would allow. "I think it's time we had a talk."

The two stopped. The man remained behind the woman. Their faces were expressionless, like statues.

The woman looked down at Vanessa's hostage, and she spoke. "We came swiftly, hoping to stop anyone else from finding out about this." She was clearly talking to the woman, not them. "If we leave quickly, they may never know."

"If you leave quickly," Vanessa interjected, "is up to me. It's up to you, too. If you talk, you leave."

"This woman you threaten is my sister," she replied. "Her name is Þalía. My name is Sía."

Just as Vanessa hadn't considered the huldufólk had families, she hadn't thought about them having names, either. Or if they did, she imagined they'd be something unpronounceable and archaic. Aside from sounding distinctly Icelandic, they were mostly normal.

Sía looked over her shoulder at the man. "This is our brother, Yngvi."

So, this *was* the brother she was trying to "protect." From Vanessa, apparently.

"You obviously know who we are." Vanessa pressed the knife tighter. "If you want your sister to live, talk. And fast, if you want to get out of here before your people find you here."

She would use every bit of leverage she had. Obviously, they were more afraid of their own than they were of humans.

Sía curled her lip. "Yes, we know who you are. We hoped never to see you again, but fate does not heed our wishes."

Vanessa glared at her.

Yngvi stepped forward. "Do not hurt Þalía." His voice was airy like the others, but deeper. "She was only trying to make sure I did not behave rashly. She was not trying to hurt you."

His eyes changed to human eyes. As they did, Vanessa's breath caught. Yes, she knew this man. But *how?*

"She was not to go near you," Sía said. "None of us were. If the Council finds out we stand here with you, we will be burnt. Let us go, before they notice us."

"You're not going anywhere without answering my questions." Vanessa remained determined. "We all have questions, and a few demands, on top of it. I don't want to hear any 'we're not allowed to tell you' bullshit. If you're here, you're already breaking the rules, so you might as well be honest."

Yngvi's expression was disturbingly human, and he seemed longing and distressed.

Gunnar drew up his shoulders. "Where is my wife?" His tone had gotten a little braver. "The one you took away from me. Where is Hera Ívarsdóttir?"

Vanessa looked at him, then back at the other two.

Sía lifted her arms, hands open. "She is right here."

They all looked around. Not another person was to be seen. Maybe she was talking about her spirit? Was she a ghost after all, hanging on the air?

Vanessa looked back at them, frowning. "Where?"

Sía lowered her hands. "You. You are Hera Ívarsdóttir."

Vanessa stared at her. Then she blinked.

"I'm Vanessa Evanston."

"Vanessa Evanston is dead."

Chapter Twenty-Two

Gunnar stared at Vanessa.

She looked back at him, bewildered. "What the hell are you talking about?" she demanded of Sía. "Yes, I've heard her voice. I've seen visions of her. Do you mean she's inside me, inside my head?"

"I mean you *are* her." Sía clasped her hands in front of her. "You have always been Hera Ívarsdóttir. In mind, body, and soul."

Of all the strange things Vanessa thought she might hear during this meeting, this wasn't one of them. "Stop messing with me." She growled. "I'm through having my mind screwed with. I'm not going to take this!"

Sía heaved a sigh. Her eyes changed to human ones. "If we tell you everything" —she nodded to Þalía— "you must let our sister go, and you must do so with haste." She looked to Yngvi. "Is this acceptable? We are already in grave danger if we are discovered, it does not matter if we tell her."

Yngvi gazed at Vanessa with pure anguish in his eyes. "On one condition," he said. "You must leave this land, forever." He addressed Vanessa. "Never come back."

Vanessa looked at Sía. "I ... can live with that condition." She lowered the knife from Þalía's throat. "That's what I want to do anyway."

Sía stepped forward, close enough she could rest her hand on top her sister's head. "I will speak this only once, and you must listen carefully, for we must fly."

Vanessa nodded. Her muscles were stiff with anticipation.

"You are Hera Ívarsdóttir," Sía said. "A century

ago, you were taken prisoner, when you attacked and killed one of us. It was decided by the Council you should remain our prisoner for a hundred years, while your husband suffered apart from you."

Vanessa turned her head slowly and looked at Gunnar. He still stared at her, his eyes pale and guarded.

"But, my foolhardy bother" —Sia's voice rose, angry— "took pity on you. He tried to ease your suffering and help you pass the time with more comfort."

Vanessa flashed back to the cliff. The voice assuring her it didn't have to be difficult.

"I warned him many times not to act as your friend, but he would not listen." She glowered at Yngvi. "Would you like to tell the rest of the story?"

Yngvi's voice was soft. "My affinity for you grew, over those many years. It might have even become … love. But there came a time the others began to suspect, and it was hard to visit you. I knew something must be done." His eyes shone. "If they cast accusations, I would be put to death, and you would never see your home again. I had to get you out of our lands. It did not matter what happened to me."

Vanessa could barely breathe.

"I decided to take you away, where they would not find you. I would tell them you escaped, but it was most important they could not follow you. So, I took you on a boat, across the ocean."

"I knew nothing of this," Sía said icily. "Otherwise, I might have killed him myself."

Yngvi shook his head. "We sailed to a land called Newfoundland."

Vanessa stumbled back. The whoosh in her ears was more than her heartbeat now. It was realization rushing in.

"I could not allow them to detect you. In a place

called hospital, there was a woman, Vanessa Evanston. She was locked in sleep and her mind was blank."

"No," Vanessa whispered. She shook her head. "No."

"I made you look like her, I gave you her memories, and I took away your own. I had never made a changeling before, but it worked."

Vanessa trembled. She looked at Gunnar. He looked as stricken as she felt. Her boyfriend told her she was a "different person" after the coma. She almost screamed.

"It was not his last foolish act," Sía said. "Go on."

"I was a fool, indeed." Yngvi's eyes glistened. "I had hope that one day, I might be able to seek you out and switch you back, so—I took Vanessa Evanston with me, to keep her for that day."

Vanessa shook her head, wildly, silently. Tears slipped down her face.

"I should have tossed her over the side of the boat and let her sink in the ocean." Yngvi drew a breath. "But I could not give up that hope. I brought her back and hid her away, and I made her unchanging, frozen in time."

"It might have all worked out." Sía focused on Vanessa. "If not for you."

"You came back," Yngvi whispered. "Even without your memories, you were drawn home."

All the longing to visit Iceland, the almost overwhelming desire to come here...

"And when you stepped foot on this land," Sía said, "they sensed you. They knew Yngvi had done something unspeakably outrageous."

"They picked me up on the street that night," Vanessa whispered. "The Council."

"We begged them to spare his life." Sia's voice grew strained. "We argued he never had a relationship with you, never even kissed you. Only, that he had been stupidly kind and made a poor choice. Our entire family pleaded for mercy. And while this deliberation went on, for a year, you slept. That is where you have been the past year, asleep while the verdict was decided."

That explained waking up in her own clothes and looking the same.

"But they demanded he give them Vanessa Evanston, and she died when they tried to wake her. Her mind and body were too broken. So they left her on the mountain."

Vanessa clamped a hand over her mouth. The only peace was knowing her parents—or not her parents—had gotten their real daughter's body back.

"They chose not to put me to death," Yngvi said. "But to give me a much more torturous punishment. You were to be returned, as you are, as I made you, to your husband, with no memories of me. And I was to never make contact with you again. It mocks and degrades me. If ever I try to reunite with you, I will be burnt."

Her presence here is to punish another.

Vanessa took her hand from her mouth and looked at Gunnar. She was shaking. Tears slid down his face as well. He shook his head.

Þalía lifted her head and spoke. "I was watching you to make sure Yngvi did not break the boundaries of his punishment. He has already done such stupid things. I was only going to watch you until you left Iceland."

"And that is the whole truth." Sía gave Vanessa a twisted smile. "Are you satisfied now?"

Vanessa couldn't stop shaking. She looked to the horizon, and it seemed to blur and tilt. "How do I know any of this is the truth?" she managed to ask. "I'm

Vanessa. I have her mind." She touched her head. "I have—all of this is me." She ran her hands over her body.

Sía stretched her arm out. "Come closer."

Vanessa didn't move.

"With haste! I will give you your mind back. Come here."

Vanessa looked at Gunnar. He blinked a few times, his eyes wet. He opened his mouth as if to speak, but nothing came out.

"Now!" Sía demanded.

Vanessa inched forward. She stared at Sia's hand as she approached her.

When Vanessa got close enough, Sía put her hand on her forehead. Her skin was cold and her grip like stone.

"Hera Ívarsdóttir." She sneered. "Your presence has been the bane of my existence for a hundred years. Take your mind and go. Haunt me and my family no more. Witch!" She pushed her.

Vanessa reeled back, the sky spinning above her. Everything went white.

* * * *

"You've always been kind to me." Hera spoke softly.

The room was dark, and silent, apart from the beeping of the strange machines on the walls. The dark-haired woman lay in the bed, pale and still. Tubes and wires were stuck in her skin, some went up her nose. Half her face and one ear were swollen and discolored. Hera had seen a boy hit his head once, slipping from a wall. His face looked like that after, and he slept, like this girl, and never woke up.

"You kept me company." Hera gazed solemnly at the girl. "You kept them from demeaning me or working

me to the bone. You brought me food, and flowers, and stories. You kept me from going mad. So many years, they all run together like paint in water, but there was always you."

Yngvi stood on the other side of the bed. His hair was drawn back from his face—a face she found familiar and kind now, instead of grotesque and terrifying.

"You did not deserve such punishment." He spoke softly as well. "You were only defending yourself and your husband."

She looked out the window, at the night and the city. She'd long dwelled in sheltered seclusion, and human cities had changed so much. A frightening and dazzling landscape lay outside, with such tall buildings and electric lights. There were no horses, and the streets were all stone.

"I wonder where my Gunnar is now?" she whispered. "I wonder what he's made of his punishment?" She tried not to ruminate on such things as the years passed, as the vision of him in her mind grew dim. Perhaps he suffered, perhaps he toiled. Or perhaps, he thrived and loved again. That seemed worse.

"He will have his day, I suppose." Yngvi sounded sad. "When they are done with him."

She looked at him. His black eyes glistened, and though they were featureless she saw his emotions in them, as she always did.

"You will never know me again," she said, "if we do this." She looked at the girl. "And I will never know my home again."

"A worse fate awaits." He placed his hands on the rail that kept the girl from falling out of bed. "If they accuse us, I will die, and you will be forced to live all your days with their torture, and without me. They may let you grow old and die, or they may keep you in

perpetual youth for eternity."

She shuddered at the thought. She wanted to burn them, every last one, with fire from her own hands. She wanted to infect their empire at the very roots and watch it wither and blacken. One day, she would have her revenge. This she vowed.

Only Yngvi would she spare. He had been gentle with her. He had given her hope.

"Then we must do this." She nodded. "It's the only way, and you must return soon. What will you do with her, after you put me in her place?"

He rested his hand on the girl's shoulder and was silent a moment.

"Her mind is gone. Her body is a shell, but her memories are there for the plucking. I will take her with me and toss her in the ocean. She will never be found."

"At least I can taste the world again."

So many years in isolation, a prisoner, had made her a strange and twisted being. She hadn't spoken to another human since she was taken. Even seeing one now, it was an unfamiliar thing—she was so used to the faces and presence of the huldufólk.

Yngvi spoke softer yet. "I ache at losing you, Hera Ívarsdóttir. But I ache more at the thought of your torment."

Hera rose from the chair. "I won't be gone from the world, I'll just be different." She walked around the bed to him. "You aren't like the others. You shouldn't stay with them. Free yourself of their bonds as well."

She slipped her arms around him, and he held her. He was cold, but so was she. She'd been cold for a very long time.

She drew back and looked at the girl again. "She is going to die?"

"She will never wake."

"Well, then." Hera heaved a sigh. "I'm also giving her family a gift. They will not lose their daughter."

Yngvi's eyes shone. "You must never return. Even with the memories of yourself gone, you must hold on to the one that tells you never to go back to Iceland. If you set foot on it, they will know it is you, even in a different body. Hold on to that thought. Do not come back."

She nodded. Keeping any part of her own memory was too dangerous, they'd decided. It would make her too detectable.

"Iceland," she murmured. "I will hold on to Iceland. Never go there."

He stroked her hair. She was unchanged since the day they took her. She had long ago stopped paying attention to her body, what it looked like, how it felt, that it was hers at all. It was just a stationary object inside which she lived. She didn't mind having a new one.

"I love you, Hera Ívarsdóttir," he whispered. "Enough to let you go and see you safe."

She gazed at him with fondness. "And I love you, Yngvi. Enough to say you're an angel, not a demon. Thank you, for everything you've done for me. If you see my Gunnar someday, will you tell him I thought of him often?"

He nodded. "Goodbye."

She closed her eyes. He pressed a hand to her forehead.

Everything went white.

* * * *

Hera opened her eyes, chest hitching, limbs shaking. The sky above her was blue and clear. The wind flowed across her skin. She lay on the hard, muddy ground. She was alive.

A face, pale and handsome, moved into her

vision. His blue eyes, his golden curls.

"Gunnar."

He gripped her shoulders. "Hera," he gasped.

She struggled to sit up, and he pulled her the rest of the way, into his arms. "My Gunnar!" She clung to him. Though so many years had passed, he felt as she remembered him, even smelled the same. Memories of him swept across time and filled her frozen heart to make it beat again.

"I can't believe this." He shuddered, gripping her hair. "Oh my God!"

She stared over his shoulder at Sía. The huldufólk woman's face was twisted in anger, but fear shone in her eyes. Oh yes, like the Devil, Hera knew this one. She had met her many times. She was always cold toward Hera and enjoyed lording herself over her, forcing her to do humiliating and tasking things. Hera seethed.

"Release my sister!" Sía demanded. "We must go."

Hera pulled away from Gunnar and then crawled across the grass like a stalking wolf, staring Sía down. A century of oppression twisted in her guts. She had no benevolence left in her, they had diminished it long ago.

Her head felt split in half, into two separate people. She was herself, her memories of the long years of isolation intact, her life before that a distant memory. But, Vanessa was also there, her life, her experiences. Two sets of thoughts that worked simultaneously.

This was still Vanessa's body, too. It didn't matter. Hera's body hadn't mattered to her in a long time, ageless thing that it was.

"Wait." Aedan held his hand out to Sía. "There's something else we want. Release me from my task. Do that, and we'll let your sister go."

Sía snarled at him. "I have no such power!"

Aedan raised his voice. "I'm done doing dirty work for you!"

Hera struggled to her feet. Gunnar helped her up, but she pulled out of his grasp again. She would have all the time in the world for him, soon, but right now she had other matters to attend to.

"I do not have the authority to release you." Sía sounded frantic. "Only the Council can do that. Give us our sister. I gave you what you wanted!"

Hera grabbed her knife from the grass. After all this time it was still sturdy, if not sharp. She advanced on them.

"Hera!" Gunnar said.

She stopped behind Þalía. She had not known this woman well and bore her no specific ill will, as she had never tormented her. But she would still kill her, if it made a point.

"I should slit her ear to ear." Hera jerked Þalía's chin back. "I should bleed her out like a slaughtered lamb."

"Please." Sia's eyes went black. "They are coming."

"Don't." Aedan touched Hera's arm. "Let them go. We'll deal with them later. When we go see the Council."

"No, she said she would leave this land!" Sía shrieked. "That was the deal."

"That was your deal with Vanessa. Vanessa is dead." Hera looked at Aedan. "Oh, I know all about the Council, trust me."

Sía lunged forward and grabbed the chain around Þalía's throat. She hissed and jerked back. "Take this off!"

Hera was done taking orders from them.

Yngvi stepped forward. "Hera, please." He

clasped his hands, eyes pleading. "If they find us, I will be put to death. You know that."

Only this made her fury ebb. She looked into his human eyes, and she saw the man who made her life bearable through years of torture, the man who kept her from a worse fate. A man, who, deep down in her soul, she felt true affection for. This made her head clear. Also, perhaps, it was Vanessa. She spoke loudly in Hera's mind, telling her not to strike right now, not to give in to rage. Time would bring her the things she desired.

"Please," Yngvi said again, a whisper. "If you ever cared for me, let me flee, before I am punished."

The years of darkness stretched between them, and the light of his kindness, a dull glow in the murk, cut a path through it.

She couldn't allow him to die at their hands.

She dropped the knife and started working the chain off Þalía's neck. As she slipped it off, Þalía tumbled forward and Sía caught her. Hera used the knife to cut the bonds off her wrists. They were red and raw, smeared with blood. Good, *good* that she suffered. Good that Vanessa had the guts to do it. She had no clear recollection of doing it herself, though Vanessa seemed to think Hera had influenced her.

Yngvi and Sía dragged their sister to her feet between them. Sía still glared at Hera, her gaze more intense for her black eyes. In that moment, they both seemed to know this wasn't over. The knowledge arced between them, hard and bitter. A century's debt would have to be paid.

"Thank you," Yngvi said. His gaze was more tender, and then his eyes went black as well. "Goodbye, Hera Ívarsdóttir."

Hera lifted her hand. In a second, all three of

them vanished, like smoke on the wind.

Hera stood, arm outstretched still, gazing at the empty spot where they'd been. The chain lay on the grass. Her punishment was over. Her years of darkness had ended in this bright, vast world that stretched out around her. Would she ever see Yngvi again?

For his sake, she hoped not.

She lowered her arm. The wind tugged at her hair and clothes. She hadn't experienced the world like this since she and Yngvi crossed the ocean together. She gazed toward the horizon, where the mist clung to the fjords, pink with the morning sun.

She was free.

She turned to the other two. They stared at her. Aedan was a tall, strapping young man. She felt Vanessa's fondness and pity for him.

And Gunnar was a vision. She didn't need Vanessa to tell her that. His mouth hung open, but he didn't speak. His eyes were wide and bright. Her heart swelled. He was so beautiful, and yet he didn't seem real. Did he actually stand before her, whole, now, after all this time?

She pushed her fluttering hair back from her face. Vanessa's hair. "Hello, my husband." She spoke in her own language.

He drew in a breath, his golden eyelashes fluttering. "Hello, my wife."

Chapter Twenty-Three

Twilight sat on the land. The sun was an orange ball on the horizon, below the mantle of the deep blue, cloud-scattered sky. The water stretched beneath it, deep blue as well. The wind held a chill, but not so much Hera shivered. She was used to being cold.

It was surreal to sit there, to breathe the free air, to not feel confined or to be constantly on guard, waiting for one of them to put her to task. Though this wasn't her body, she was becoming aware of it. She gazed at her fingers and wiggled her toes. She raked her hands through her long dark hair. She touched her cheekbones and lips.

Vanessa sat in the back of her mind, bemused.

She'd changed clothes, because the clothes Vanessa wore felt too strange. The only thing Gunnar had to offer that wasn't clingy or confining was a long shirt and a bathrobe. He said it was an absurd outfit to go walking around in, especially outside, but she couldn't wear those jeans, because they made her legs itch. The shoes Vanessa had on were also ridiculous. She was barefoot now.

For many long years she'd worn little more than what she had on now—just a shapeless gown, and sometimes a robe, more voluminous than this one, when it was cold and Yngvi would sneak it to her.

Gunnar's clothes felt comforting. So long since she'd smelled his scent on her. She turned her face to the shoulder and inhaled.

Like Vanessa had.

Gunnar strode over and sat down next to her, on the broad, smooth rock she'd found. He held a mug out. Steam rose from it.

"Thank you." She took it and cherished the warmth between her palms.

"It's warmer inside. You could come in there."

She shook her head. They were at the foot of a hill behind Gunnar's house, overlooking the town and the fjord. It was a good vantage point to take it all in. "I've spent too long a prisoner. I want to breathe." She took a sip. The coffee was hot and bitter. She frowned at it. It didn't taste like the coffee she remembered, not as hearty or strong. But then, it had been a very long time since she drank anything other than water, and an occasional sip of wine, another gift Yngvi brought her in secret.

Gunnar sipped his own coffee. "I have so many questions, but I don't know if they're appropriate to ask right now. I feel like I should give you time."

Vanessa fluttered in Hera's head. They were speaking Icelandic, which Vanessa didn't understand, but she *did* understand. Hera smiled to herself. *I will teach you so many things, silly one.*

"It's all so strange." She huddled into the robe. "I was kept hidden away. I didn't see the world change. Everything is odd to me, so many things I've never seen before. The boats with their motors. The cars. The lights. Even the way the houses are built. I don't recognize these things, and yet, Vanessa knows them, so I know them. When I see something I don't understand, she explains it to me and it feels familiar."

You're teaching me things too.

"I can't imagine what it's like. It must feel crazy."

"Indeed. But I've lived through a lot of crazy things."

They were both silent a moment.

"Is she—really inside you?" Gunnar hesitated. "Is she … alive in there? Or is it just a memory?"

Hera peered at him. "You had sex with her."

He blinked. "Yes. Well, you haven't been around for a hundred years." He glanced away. "I thought I would never see you again." He looked back at her.

"You've slept with other women." Her tone was deadpan. "Had relationships with them."

"A hundred years, Hera!"

She smirked. The concern on his face faded, as he must have realized she was only playing with him.

"You said I made you laugh." She wiggled her fingers around the cup. "Am I making you laugh right now?"

He sighed. "This is too confusing right now to laugh. I'll laugh when I realize it's actually happening."

"It's happening."

They were silent again, gazing out at the water.

He shifted toward her. "Will you tell me where you've been?" He spoke softly. "What you've been through? I can hardly believe you're here right now, after all this time, by my side again. I just want to know what it was like for you."

She looked down at the dark liquid in her cup. "My hundred years was not quite so productive and carefree as yours." She didn't mean to sound accusing. It was a fact. "Despite both of us spending a hundred years in their toil, our experiences are quite different."

"I'm sorry." His voice grew even more hushed. "I'm sorry that—"

She held up a hand. "It's not your fault. All fault, all blame, is theirs. Don't apologize."

He lowered his gaze and spoke, anguished, "I thought you were dead. I didn't believe they would let you live after what happened. And if they did, I couldn't imagine they would let me see you again. I had hope, for a while, and it came back now and then over the years, but it seemed a very distant light in a very dark world."

His eyes shone in the twilight, and she wanted to kiss him—or did Vanessa?

"That part of our experience, then, was much the same." Her feelings were conflicted. She knew him, but he was a stranger. Vanessa also knew him, in a different way. Admittedly, over a hundred years her grief faded as well, as he'd expressed to Vanessa about his own. Her thoughts were consumed with her situation and torture. She wasn't sure she even still loved him, or if she was only remembering a long-ago love.

Maybe she'd learn to love him again in the present, though.

"Hera." He took one of her hands, drawing it away from the cup. "I can't comprehend how difficult this is for you, but it's difficult for me too."

His hand was warm. She looked at it, joined with her own. Vanessa's fingers were longer and slenderer than hers.

"But I think" —he held her hand tighter— "in time, we can come to understand all of it, together."

She only understood one thing right now—the desire for revenge. She didn't express that, though. After all, hadn't her rage caused all of this to begin with? "Why did you keep my knife?" She'd been perplexed by this since she found herself holding it again as she faced Sía. "Why did you keep the instrument that started this?"

"I didn't know it was yours." He looked down at their joined hands. "After—you went away, I couldn't stay in our home. Your parents cleaned the house out and gave our possessions to me. I was staying in the shack on your father's land. The one by the stream, do you remember? I just stayed there until I could figure out what to do."

"Where we kept the old tools?" She snorted.

"That run-down, leaking excuse for a building? Why on earth would you sleep there? My father should have knocked it down."

His stricken look made her instantly regret being so harsh.

"I couldn't stay in our house," he said softly. "I—every time I walked in the door, I saw you, everywhere. At the hearth. Cooking at the stove. Standing next to our bed."

She remembered their little house. It was cramped, and sagging, and cold air came in around the windowpanes even in summer. That was why Gunnar wanted to build a new one. She had a braided rug on the floor in the kitchen, to cover a gaping hole. Every time it rained she had to put pots in the corners to catch leaks. And it rained *a lot* in Iceland.

"The knife was in a box." He rubbed her hand. "I didn't know it was the knife you used that night. They must have found it in the kitchen, where everything happened. I didn't even know you'd bought a knife. It ended up in the collection of iron knives I amassed over the years."

She tilted her chin up. "You wanted to fight them too."

"I used them to ward them off." He let go of her hand and took a drink of his coffee. "That's all."

"I will tell you what happened to me." She reached out and played with his fingers again. "I will tell you what it was like, all of it. And I'll tell you about them. But right now, I don't want to dwell on it. I want to breathe in my freedom."

In truth, it was much to tell, and she wasn't sure what was important enough to include. The small details seemed irrelevant in light of the whole, now that she was no longer their prisoner. It would all be taken as one terrible, limitless crime, and she would exact her judgement on it at the first moment she could.

"All right," he whispered. "I understand that. And I suppose I'll tell you about my hundred years too. It wasn't just women and relationships, you know." He flicked his gaze to her lips. "I still love you."

She was curious about Aedan. She knew only what Vanessa knew of him. That was one thing about Gunnar's hundred years she *really* wanted to know more about. She spoke lowly. "I will tell you this, in short. I know many things now—their limits, their weaknesses. You have little reason to fear as you do. Vanessa was right, they can't kill humans."

Gunnar's face lit with surprise. "They can't?"

"It's forbidden in their culture, for practical reasons. Killing a human weakens them of their powers."

Gunnar stared at her. "Are you certain?"

"Have you ever heard of them actually killing a human?" She gave a rueful laugh. "Do you not think they would have killed me if they could have? Why do you think Sía is so bitter? She hates me, and the chaos I caused. She wanted me dead for ages. She hoped out loud for me to end my own life, many times. I wouldn't give her the satisfaction."

Gunnar's brow knitted. "But why does it diminish their power? How does that work?"

She didn't answer. Instead, she set her cup on the ground and stood. She moved over to straddle his lap, facing him.

He quickly put his cup aside and stared up at her, eyes wide. "Hera?"

"I want to feel you again." She smoothed her hand over his crotch, and then undid the button of his pants. "I'm your wife, and you desire this body, don't you?"

Long ago, she would visit him in the pasture while he worked, to bring him food. When it was warm, and he was working alone, they'd find a spot and she'd raise her skirts and sit down on him. It was urgent, and fruitive, and it was the way a man and wife were supposed to behave. Though, if her mother ever found out she'd have her in church.

"Hera…"

He wasn't fully stiff when she pulled him out, but he wasn't soft, either. She remembered the feel of his prick. It was a nice one, she'd gotten lucky. She undid the sash on her robe.

"You remember?" She gazed down into his eyes. "When you were working?"

"Oh yes." His voice was hushed. "I remember."

She needed to feel him. She needed to experience a sensation that would reconnect her with her numbed body, though it wasn't her body. She licked her palm and rubbed between her legs, like she had when she wanted him immediately and couldn't wait for him to get her oiled up. Then she licked it again and worked him up. He didn't resist. It hurt a little as she eased down on him, but that sensation was one she welcomed too. Any feeling, at all, was good.

He clutched her around the waist. "Jesus."

"Don't blaspheme."

She rode him urgently and silently. Swift and hungry. It was good, having him up in her, but she still struggled with the disconnect between her body and mind. No matter, it would come, or not, it was all the same.

He shuddered, his eyes bright as he gazed up at her. He, at least, could feel emotion.

"Don't empty yet," she commanded. "Not yet…"

She hadn't experienced release in a century.

She'd been in Vanessa's head when she had sex with him, but it was distant and vague, like a dream. As the orgasm swept through her, making her shudder and clench, it was pleasant and yet profoundly strange. Was this what it had been like to know pleasure? She was barely able to recall the feeling.

He moaned against her neck and licked the sweat there. "Hera, my wife."

She kept bouncing on him, urging him to his own finish. He was always good about letting her go first.

"I'm nearly there," he gasped.

"Yes, come inside." She urged him on with her hips.

"You're going to get pregnant."

"I'll wash out after."

Vanessa screamed in the back of her head. *That doesn't actually work!* She told her about birth control.

Nevertheless, Hera held him tight and squeezed around him as he filled her. His groans were lusty and made her smile.

She looked down at him.

Emotion strained behind his eyes. "I missed that," he whispered.

"So did I."

She slipped off him and stood, and pulled her robe shut. His release streaked down her thighs, another reminder of those long-ago days. She'd never gotten a baby before. She would take her chances now.

Gunnar tucked himself away and did up his pants, then stood as well. He took her arm. "I think we won't have much trouble reconnecting."

Before she could reply, a movement caught her eye. Not far off, near the base of the next hill, a shadow among the shadows. She froze.

Gunnar looked too. "What?"

Tingles rushed across her skin. Surely, they weren't coming to try to take her back.

The movement again, and this time it was clearly a figure. A dark, robed figure. It stepped out from behind an outcropping of rocks and into the twilight.

She pulled away from Gunnar. The knife was in the pocket of her robe and she clutched her fingers around it.

Then, the figure stepped forward and she recognized the stance and stature, even before she could make out a face.

"Yngvi!"

"What?" Gunnar frowned. "Has … he been watching us?"

"Probably." She didn't have feelings about it one way or another. She started toward him.

"Hera!" Gunnar rushed after her.

Yngvi would not hurt her or take her back, she was sure of it. She hurried toward him, and he to her. They met.

"What are you doing here?" She kept her voice down. "If they find you, they'll put you to death!"

Yngvi's face was a pale mask of consternation. His eyes were human right now, and he looked sad. She was so used to seeing his black eyes. The only black eyes that didn't fill her with malice.

"I had to speak to you." He was quiet too. "No one knows I am here, not even my sisters."

"Yngvi, you fool." She took his hand. In contrast to Gunnar's, it was cold as winter. "You must not risk your life for me."

"I may never lay eyes on you again, Hera Ívarsdóttir. I did this to you, and my parting apology must be to make it right."

She didn't understand what he meant. Footsteps

approached through the grass behind her and she looked over her shoulder.

Gunnar stopped a few feet away, staring at Yngvi.

"What do you mean?" She looked back at Yngvi. "You didn't do this to me. You were always kind."

"No, I mean this." He gestured to her body. "I put you in this form. Let me put you right."

She didn't know how to reply. She hadn't expected such an offer and already accepted this was how things would be.

"Not just your body, your mind." He clutched her hand. "You cannot live in two minds. It will drive you mad eventually. Let me take Vanessa away, so you can be yourself again." He paused, and his words turned strained. "Or, if you prefer, I can take away … you. It would be a blessing, perhaps. You would forget your years of punishment. You would forget about us. You would know peace."

She expected this even less.

Vanessa rattled in her head.

If Hera was rid of Vanessa, she would be herself again, but *who* was she now, really? Just an angry, empty shell. She'd become accustomed to pain and strife, and it would be a long, hard road to experience anything else, and to heal. In truth, she might never heal. She might never be the person she was before the night they took her away.

On top of that, she would be a girl of a hundred years ago in this modern world without any understanding of how it worked, of what anything was. And she would be at the side of a man she barely remembered, who could only attempt to help her grasp things. She would be othered, out of place, walking the earth with no purpose.

"Please, choose." Yngvi's voice was urgent. "I cannot stay here long."

However, if she lived as Vanessa, the hope to ever get back what she once was, even if that chance was small, would be dashed.

She shook her head. "I can't make such a choice!"

Gunnar stepped closer. "Hera … this could be a chance to forget everything they've done to you."

She glared at him. Did he want her to be Vanessa? Was he already in love with the girl?

"I don't know that I want to forget." She looked between them. "And do you want to lose Hera again so soon, after you've just found her again?"

Gunnar swallowed, and his eyes glittered, but he didn't reply.

She looked at Yngvi. He seemed desperate and torn. He couldn't stay here long, but she couldn't make such a decision so quickly.

"I can't make this choice now. This is such a thing I hadn't even considered."

"Hera." Yngvi pulled her closer. "Sweet, strong Hera. You must listen to me. Being of two minds will drive you into dark places. It will make you lose yourself, all of you. I do not want this for you, after all you have been through. Whether I lay eyes on you again or not, I could not bear the thought this might be your fate. I could not bear the thought that I was the one who did it to you. You must let me fix this."

Her stomach clenched. Still, she could not say which she wanted more, on the spot. "I must think about it. I don't want to put you in further danger—it is so selfish of me to ask. But I can't decide now. Can you return? I must consider." She would understand if he couldn't, but she would not be able to decide right now.

She would have to pick madness.

"Hera, I cannot."

"Please. If you won't, then I won't choose."

He was silent a moment, stern-faced, then nodded. "Very well. In two days, I can return, when the sun begins to climb. Come to the water." He turned, still holding her hand, and pointed to the waters of the fjord. "Row out and I will come. It is harder for them to detect me on the water."

Could she even make such a choice in two days?

"Go, Yngvi." She pulled her hand from his. "Go, before they find you here. In two days, I will meet you."

He nodded once, and then vanished.

She stared at the spot where he'd been, stricken, disbelieving. Then she turned to Gunnar. This was not something she'd prepared herself for. Would she allow herself to go mad as well, after all she'd been through?

"Hera." Despair filled Gunnar's voice. "I didn't realize one of you has to go."

"I didn't either," she murmured. "This is a choice I don't know how to make." She couldn't lose herself. She couldn't lose her anger, and she couldn't lose the knowledge of what she'd been through, even if it was terrible.

Vanessa whispered inside her: *don't let all that's left of me die.*

And Hera found she didn't want to lose that either.

Chapter Twenty-Four

The morning sun had begun its climb into the sky. Thick clouds covered it, but its light shone orange on the undersides like a fire in the heavens. The air was chilly but fresh. Hera stood on the prickly grass of Gunnar's yard, feet bare, wrapped in a sweater and long dress. They'd bought her some clothes of her own. She hadn't worn shoes in so long they felt odd on her feet, so she wouldn't put them on even now.

Out on the water, the island rose from the mist. She would row toward it and pray Yngvi would come. She wanted to be assured, mostly, that they hadn't found out his crimes and killed him. She felt terrible for asking him once again to risk himself.

Gunnar and Aedan stood outside as well. The morning sun fell on Gunnar's curls and shone in his eyes. Every time she looked at him, she knew him a little more. He was as beautiful as when she first met him, and when she'd said her vows to him beside the ocean. He used to have such a laugh, bold and bright and ridiculous, and it made her laugh too. She was yet to hear that laugh again.

"Be careful," Aedan said. "The rowboat is at the dock."

Aedan was a beautiful man as well, and in the past couple days, his ferocity had come to charm her. He was angry, like her, and this made him easy to commiserate with. He'd made a decision—he would no longer receive their messages or work for them. Her revelation that they didn't kill humans made him bold. However, she wasn't so sure about the half huldufólk. She didn't know their fate, as she hadn't been privy to that during her imprisonment. She knew they existed but had never seen one until she laid eyes on Aedan.

Her iron knife was tucked in the pocket of her sweater. Not for Yngvi, but if others showed up.

"Hera." For all his beauty, Gunnar also looked tired and gray right now. Neither of them had slept much last night. She sat on the couch, staring out the window, her thoughts churning. He'd walked the house, silent and restless.

"I will be back soon." She gripped his arm. "Don't be afraid."

"I should come with you." He took her hand and held it in both of his. "What if it's a trap? Or an ambush?"

"Yngvi would not lead me into a trap, I tell you this with all my heart. If they follow him, they will. They cannot kill me. But I can kill them."

He said nothing, but the trepidation in his eyes was apparent.

"I fear more for him," she admitted. "But I could not make such a choice on the spot."

She had not told Gunnar what she chose—truly, she didn't know herself until a short time ago, as she came out of a doze and saw the sun lifting off the horizon. Vanessa had weighed in heavily over the past two days, and Hera listened without bias. What dwelled inside Hera wasn't an entity, though. Vanessa, her mind and body, was dead. She was only a memory. Still, perhaps it was a memory that deserved to live on.

"I have to go," she said. "I will return as fast as I'm able."

"Hera…" Gunnar still clung to her hand. Desperation flashed across his face. She knew he wanted to ask her decision, but she wouldn't speak it except to Yngvi. She didn't want anyone else's opinion to influence her.

"I will return soon, I promise."

She slipped her hand from his. They gazed at each other a moment, and he couldn't mask his pain. How terrible for him, to have his wife back and think he might be losing her again. This had to be wholly her choice, though.

She leaned in, kissed his cheek—breathing in his familiar scent—then turned and walked down the hill toward the water.

The tiny rocks on the street bit into her feet, but she ignored the pain. The wind snaked up under her dress and made her shiver, but she didn't care. Comfort and warmth were not things she'd known in a long time. Maybe someday, she'd indulge in them again.

She didn't look back. She wouldn't allow herself the weakness.

The rowboat waited at the dock, tied with a rope on the beach. No one was about at this hour, not even the early-morning fishermen, as they had already gone out.

She gazed across the water but saw nothing. If Yngvi was about, he gave no indication.

She began untying the boat. The oars were inside.

As she pushed off, she smiled at Vanessa in her head. Vanessa didn't know how to launch or row a boat and she was excited about this. Hera sat down, in the front. She then used one of the oars to push herself along the shallow bottom until she could row properly in the open water.

She'd been doing this since she was a child.

Vanessa was amazed.

Hera chuckled. "We learn so many things from each other."

Hera quickly grew frustrated, as Vanessa's arms were not as muscular and powerful as her own. They simply couldn't work the oars like she would have been able to in her own body.

Sorry, Vanessa lamented in her head. *I should have gone to the gym more.*

"We should put you to work on a farm." Hera grunted. "This world has made people soft."

Never mind I kicked Þalía's ass into submission for you.

"Point taken. I hope you're willing to do it again if need be."

Bring it.

The wind blew harder as the boat bobbed across the water. The blazing clouds hung above, and the world encircled her. She hummed an old rowing song, one her father taught her. She wasn't afraid, even all alone, out there in the great engulfing expanse.

Near the island she stopped rowing, pulled the oars into the boat, and lay them on the floor. Here she would wait, she decided. She pulled her sweater tight around her. Her hair whipped around her face. It still startled her when she saw it, as it was dark. She'd never envied the dark haired girls. She liked her golden hair just fine.

"Yngvi," she said to the air. "I am here. I will wait."

Apart from the wind and the lapping of the water against the boat, all was silent. The island rose from a ring of mist and birds circled it. Two days ago, she'd found herself in mind and spirt there. Five days ago, she'd been given her freedom there but didn't know it yet.

Whatever happened today, it would happen within sight of the island, again. And so, it must be a sacred place. It already was, in her mind.

The minutes passed. She sat huddled, gazing toward the horizon, the sun warming the back of her neck. Anxiousness knotted her stomach. Not for herself, but more in the hope Yngvi had not been found out and punished.

Vanessa was far more bored than she was, fidgety and wishing she had a phone to distract herself and play with while she waited. Such a curious modern mindset. Hera used Gunnar's phone, while Vanessa told her how it worked. Hera laughed at it. Everyone in the world knew each other now, and could speak through the air, even in typed words. A letter to Denmark that had once taken a week to arrive now took seconds, and strangers could know each other in a minute. She found that both amazing and frightening.

The world seemed much vaster than it had been in her day. Back then, you only knew the world as far as you could ride a horse. She'd seen automobiles in cities, but they were noisy, clunky things and didn't seem practical. Now, they were not only practical, but common and often necessary. She hadn't seen a single horse and wagon since she'd been back.

Such striking differences, and it only underlined the decision she'd made. She would do what benefitted her most in this new world.

More time passed. Her anxiousness grew. And then, finally, she heard a faint splashing in the water nearby, unusual enough it caught her attention.

It was not the normal lapping of waves, and she turned her head toward the sound, expectant. Just a fish?

A long, pale shape glided up to the boat, just below the murky surface. Her breath caught.

A white hand gripped the side of the boat, and then a person pulled themselves up over the side, swift and smooth like an eel. She let out her breath and released her grip on the knife in her pocket.

"Yngvi, you've come."

He sat across from her. His black hair ran with water, his robe heavy and dark with it. His eyes changed from black to human. His expression was worried and tense.

"You're alive." She smiled. "I'm so glad."

"I cannot stay here long." He spread his robe around his legs, and it was already starting to dry. "My sisters have kept close watch on me, and I had to escape to come. There have been whispers that we disappeared from the community without explaining our absence. I do not know if these whispers have reached the Council yet."

Hera swallowed. "I shouldn't have asked you to come, but—I could not choose as you were asking me to do in that moment. It is such a choice."

"I know." He spoke softly. "You are the only one I would take such risks for, Hera Ívarsdóttir. I will not see you further tormented with madness because of me."

She lifted her hands and stretched them out to him. He took them. His skin was cold, but not wet. Her hands were warm from having them tucked in her sweater.

"You must promise me," she said, squeezing his hands, "that you will try to escape them for good. You don't belong amongst them, gentle Yngvi. Promise me you will try to get away."

"Where could I go?" His gaze was sad. "There is nowhere they would not find me. If I left Iceland, maybe, but even then, they might discover me. Where would I be safe?"

Her heart ached—and she still had a heart, for things like this. "You must try. You cannot spend your existence with them. Promise me."

He sighed. "You must promise me you will leave as well, no matter what you choose. You are not safe here."

She could not make such a promise, not with the thoughts currently in her head, and so she quickly avoided a reply. "What do they do to those who are half huldufólk?" she asked. "Aedan doesn't want to maintain his duty. Will they kill him? Can they?"

Yngvi frowned, deeply. His dark brow furrowed. "I do not believe they can. If they can, I have never heard of it."

This was some relief to hear.

"The ones who are born of a human parent," he said, "they send them away. They send them off the island, so they cannot grow up here and know their roots or try their powers."

"Away?"

"Yes, they abandon them in other lands. Some, I'm sure, are found and thrive, as surely as some must suffer and die. Not all are discovered in infanthood. Some grow to adults. That is why they need abominations like Aedan to detect them."

The word was foul, but he would know no other descriptor, so she didn't correct him. This might be hope for Aedan, however.

"If he will not do as they say," Yngvi spoke gravely, "they will take him away and leave him somewhere as they do the others. The older ones they sometimes leave in frozen, isolated places so they will not survive or find other humans to help them. He will not know his home again."

She would see about that.

"And what of Gunnar?" She gripped his cold hands tighter. "What of my husband? When will his punishment end? Now that I'm returned to him, shouldn't his hundred years be ended now? Our sentence is served."

Pain flashed across Yngvi's features. Being returned to her husband must be torture for him, but she didn't say "husband" out of a sense of love, or any shadow of love she still felt. It was simply a fact—Gunnar was her husband.

"I cannot say. His release is in the hands of the Council. I cannot do anything for him." His gaze darkened and grew more serious. "Another reason you must flee. If they find you with him, as Hera, they will want to know how you came to have your memories back. It will be the downfall of my family. Unless, of course, you do not want to be Hera any longer…"

She slid her hands from his and placed them in her lap.

"What have you decided?" He looked across the water. "I cannot linger. I must return before my sisters find me gone. Have you made a choice? You must, for I cannot return again. It is too risky."

She looked down, at the floor of the boat, then back up at him. "Yes, I have decided."

He sat up straighter. His hair and clothes were now dry, and the morning sun cast an orange tint on his alabaster skin. It shone yellow in his human eyes.

"What is your choice?" He gripped the sides of the boat. "Will you have Vanessa expelled, or will you forget your years of torment?" His voice was steady, but despair hung on the ends of his words.

"If I let you expel Vanessa," she said, lacing her fingers together, "I will struggle in this new world. I don't know the things I see around me. I don't know how society has advanced. The things I've learned about the modern world already seem like magic." She let out a soft laugh. "She's there in my head though, to tell me, to show me. She keeps me from fear and confusion. Also, she's a bridge to Gunnar that has long collapsed for me.

Without her, he'd be scarcely more than a stranger."

Yngvi nodded and cast his gaze down.

"Without her, I could not live in this world. I could not live by Gunnar's side. What good would my freedom be? To be outcast and confused for the rest of my life?"

He brought his gaze back to her face. "So, you want to forget Hera." He nodded. "I do not fault you. You have suffered so much and known so much darkness."

She tilted her head. "No, I don't want to forget myself, either. Why should I give myself away? I don't want to forget what they did to me. It's fuel for my fire. I want those memories. I want myself."

He raised his eyebrows. "Then—what do you want?" His deep frown returned. "What is your choice?"

She drew in a breath of the cool, damp air. She only hoped he cared for her enough to honor her wishes.

"My choice is neither." She spoke with confidence. "I don't want you to do anything. I want you to leave me as I am now."

He stared at her.

She gazed back, placid, sure.

"Hera Ívarsdóttir." His voice was anguished. "You cannot choose such a thing! You cannot live of two minds. Eventually, it will drive you to madness. It will eat your mind!"

"How do you know that?" She remained calm. "Have you seen it?"

He seemed to tremble. Maybe it was only the rocking of the boat, though.

"I have heard of it." He shook his head. "They have used it to torture humans before. I cannot live with myself, if you succumb to such a fate. I did this to you, and it would be my fault."

She reached out again and took his hands. They did indeed tremble.

"This is my choice." She looked him in the eye. "I don't want to lose Vanessa, and I don't want to lose myself. You've given me a gift in her, and I thank you for it. The decision is mine. If I fall into madness I will never blame you."

"You must not make this choice." He clutched her hands. "I want you to be whole and well, and get out of this place, far away from them. I want you to be safe."

She pulled one of her hands from his and leaned forward, so she could touch his face. It was like touching marble, and she was not afraid.

"Dear Yngvi," she murmured. "You have been so good to me. I ask you this one last thing, to leave me as I am, and go. And then you must also flee, far away from here. I alone will deal with the consequences of my decision, and you are never to be blamed."

Despair filled his eyes and twisted his face. She thought he might weep.

"Hera Ívarsdóttir..."

"I only ask for one favor, before you leave me forever." She drew her hand back and looked at Vanessa's long fingers. "Would you grant me that?"

He gazed at her with bright, shining eyes. "I would do anything for you."

She flexed her fingers, then curled them. The dark strands of her hair fluttered in front of her eyes. Vanessa was silent inside her head. Perhaps she didn't care, or perhaps she was too scared to speak. That was all right. Vanessa was, after all, dead. This was Hera's existence and she made the decisions.

"What favor can I grant you, Hera Ívarsdóttir?"

* * * *

Hera dug the oar into the soft bed beneath the

water and pushed the boat up onto the beach. She put the oar down and stood. As she got out, she wobbled. Her legs were unsteady after being out on the water, and perhaps for other reasons. She hopped into the shallow water next to the boat and then splashed up onto the dry rocks.

People were on the dock now, a few men unmooring their own boat. They gave her curious looks but nodded in greeting. She nodded in return and began tying up the boat.

When it was secure, she tugged her sweater around her, drew a deep breath, and walked up the beach toward the town. Less than an hour had passed, she reckoned. The sun was a little higher in the sky and the wind a little warmer. It was going to be a lovely summer day. She hadn't been able to enjoy one of those in a long time.

She climbed the breakwater up to the road, still a little unsteady. She then plodded toward Gunnar's house, her feet slapping on the pavement. Her wet dress clung to her ankles, a little longer now, her sweater baggier. *Gunnar's house.* Her house? She would need a place to live, after all, and where better than with her husband?

As she came in sight of it, she noted a figure outside, sitting on the back steps. A flash of golden hair. He was waiting for her.

She smiled and walked a little faster. He'd waited a long time for her, like a good husband should.

As she drew closer, he noticed her and slowly stood.

She squinted against the sunlight and waved, so he would know it was her and not his eyes playing a trick. She reached the grass and crossed the yard toward him. Her heart raced, from expectation and the effort of her walk.

He ran his fingers through his hair and then gripped it in both hands, staring at her, his mouth open. He looked both shocked and amazed, and she laughed.

"Hera," he gasped as she reached him.

She stopped and sifted her fingers through her own hair, bringing it over her shoulders. It lay thick and blonde down her chest, a shade darker than his, clean and silky, which it hadn't been in some time. She was shorter now by a few inches, thicker around the waist and hips, her legs and arms well-muscled. She was a "hardy girl" as her father always put it, and she didn't mind the description. Vanessa had been willowy in comparison.

"You—" Gunnar lowered his hands. His eyes glistened and tears slipped down his cheeks. "You chose—"

"I chose neither." She lifted her chin. "Vanessa is still here." She clutched a hand to her chest. "I will take the risk of madness. But I wanted my body back, for it is mine." She had been disassociated from it for so long, but already, it was starting to feel real again, and she wanted to know it.

He grabbed her, pulled her to him, and crushed her mouth in a deep, warm kiss. Her mind opened with both affection and recognition. She gripped his arms and let herself be caught in the moment, the memories.

He broke away and held her face between his hands. He pressed his forehead to hers. "My Hera. You're back with me."

She smiled, and her own eyes pricked with tears. "I have been back with you for days, fool."

"It didn't seem real until just now, when I saw you in the flesh."

He wrapped her in his arms. She held him in return and kissed him back as he kissed her. He extended the kisses all over her face, and his hands explored her, as if trying to make sure she wasn't a ghost.

Vanessa took delight in this as well.

"Are you sure?" He spoke softly against her hair. Her cheeks were wet with his tears. "What if it destroys your mind, like he warned you?"

"I like to think my mind is stronger than that. I endured nearly a century of their punishment and never went mad." She tightened her grip. "And now, I'm home."

He clung to her, buried his face in her hair, and wept.

She closed her eyes and tears slipped from beneath her lashes as well. She could feel again, and it was so poignant and intense she could only cry with him. But it was not sadness, pain, or weakness—only joy, triumph.

And then he laughed, and it was as beautiful as it ever was.

The past was behind her, but it was not forgotten, nor forgiven. What the future held she didn't know, but she looked toward it with the eagerness of a child born once more into the world.

Chapter Twenty-Five

Hera lay on her back, staring at the ceiling. Light shone through the bedroom windows, deep blue and rich. Shadows gathered in the corners and draped thick on the bed. She'd stopped caring about the months of darkness and light going through their cycle long ago. But like everything else she'd forgotten or lost, it was starting to resonate with her again.

She rolled her head on the pillow and gazed at the man asleep beside her.

Gunnar lay on his stomach, his face half buried in the pillow, curls tousled. He was bare from the waist up, the sheet wound around his hips.

She wore one of his t-shirts. She was still wet and tingly between her legs. He'd had her properly this time, on her back and from behind, which she liked almost as much as riding him. Soon, she might actually find some emotional connection in the act, like he did. She'd rediscover what it was truly like to lay with her husband.

The night was quiet, so much so that every gust of wind around the windows could be heard. She was also keenly attuned to sounds inside the house, no matter how soft. She'd heard footsteps earlier, in the hallway.

She stared at the ceiling again. Sleep hadn't come easy over the past few days and was scant when she managed it. She'd never truly slept well among the huldufólk. They themselves didn't sleep, not like humans, though they sometimes lay dormant. She was of the mind that was when they were at their weakest.

She'd been thinking a lot about their weaknesses.

She sat up carefully. Gunnar didn't stir. She slid out of bed and found her pants—Vanessa called them lounge pants—and pulled them on. She was still trying to get used to the feel of them. She'd never worn pants in her life before. The closest to them was the long, thick underclothes she wore beneath her skirts in winter.

The pants were a bit too long and baggy now. They'd bought them for Vanessa's body.

She left the room and walked through the darkened house. Modern houses were much cleaner and roomier than houses had been in her time. Gunnar said this was a simple and cheap house by modern standards. When she was young, only wealthy people had houses like this.

Vanessa chuckled when Hera thought these things. Perhaps the only madness Hera would succumb to was Vanessa's taunting. She would start yelling at herself to shut up, like the old women who huddled on their benches muttering to themselves.

In the living room she stopped and gazed across the room at the shelves in the corner. She walked over and picked up her picture.

A man with a camera had come to their farm, and her father paid him to take pictures of their entire family. She was two years younger in this picture, and she'd given it to Gunnar when he started courting her. The only other picture she'd had taken in her lifetime was with him on their wedding day. She wondered where that picture was now.

A mirror hung on the wall, near the fireplace. She walked over and looked at herself, comparing her face to the picture.

She was twenty when they took her. Her hair hung messy on her shoulders right now, though not the snarled, matted mess it had been during her imprisonment. Her face was tanned from working in the sun. She had a broad face and thick lips, and never thought of herself as particularly attractive—she was much too plain and a rugged country girl—but Gunnar insisted she was a thing of beauty. He was utterly smitten by her lack of grace and refinement, and she found it amusing.

Vanessa had been svelte and delicate, striking with her green eyes and dark hair. But Hera couldn't live the rest of her life in that body, no matter how pretty it was.

She put the picture back on the shelf and peeked out the window.

A person sat on the porch, his back to her.

Quietly, she opened the door and slipped out.

Aedan looked up but didn't seem startled by her sudden presence.

She walked over and sat down next to him. "I can't sleep either." She wiggled her toes in the grass. "Do you sleep? The huldufólk don't."

He shrugged. "A little. Not as much as humans do. A few hours, here and there."

She nodded and was silent for a few minutes, staring toward the hills. "You're thinking of going back to the island, aren't you?" She'd been observing him and noted the way doubt seemed to grip him. "To receive their messages. Going back to doing their bidding."

"I don't want them to take me away from Gunnar." He rubbed his hands together. "He's the only father I've ever known. I don't remember my own father. I barely remember my mother—and what I do remember frightens me. She was mad. Gunnar is the only thing like a parent I've ever known. He raised me, protected me. He understands me."

"How old are you?" She sat back on her hands.

"Nineteen." He paused. "In human years, anyway. I don't know how the huldufólk age. Maybe I'm way younger in their eyes."

"I'm twenty." She kicked her feet idly. "And ninety-eight, but who's counting?" She smirked. "I barely remember my parents. I know they're dead now. Gunnar says they searched for me for a long time. I wish there was some way to go back and see them."

"I don't want Gunnar to have to search for me. He's the only stable thing I've ever known."

"He always seemed like he'd make a good father." She pondered that. Would they go on to have children? She wasn't even sure right now they would stay together, or that she wanted to remain his wife. And the idea of having children now, bringing them into a world haunted by huldufólk, made her flesh crawl.

"He wants us to leave Iceland," she said. "He thinks it would be for the best. To get out of this cursed country."

"If I leave voluntarily, they might give me peace."

She continued kicking her feet, brushing them across the top of the grass. "His punishment is not lifted, though. I have no idea what will happen in two years, when it comes to an end." She stopped kicking. "He may wither and die on the spot."

Aedan looked at her, the angles of his face hard, his expression stony.

She sat up. "I don't want to leave." She looked into his eyes. "Not only because this is my home, but because I'm not done with them. I'm not going to allow their sins to go unpunished. They must pay for what they've done, to all of us."

He seemed to soften and grow interested. She was speaking his language.

"I know things about them." She touched his arm. "I know their weaknesses. I've had a century to sit and study them. Believe me when I say, they want me out of this country, or my mind taken from me, because they know I'm dangerous."

A glint filled his eyes. She liked seeing it.

"It wasn't just a punishment to Yngvi that I should be left as Vanessa and dumped with my husband. They didn't want me to remember the things I know. They didn't want me to feel the fire in Hera's veins. It was a perfect solution for them. It would torment Yngvi, but more importantly, I would think I was Vanessa and leave."

"They didn't count on Sía giving you your memory back."

"And I'm sure if they find out, she'll be put to death." She lowered her voice. "So, it's very much in her interest to make sure they don't find out. And that means, I am Hera without them knowing. I have the advantage for as long as they don't realize I live and thrive again."

He narrowed his eyes. "Do you think that's why Yngvi wanted you to choose between the two minds? Do you think he was hoping you'd pick Vanessa for that reason?"

"I believe he wanted me to pick Vanessa, but only because I would be safer that way, and more likely to get out of here." She smiled faintly. "Yngvi is a good man, and kind. There are others like that, and they're usually shunned for it. If I had not known his kindness for so long, I would not have believed some of them can be good. But the ones in charge—they're not good, and they dictate everything. They're old and powerful and hard to argue with."

"How does their society work? What is the Council?"

She touched his arm again. "I'll tell you all about it. You can write it down like your mother wrote things down, so other humans have a guide. But it's a lot, and we must devote some time to it."

He nodded. Gunnar, she knew, would be hard to convince. But this one, he would stand by her side and fight, she could already see that. She had to be careful, and make sure Aedan didn't get snatched away. They had to put up defenses to make sure.

"I will protect you, as well as I'm able." She squeezed his arm. "Maybe one day you'll think of me as your mother, as you think of Gunnar as your father."

He gazed at her a moment, then his lips broke in a hesitant smile. "Thank you."

"I have plans, ideas. I don't think Gunnar will like them, but he'll come around. I still know how to convince him."

Aedan smirked. "Yeah, he's cautious. Can't say I blame him."

"Me neither. I suppose one of us needs to have some good sense." She rose, patted Aedan on the shoulder, and went back inside. She went to the bedroom, slipped her pants off, and climbed back in bed beneath the sheets.

Gunnar stirred. "Hera?" He slipped his arm across her waist.

"It's fine, I'm just restless." She placed a hand on his thick forearm across her stomach. "I got up to speak to Aedan."

"Where is he?" He sounded a little more awake, and worried.

"Just sitting outside. He's fine." She rubbed his arm. "Don't worry, I won't let any harm come to him."

"You might not be able to stop it." He rolled onto his side, pulling his arm across her. "He shouldn't be outside alone. They could come and take him."

"They're not around. I don't feel them, anyway."

Gunnar sat up on one elbow and ruffled his hair.

She smiled up at him. He was handsome even with sleep clinging to him, and such a frown on his face. "Don't fret. I know it's hard." She poked him in the ribs. "Do you remember the first time we made love?"

He lowered his arm and blinked a few times. "Yes, I do."

"We were sinful, not waiting until our wedding night." She grinned. "If my mother had known, she would have fallen over. On our wedding day she gave me all sorts of advice and it was hard to keep a serious face."

He chuckled. "I'm just glad you didn't get pregnant."

"So am I, for other reasons now." She turned serious. "I can't imagine the fate of such a child, after what happened. You would've had to raise it alone, and it would have died by now. How strange it would've been to grow up with a father who didn't age."

"Unsettling to think about."

She rubbed her hands over her stomach. "I don't know that I'll ever bear children. I wouldn't want to live in fear of the huldufólk descending upon them. I'm sure they would love to torture me further by snatching my children away."

Gunnar grunted, and rolled back onto his stomach, but stayed up on his elbows. "Another reason we should leave Iceland. The sooner, the better."

"We should stay until your punishment is lifted. They have no reason to keep you under it now. Maybe they'll come sooner and end it."

"And they'll find you with me." His tone serious. "And we'll all be in trouble, especially your friends."

"Friend," she corrected. "Sía and Þalía are no friends of mine."

"Still. If they know you're back to yourself, it'll

be trouble. That's why at least you have to get out of here soon. If I must stay, I will. But I want you to take Aedan and go. It's safer that way."

He spoke sense, but she had no intention of leaving. She might part with him until they lifted his curse, so that Yngvi wouldn't be found out and punished, but she would not leave Iceland. Aedan might be safer if he did though, at least for now. At least until she had a full plan in place and a way to protect him.

"This is my home," she said. "They don't get to torment me for a century and then run me out of my home. I will deal with them."

"Hera." He shifted toward her. "You're not going to fight them."

"Only I can." She sat up and looked him in the eye. "I know their secrets."

"Last time you fought them, I lost you for a hundred years." His voice climbed. "Now that I have you back, it's not happening again."

She felt for him, for his pain, she did. But her pain was of a kind he couldn't imagine. It was deep and powerful and fueled her every thought and move. "I will leave you and go south, so they don't find out I'm here." She kept her voice even. "You have to call out to them, summon them. Tell them Vanessa went home. They don't know you know the truth. Maybe they'll lift the punishment. I think the only reason they don't lift it now, of course, is they think you don't know who I really am. They'll let the last two years play out, and then tell you some lie that Hera is dead. But perhaps if they think I left Iceland, they'll lift it sooner."

He shook his head. "I'm not summoning them. I'm not messing with them. Unless, of course, I know you and Aedan are both safely out of Iceland first."

She could lie to him, tell him that she and Aedan

were leaving, but stay. It would be dishonest, and dangerous, but it would put him at ease and he might do as she asked. It was a hurtful thing to do after they'd been so long apart, but it might be necessary.

She looked into his eyes, bright in the shadows of his face. "Do you really think I will turn my cheek and go on with my life? I deserve retribution."

"And what is your idea of retribution? Will you kill all of them? How many are there, do you even know? And would it even be possible? You speak of paying them back, but how exactly will you do this, and what is enough?"

She scowled. He was speaking sense again, but it didn't matter.

"Not all of them, but a few, who deserve it." She hadn't thought things through yet, and not being able to give him a clear answer aggravated her. "*Enough* is when they stop tormenting humans. When they stop punishing us for mere slights, and they stop inflicting terror, imprisoning people, and snatching away half-children. When they agree to leave humans in peace and exist without interacting with us."

Gunnar let out a dry laugh. "So, you want to reform the whole of huldufólk society and tradition? What great power do you have that would bring about such sweeping change?"

Her aggravation increased. She had little patience, and little ability to control her anger now. Both had served her well, fueling her will to live.

"Do not doubt me, Gunnar Heimirsson." She spoke in warning. "I am not the same woman they dragged away into darkness. They tempered me with their cruelty, unwittingly. And now I'm a sharp weapon, one that can cut through them with precision."

She expected him to scoff, but he didn't.

He looked down. "I won't lose you again, Hera," he whispered. "You're angry and wronged. I urge you not to act until your head is clear. Give yourself some time to adapt to being back, distance yourself from the past. At least allow yourself some rest, and see what you stand to lose all over again."

It was sound advice. Hard to swallow right now, but she knew he spoke the truth. She glared across the room, toward the windows, and held her tongue.

"If you want to start a revolution," he spoke lowly, "then start small and discreet. Don't walk directly into a nest of venomous snakes with only a rake and expect to cut all their heads off, just because you're mad enough to try."

She glared harder.

He sat up next to her. "Usurp them quietly. But..." He cupped her cheek. "Not right now. You and Aedan get out of Iceland. Stay away, until my curse is lifted. Then you can come back and put some kind of plan in motion, if you want to. You'll have time to distance yourself and think rationally. You have to do this for me, and Aedan." His next words were pained. "Please, Hera, he's my son."

She knew this was right, though it pained her. Gunnar would suffer if she didn't obey his wishes, and if something happened to Aedan because of her, the guilt would crush her.

She gripped his wrist. "Perhaps I should go to America, then. I can visit Vanessa's family. I know where they are, after all."

He crinkled his brow. "I don't know what you would say to them?"

"Nothing, maybe. I just want to see them. She wants to see them." Indeed, Vanessa still longed to go home. She thought of it often enough to be distracting.

Yngvi's warning rang in her head. Would it eventually become unbearable?

He withdrew his hand from her face, and she held it in her own, between them on the bed. This would be difficult, for more than one reason.

"I don't know what will become of you." She looked into his eyes. "I don't know what will happen when your punishment is lifted. What if you age and die? What if they would rather put an end to you than to ever risk you finding out I'm still alive?"

He leaned forward and pressed his forehead to hers. "Then I will have seen my wife again. I'll have had this with you, and that's enough to let me die in peace. And I will know Aedan is safe in your hands."

She closed her eyes. "If you die, my anger will be a thousandfold. They will never know peace until I'm in my grave. I will kill a hundred in your place."

He put his arms around her and pulled her close, drawing her back down on the bed with him. She wrapped herself around the firm warmth of his body, hands on his skin, legs wound with his.

"I still love you," he whispered. "Despite anything I said to Vanessa, I have always loved you. I didn't give up hope. Trying to forget you would have been impossible."

She stroked her fingers through his curls, as she often did at night in their marriage bed. He'd smelled of the land and sea back then, and though he didn't now, the essence of him remained. He was still her Gunnar: earnest, fierce, sensible, and tenderhearted. She'd never met a more practical man, and that's why she'd married him. Maybe one day, she would be herself again too: erstwhile, caring, devoted, and yes, even funny. She'd snatch back the things they'd taken from her, body and mind.

"I love you too," she murmured. "In the darkness you were the light, and you are the light who will guide me back home once more." She clung tight to him. "Fear not, we are reunited forever."

She shifted her gaze over his shoulder to the nightstand where her knife lay, glinting. It was old, like her, but not broken or useless, only a little blunt and in need of sharpening.

"They will never part us again," she whispered.

The End

www.meganmorganauthor.com

MEGAN MORGAN

EVERNIGHT PUBLISHING ®

www.evernightpublishing.com